KAYLA ROSE

LOVE, MILO

*For those who dreamed up the
perfect partner, this is for you—
May you meet them in these pages*

1

RAELYNN

I've always been good at telling lies.

But you know what they say: the truth always has ways of escaping the shadows.

My parents are currently downstairs in the lobby. I don't know what to do. I regret giving them my address in the first place. What was I thinking? I thought they might show even an ounce of pride if they knew I now live in an apartment building that sits snugly in the part of Manhattan where celebrities walk the sidewalks, old cobblestone roads still exist, and people who wear expensive designer stroll carelessly around—a location worth gloating to their sorry faces about.

I have it all planned out for them—the perfect job, the perfect apartment, and their favorite one, the perfect boyfriend. One of the three is the lie that might very well put me six feet underground alongside my dignity.

They've been hounding me daily about meeting my boyfriend.

You see, I would have no problem showing him to them.

If he were real.

My phone almost drops front-first onto my floor seconds after answering my mom's call, but I catch it, letting out a long sigh. I may live in a wealthy area, but I sure as hell don't have new iPhone money. I wedge it between my shoulder and cheek as I slip my socks on.

"Oh honey, I can't wait to meet you and that boyfriend. I can't believe it! *Ugh*," Mom laughs. "You're so grown up and finally settling down after all the stuff I had to go through with you in high school. Do you remember the boys and the arguments—"

"*Mom*," I blurt out, cutting her off before she begins taking yet another stroll down memory lane.

I made up my non-existent boyfriend around a year ago. If someone asked me how I got so far buried under my lie, I wouldn't be able to answer them.

"Haven't we taught you that interrupting people is rude, Raelynn? Have manners, you haven't seen me in a year, and you're already disrespectful."

I grind my teeth, closing my eyes as I shuffle on my shoes. "Sorry, Mom. It's just that I have to tell you something when I get downstairs."

She sighs, an unsurprising hint of disappointment dripping from it, and speaks to my father in a hushed voice, not knowing I can still hear every word she says. "I knew this was coming. They broke up, I bet you." It's barely audible, but I still hear it, and it makes my skin burn with anxiety.

I always let them down, her more than dad. Mme getting a new apartment and moving in with my new "boyfriend" was something they were finally praising me for.

Sometimes, I wish I had it as easy as my sister, Gia. She's getting married, and it's all everyone in this family ever talks about. Especially my mom. Gia this, and Gia that,

"Raelynn, when are you going to settle and get married like Gia?' And *'Raelynn, don't get pregnant with some dead-beat again; abortions aren't free, y'know, we never had this problem with Gia".*

She's the definition of an angel child. While I got put down for living my life the way I wanted to.

"I'll see you downstairs, Mom. Bye." I hung up before she could get another word of disappointment out.

I grb my keys from the bowl beside the door and look in the mirror on the wall beside me. I cringe at the sight of my hair. It's curly, wild, and a damn mess. I pull off the purple scrunchie from my wrist and collect the ringlets that brush my boobs into a high ponytail.

That'll have to do. I'm bound to get at least one comment from Mom about how my hair is a disaster, but I couldn't care less now.

I open my front door and slip my phone into the pocket of my overalls, still covered with dirt. One of the straps stays on my shoulder while the other hangs unbuttoned, showing the white crop tank top underneath. The half-visible print on it states, *Fuck off.*

Hopefully, my mom gets the hint.

Walking towards the elevator, I click the button, calling it down—my hand fiddles with the rings on my hands. I always hate meeting with my parents, but I hate taking elevators much more. I didn't consider how many stairs I'd have to take when I signed the lease for an apartment on the twenty-third floor. Now, I'm stuck taking the elevator, hoping that I don't fall into one of my claustrophobic panic attacks every day. My arm hairs stand on end. I can't be the only one who hates these suffocating steel cubes.

The dunning of the elevator's arrival yanks me from my thoughts, and the doors open, allowing me to walk in. I press the L for the lobby, and the doors close.

Twenty-three floors and around a minute till I have to face my parents. I can do this; I can tell Mom I'm boyfriend-less, and in the past year, I didn't do all the romantic things I told her I did.

The elevator stops at floor twenty-two, the one right below mine. The steel doors open, but I'm too busy looking at the ground and stressing over what I will say to Mom to care about the person who entered. My head hurts from the stress. I need a fucking ice bath after this visit.

My attention returns when the man beside me sighs as if he's also stressed. I'm glad I'm not the only one.

We both stand facing the elevator doors as they close shut. Out of sheer curiosity, I look at him with my best-undetected side-eye.

He's wearing a nice icy white ribbed sweatshirt and creamy khakis that match it, his hands buried in their pockets. His clothes fit him perfectly. I can only make out his side profile, but from the looks of it, this guy is from the fucking deepest parts of Heaven. This is a guy I expect to be walking the streets of a neighborhood like this one, but I never exactly realized I'd be sharing elevators with them. I take his sharp jawline and force my mouth not to fall open at the sight of it. *Geez-Louise.* The temptation to go back up and grab a knife to compare it to his jaw itches at the back of my head, but I don't. The elevator starts moving down again.

He shuffles his feet a little and leans his shoulder against the wall at his side. He's pretty tall, considering his chin could easily touch the top of my head, and I've always been considered tall for a woman.

As if my eyes controlled themselves, they lowered towards his groin, noticing the unavoidable print of his crotch between his legs.

My eyes widen. Jesus... is that him on *soft*—

His eyes dart sideways to meet mine. "Are you checking me out?" He says cockily, an accent I immediately recognize as British lace his words.

My cheeks immediately burst into flames as I dart my eyes up to look at his face and then away at the elevator door. The tick of the elevator traveling down floors sounds.

"What? No?" I blurt out with an awful, uneven laugh.

I fiddle with my rings again, clearing my throat. Meeting my parents isn't the worst thing at the moment.

"Hm," he hums. "Really? Because it looked like you were staring at my dick to me."

My heart stops as fast as my breath does. I snap my eyes towards him, widened and shocked by his words. "No, *no, I was*—I was looking at—"

Cutting me off, the elevator floor between our feet shakes, and I stifle, losing my balance. I yelp, flailing my arms to balance myself as the eerie sound of metal screeching scratches my ear drums. This cannot be happening right now. My heart races more than it was seconds ago. One last long, irritable screech makes my eyes shut tight, and I nearly fall to the floor but am humiliatingly caught by the man beside me.

A whimper of fear leaves me.

He grips my arm as I breathe like an Olympic runner out my mouth. What the hell is going on? If this guy weren't here, I'd for sure be screaming my ass off.

"You're okay. This happens sometimes," he says loudly, just as the elevator comes to a stop. Yet, the doors don't open. Why haven't the doors opened? Don't tell me we're fucking stuck. We're stuck. No, we're not—*Yes, we are*. We're trapped together in a box the size of a New York apartment bathroom.

I gasp in a sharp breath, gripping my shirt over my heart, and find the will to breathe again.

Is there even oxygen in here?

"It's stuck," the guy states the obvious. I turn to him as he lets go of my arm. "Give it about fifteen minutes before whomever the hell comes to fix it." He presses the emergency help button, and it glows red.

My brows curl up as I feel myself begin to cry. I shake my head, swallowing. "No, I can't."

His head tilts, and his brows furrow at seeing me, but I can't find the energy to explain this to him. I'm already starting to feel it. It sores through me like electricity, clogging my veins and arteries: the feeling of being locked in this small space, the four walls surrounding me—a gray room from hell. Everything's getting smaller, or maybe I'm getting bigger—too big for this space. I shut my eyes, and my back finds a wall to slide down. My legs will collapse from under me if I don't sit.

I was okay with the two minutes in an elevator daily, but getting *stuck* in them is entirely different.

"Hey, *hey*?" The man consults. I don't open my eyes. "What's the matter? I said it won't last much longer. You don't have to go all crying mode on me; I get enough of that daily."

His voice gets closer as if he's just crouched beside me.

"Talk to me," I blurt out, my mouth running dry with how many breaths I'm taking a second.

"I hate to ask, but I'm bad at noticing these things. Are you flirt—"

"*Please*, just... Talk!"

"Okay! Geez, I'll talk." He laughs, but I can't seem to find the punchline.

It's bad enough that I'm trapped in an elevator, it's downright torture that I'm trapped in it with a man.

He sits beside me as I dig my forehead into my knees. From the side, I see his feet planted down, and his arm brushes mine as he rests his arms on his knees, sitting in the same position. I sniffle my running nose.

"Well," he starts. "I just got a message from one of my student's parents telling me their kid is sick and can't come to school this week." A rush of hair leaves his nose, and I'm utterly confused. "It's a normal thing, of course, and probably just a cold, but I *really* hate it when my students are ill." The British accent dripping from his words massages my ears. It's now that I bring my undivided attention to it. I don't think I've ever met anyone with an accent that wasn't American before. Each word comes out of his mouth like melted butter.

I don't speak for a moment, then turn my head so one eye peeks at him. I see him blurry through my tears. I blink a few times so his image clears up. An extremely light stubble dresses his chin and top lip like he shaved a day or two ago. He looks young, nothing like what my teachers back in college or high school looked like. They were all old and wrinkly. He, however, looks like a man that could still be in college.

"You're a *teacher*?"

He nods, his deep brown hair falling over his forehead. He lets it sit there, making my gaze wander to the gray of his eyes. Oh, *wow*.

"Yeah, a first-grade teacher. Kids make me go fucking insane." His voice goes raspy as he chuckles, and it vibrates a little something in me.

"How old are you?"

"Twenty-six," he answers. "You?"

"Twenty-five."

"Hm, so old, yet still scared of... *elevators*. Interesting."

I squint at him. "I'm claustrophobic, not that I need to explain anything to you. If I weren't, I'd be perfectly fine with waiting here."

"If you weren't, you'd also still be staring at my dick. Not complaining, though."

My body stiffens again, the heat returning to my face, boiling at the rounds of my cheeks. For fucks sake, can he just drop that already?

"I wasn't *staring* at your dick."

"No, definitely not. You were just *observing* it."

I press my lips together, "That's the same thing."

He nods and smirks. "My point exactly."

He's repulsive. I shake my head, closing my eyes and letting my head deadfall onto my arms once again. "Don't talk anymore. I change my mind."

I don't truly want him to stop talking. Whatever it is that that voice is laced with is getting me high, distracting me from the situation we're in. I don't know how long it's been, but he's good at chatting. Does it have anything to do with his job with children? Most likely.

I should ask him to do ASMR videos with his voice— *No, Raelynn.*

"Fine, go." He shifts his butt on the floor to face me and crosses his legs, and for some reason, I'm worried about the filthy elevator floor dirtying his expensive-looking clothing.

My eyes dart to his. "Go?"

"Talk."

"Okay..." I say slowly, leaning against the elevator as I stare up into what I would like to imagine as space and not the corner of a metal box. I'd much rather be looking at clouds and the blue sky. "I have an imaginary boyfriend."

He snorts, looking at me through his lashes. "Imaginary? Like from your head imaginary?"

"Well, are there other types of imaginary boyfriends that *aren't* in heads? If so, please tell me. I'd *love* to know."

He shakes his head. "Nope. Maybe a therapist can help you with that one."

I squint as he grins. My gaze shifts to his mouth, inspecting his pearly whites. They're surrounded by lips,. *obviously*. Just lips. Not pink, perfect, and plump, or shaped really nice—

I shake the thoughts out of my head. "I don't imagine him for my enjoyment. I'm not *insane*. He's a lie."

"A lie," he repeats as if struggling to follow along. That shows how irrational this story is, considering he doesn't even know a quarter of it yet.

I nod, glancing at the floor momentarily, playing with the loose strap on my overalls. "Yeah, a lie to my family."

One of his eyebrows rises when I look back at him. "I don't... Why would you have to…"

"Lie?" I finish his question, "Because I'm twenty-five and single with no boyfriend and have a... *history* that runs through my family. They're religious, and I'm not exactly the Virgin Mary. I wanted to show them I could keep a relationship when in reality, I couldn't keep a relationship for shit. I still can't. They only leave me heartbroken or breaking hearts," I say bitterly. "So, I made up this *lie* and said I had one. And guess what?"

"You don't," he answers correctly. Now he's following along, it seems.

I drop my eyebrows, miserable with the past circling my head. "Bingo," I whisper. "The funny thing is my mom and dad are going to be waiting just outside the elevator door when it goes back down, and they're expecting this imaginary amazing boyfriend that I don't have."

I turn to him, and he's staring at me intently, listening as if genuinely fascinated. Another teacher plus, I guess—a great listener.

"What does this imaginary boyfriend look like to them?"

I shrug. "Never described him, obviously didn't show any pictures over the past year—"

"Love, a *year*? You've got to be some kind of a pathological liar.

"*Hey*."

He smiles. "Kind of hot." Then leans back on the wall, mirroring my position beside me. Our shoulders touch, and I roll my eyes, feeling goosebumps on my arms rise from his complement. If that even *was* one? He's only trying to distract me with his obscured comments.

"Stop with the flirting. You've met me only minutes ago."

"Yeah, and you knew me for zero minutes when you stared at my—"

I shuffle to stand on my knees, aggravated, and point a finger at his chest. "Say it again, I swear I'll... I'll..." My words are lost in translation as I follow his rain-cloud-like eyes to my finger, now pressing against his chest. He looks down at it for a long time, then takes a drawn-out look up at my chest that sits

my cleavage. His eyes bounce from one boob to another for a moment, then he views my face with that stupid smirk on his.
"Sorry, I got distracted. What were you saying, love?"

2

Raelynn

"Look who's checking who out now," I say, shifting away from him and crossing my arms over my breast.

"You got me. The only difference between you and me is that I'd admit to checking out someone I find attractive. You clearly won't," he banters.

This guy, who I have not even learned the name of, is bolder than any man I have encountered. Confident also, *too* confident.

I stand up, ignoring the pounding in my head and the pain in my throat from my dry throat. God, I need to get the hell out of here.

"Thanks, but I pass." I breathe out, long, deep breaths following. Breathe in through the nose, breathe out through the mouth. *Simple, Raelynn.*

He stands up and stands opposite me, tilting his head. How is his face just so— "Pass on what?"

I look at him—with more of a glare. His brows are thick but maintained, and they're drawn together. If I don't exit this elevator in the next minute, my parents are going to have to meet my corpse.

I wave a hand around between us, dismissing him. "Your sad attempt at hitting on me. I pass." I smile bitterly.

He barks out a laugh, and I squint my eyes. "Darling, just because I flirt with you doesn't mean I *want* you."

I press my lips together, my brows jumping up. "Wow. *Charming*. You seriously won me over with that one."

He smiles at me, crooked and almost arrogant. If I was Raelynn a few years ago in college or high school, that comment of his might've hurt me. *It would've* hurt me. Some try to change the past; others try to cut it out of their lives. What I've learned is that you simply have to deal with it. The past can't be changed. No matter how often you cry into your pillow, wish upon a star, or pray for a miracle. Trust me, I've tried it all. I like to think present Raelynn is different; I'm not careless and obsessed with the opposite gender anymore. I'm not out past three in the morning getting drunk. I'm not having careless sex with anyone who much as flirts with me or being a pain in my parent's neck—going to jail for silly crimes. That might be someone's proud life, but it's not mine anymore. It hasn't been for a couple of years. And this guy, whoever he is, won't break my streak.

Besides the perfect, flawless one I made up for my family, no guys or boyfriends can distract me.

No matter how tempting they are.

A beep breaks our peaceful silence. "Sorry for the inconvenience. The elevator is up and running and will be moving again shortly." A helper guy speaks through the speaker near the floor buttons.

I sigh a breath of relief. Thank the Lord.

"See, I told you it'd be done quickly," No-Name says. I cross my arms, ignoring him as the elevator gracefully begins to travel down. Hearing the elevator move is like music to my ears. The glowing descending numbers keep my attention undivided.

Then a ding sounds, and the doors open.

At the far end of the lobby, my mom and dad sit in the chairs, a book in mom's hand and dad looking over her shoulder to read it. They both wear casual clothing to accommodate this warm April weather. I swallow the dry lump clogging the center of my throat.

I immediately feel pressure on my chest, head, and heart as I take my first step out of the elevator.

Please, don't be disappointed in me.

I leave No-Name behind, forgetting his existence with my steps toward the middle-aged people before me. Their brown skin shines in the light above, and my mother looks up at me above her glasses.

She gasps and smiles. "Raelynn!" She stands up, and so does Dad, but I try not to meet his eyes. Dad and I haven't been on very good terms for quite some time now. Since I can remember, my dad has always been strict, and unlike Gia, I haven't been one to listen to him—at all. I guess I should just be glad he's here. It's a step in the right direction.

"Hi, Mom," I say blankly with an attempted smile, hugging her.

"Ugh," she scoffs, pulling back and picking at a curl dropping over my face. "Your hair, it's a—"

"Mess," I roll my eyes. "I know."

"Your boyfriend must really love you; having your hair so wild would scare off anyone who doesn't." She cackles, and I blink at her, shifting my jaw from side to side.

Sometimes, I wonder if she knows how rude she is. My hair isn't even that wild. It's curly and in a ponytail... may the Lord be with me, how *terrible*.

"Actually, Mom, that's what I wanted to tell you ab-"

I watch her brown eyes trail away from my face and to somewhere behind me. She beams, "Speaking of your boyfriend, would you look at *him*."

My brows drop in confusion. But a second later, a warm, hard hand threads with mine.

I flinch at his contact and turn to see elevator No-Name.

My eyes widen and he looks at me with a bright smile. Is this his way of getting back at me for turning him down? Playing some sick game with my problems?

He turns to my parents and gives them his most appealing smile. Big and white all over. My eyes trail down to our hands connected, and I flex my hand. The feeling of a male makes me repel. He closes his grip on me tighter.

"It's so nice to meet you. I'm Milo Evans."

Milo. So, No-name isn't nameless after all.

Milo extends his hand to shake my mother's. She returns it gladly. Then he turns to my dad and attempts to shake his, but dad only stares at his hand, a low flame burning behind his dark brown eyes.

I tug at Milo's other hand, and he drops the gesture, slipping the rejected hand back into his sweatpants' pockets.

Over the years, my dad has come to hate every one of the guys I've brought home. He didn't trust them, and he had good reason to. They were all a bunch of jerks who used me for one thing and one thing only. I was too stupid to realize that then.

This fake boyfriend Milo's filling in for doesn't change anything in Dad's mind. His guard's still up when it comes to my so-called boyfriends. Mom, however, looks over the moon.

She grips Milo's shoulder. You're one handsome man, I didn't think Raelynn was capable of—"

"*Mom*," I hiss through my teeth. Do I reveal what I was going to or keep this charade up?

She waves me away. "So, Milo," she starts.

"Yes?" His voice is deep, smooth, and so... British.

My mom closes her eyes. "Your accent is killing me." She turns to me. "You mess this one up, I'll end you myself, Raelynn."

I swallow, biting my tongue to stop the urge to tell her off for how bad she makes me feel. This stranger she's just met, and she talks to him better than her daughter, who's standing right in front of her.

I turn away and stare at the wall just as I feel Milo's thumb rub back and forth against the back of my hand.

A knot forms in my throat, listening to their conversation.

"So, how long have you known Raelynn, Milo?"

"Oh, for around two years," he says, remembering what I've told him in the elevator. "Isn't that right, love?"

I realize he's just spoken to me; I turn to look at his fake smile and grill him for a split second before I go along with his lie. "Mhm, two fantastic years."

"What are your intentions with my daughter," my dad asks. He's overprotective, extremely protective, even with me being an adult. I don't know if I should hate it or cherish it. That's the thing about religious parents. You either want to get as far away from them as possible or give in to them.

Milo stares blankly. "Um—"

"Have you thought about marriage?" Dad quizzes, "What is your career path? Are you a criminal—"

"Mom, Dad, we *really* got to get going," I unintentionally dig my nails into Milo's hand, and when he flinches, I soften my grip.

Mom smiles and sighs contentedly, turning to Dad. "Don't be so scary, David; you'll scare him away," she whispers. Then turns to Milo, "It was nice meeting you. I hope to see you both at the wedding in a few months, yes?"

Gia's wedding. The perfect angel of our little family is getting married. How could we forget?

"Wedding," Milo says before I can open my mouth. "Of course, we'll be there."

Is he out of his damn mind? I have to smile to prevent myself from cursing at him.

"We *really* have to go," I say, breaking this twisted version of a reunion up.

He bends down and kisses my mother's cheek goodbye. She softly gasps in shock and laughs, "Oh! What a gentleman. I like you," she pats his cheek and grabs Dad's arm, finding their way out of the building.

Immediately, I let go of Milo's hand with disgust and turn to face him. He slips both hands in his sweatpants pockets and raises his eyebrows. "That was... something."

"What is *wrong* with you!" I bellow through my teeth, pushing at his chest. He doesn't budge, of course. His chest feels like steel. I try not to be loud, noticing the security lady sitting behind her desk reading.

"What? Did you not need my help?"

"*No*, I didn't, and I don't. You've just made everything worse. What am I supposed to tell them now? That we broke up? In a few minutes, the entire family will hear about how great you are, Milo. What lie do I come up with? How do I even—"

"Darling—"

"And my name is not *darling* or love!" Steam practically oozes from every hole in my head as I shout. Someone exits the elevator, and I lower my voice. My heart is thumping so fast my chest hurts. "It's *Raelynn*. Drop the act."

He stands and stares at me. Silent. He searches my eyes until I break eye contact and walk past him to exit the building.

I don't have any plans; it's the weekend, and it's the morning. So, only one place comes to mind for moments like this. Moments where I need to cool off in peace.

Anything's better than standing under that heavy gaze.

3

MILO

"Bye, Mr. Evans!" One of my students calls out, waving as she holds her mother's hand.

I grin and wave goodbye to the little girl, Haven, her name is.

Today has been a long fucking day, and so has this week, and it's not even over yet.

First, it was that woman who lives on the floor above me yelling at me a few days ago, and then it was me spilling tea on myself while teaching yesterday. And today, my head has been pounding like crazy from dealing with crazy, cranky children all day.

I sit in my car and sigh, thinking about that day two days ago. My brain seems unwilling to slip from my mind as I start my car and begin driving.

Raelynn.

I wonder what she's up to. What does she do in her free time besides getting stuck in elevators? I didn't exactly think things through when I pretended to be her boyfriend to her parents. It just... happened. And it worked, so I'm not sure why she got upset with me afterward.

I bite the inside of my bottom lip, simply thinking of her face. The piercing that hung from her septum, the rings she wore, the way her breast sat so... perfectly—

A car horn honks, and I glance at the streetlight. I wonder how long that's been green for. I shake my head and the image of her out.

It's not ideal to grow a boner while driving.

Turning the key in the ignition of my car, I press down on the gas and start driving.

The streets of NYC are ones most people would call hectic. It's a fucking nightmare. I've come to miss London sometimes every time I start driving; traffic is inevitable here. I take a longer route home, avoiding the streets that would otherwise lead me into hypnotizing start-stop jams. I have no real reason to rush home. I have a few papers to fill out and lessons to plan, but other than that... I'm unsure why I need to get there so quickly.

I don't have many people anyone to converse with either.

Getting to the front of the building takes less time than usual.

Sitting at the front desk is Edna Higgins, the security guard. I raise my hand as a hello, and she grins. She's a fairly older woman in her fifties, the center of her eyes starting to wrinkle when she smiles.

"Afternoon, Mr. Evans," she greets.

I walk to her, leaning on the desk. "Edna." A huff leaves me. I glance around the lobby. "You know of that new resident? The woman? Fairly tall," I measure her height with my hand just under my chin. "Very curly hair, big brown eyes..."

She nods while stacking some papers on the desk. "Yes, Raelynn Garcia?"

"Garcia, yes. Is she home? Have you seen her... leave?" Though calm and collected has never suited me, I try to sound nonchalant.

Edna shakes her head. "She should be home right now. Should I ring her apartment phone to tell her to come down, sir?"

I shake my head. "That won't be necessary, I'll go up." Just then, the door to the stairs opens, and a familiar face pops through, walking with her gaze pinned on the floor as if her mind wandered far from this world.

Raelynn. I grin.

"Rae," my voice comes out rough as I call out to her. I clear my throat.

The thick curls falling past her shoulder blades whip to the left as she turns at the sound of her name. She wears a casual dress that flows and gives off a spring feeling. Tulips dress the dress. She carries gloves, but not ones for cold weather, but thick working gloves.

Her eyes jump to me as she halts her walk, then gives me a once over.

I hastily check my outfit. Black slacks, a suit jacket, and a white Oxford shirt under it. A light brown trench coat sits over it all. Hopefully, she finds nothing wrong with anything I have on.

I look back up at Raelynn, and she starts walking again. I follow her.

She doesn't even turn around as she threatens me, "If you keep following me, I'll have no choice but to call the police." I can't tell if she's joking or not.

I grab her wrist and turn her around before she can get to the door. "I'm sorry," I exclaim. "For pretending to be your boyfriend."

She yanks her hand away, and I refrain from frowning.

Why does she hate me?

Maybe because I told her I didn't want her. I thought I was making her uncomfortable, so saying that was the first thing to mind.

She walks through the door, and I follow her despite her protest. The moment we step out, we navigate through the swarm of New Yorkers walking the narrow streets. Everyone is in a rush, and I learned that if you're not, you should pretend to be when walking. A strong warm wind makes the corner of my coat flair, I flatten it with my hand.

I struggle to stay at her side. She's much smaller than me and doesn't bump into people as often.

"Where are you headed?" I ask her when I manage to catch up, out of breath. "I can drive you."

"Oh, was that your Tesla out front?" She says without turning around or stopping her stride. "Figured."

"What does the kind of car I have matter?"

"Nothing that your outfit doesn't say by itself."

My outfit? So, she doesn't like it after all?

I frown now. "What's wrong with my outfit?" I find her side again as the street clears up. We turn a corner, and I continue at her side. I haven't walked this fast in a long damn time.

She turns to look up at me for the first time. "Oh, nothing..." she surveys me up and down.

"*Clearly,* it's not nothing, Lo—Raelynn, so tell me."

She glares at me, darting her eyes around my face. Then stops moving. Annoyed New Yorkers give us ugly looks and walk around us. I grab her hand and pull her off to the side.

"What do you want, Milo?" She still holds those strange gloves, which I now realize are covered in dried dirt. What does she need those for—burying a body?

I look back at her. "I can't be friends with my new upstairs neighbor?"

"Are you friends with all your neighbors, or did you just decide to fuck with just me for whatever reason?"

I shrug my shoulders. "Not to the extent of friendship, but I'd say acquaintances."

She tilts her head. "Why do you talk like that?"

I draw my brows together. "Like what?"

"Like so... formal. It's creeping me out, especially with your accent. You sound like you might give me a lecture."

"Well, I *am* a teacher."

"Well, I don't think you're in the middle of giving me a lesson, so..."

I tilt my head. "Depends, do you want me to?" My tone lowers, and I smile.

She presses her lips together, her eyes darting from my face awkwardly. Her breath visibly quickens. "I'm going to pretend you didn't just flirt in some weird... teacher language."

"I'm going to pretend you weren't flustered."

She turns around and walks away. I follow her again. Where the hell is she headed?

She ignores me. "Is there a reason you're following me like some creep?"

"Not really... Where are you going?"

She finally stops when she reaches the front of a gate that's the width of two buildings, looks at me, and groans. "Since you don't seem to be leaving me alone until you know, I might as well show you." Behind the gate is, well, nature. A garden, plants, and small trees dress the entire space. In a city where green isn't so common, this is like a splash of life to the green-less world surrounding it. From here, I can see through to the other street. It's at least a few yards away.

She transfers the gloves in her hand to the other and takes a key from the purse draped across her chest. Opening the two white-painted gate doors. She walks in onto the cobblestone pavement below, and I do so, too, looking around at the leaves that hang overhead from nearby trees—creating a shallow canopy.

"You should probably not touch anything before you get your clothes dirty with soil. I'm assuming you're strict on that stuff."

I shrug off my trench coat and drape it over my arm. "I don't mind getting a little dirty. What is this place?"

She walks towards the small white table with chairs, sets her bag and keys down, and heads to the small glass greenhouse in the center.

"My garden," she answers, looking at me over her shoulders. I place my coat on the table where she placed her purse and fall in the path with her toward the greenhouse.

"You're a hot plant, Mom. Nice."

She glares at me and opens the greenhouse door—

An ear-throbbing scream leaves her.

"No!" She yells. My eyes widen as I watch her run to a tree and grab a broom leaning against it, then run back to the greenhouse, slamming the end of the broom against whatever is inside.

"What's going on?"

"The *fucking* raccoons!"

Raccoons?

Then I see the large animal, its natural mask across his eyes, running across the greenhouse plants. Dirt sprays across the air from under its feet and hits me. My heart races at the sight of it. I haven't seen one of those since I was in Central Park... years ago.

Raelynn looks terrified but oddly used to this. She stops in front of it with a broom, and it looks at her, hissing and standing on its two back legs with its legs up.

I run to Raelynn and place my hands on either side of her hips, pulling her away from that wild animal.

"Milo, stop. I need it to get out." She wiggles, and I grip her tighter.

"No, Rae, that thing is probably rabid. If it bites you, you could die."

"I've done this before, okay?" She grips the broom tightly but doesn't attempt to leave from between my hands, sitting on the curve of her hips. I feel her stomach fill and deflate with the quickness of her breaths, her dress rising a bit, crumpled in my hands. "I'm not scared of it."

"Yeah, you *certainly* don't look like you are." I laugh out against her ear, and she scoffs. I can practically see her scowl while staring at the back of her head.

I take hold of the broom and let go of her, stepping towards the raccoon. Raelynn backs away.

Lifting the broom over my shoulder, I grill the animal as it stands on its back legs, the front paws raised high, in full attack mode. I eye the foam dripping like cottage cheese from the corner of its mouth. Not a good sign at all.

"You're an ugly son of a bitch," I say to it. It hisses back in retaliation.

"Don't ego trip the damn animal; get it out!"

I tighten my grip on the broom, raise it like I do a baseball bat, and hit the raccoon across the greenhouse. It bangs into the wall, shaking the structure, then drops to the floor with a thump. We stare at it, its limp body lying still.

Homerun.

I pull my sleeves up my arm, ignoring the large dirt stains on them, and stand beside Raelynn.

"How'd I do?" I question as we look at the raccoon that may or may not be dead. "Good, yeah?"

I see a slight sadness cross her face, but she rolls her eyes. "Oh, shut up and make yourself useful. Just get *rid* of it."

4

Milo

I carry the dead raccoon in a trash bag and into the garbage bin outside the garden gate.

Raelynn seemed upset that it was dead. It confuses me; isn't that what she wanted in the first place? For it to be gone?

It was going to die either way, unfortunately. It had rabies.

I walk back into the greenhouse to find her brushing the dirt into a pile on the floor, scooping it up with her hands, and placing it back into the flowerpots. A broken flowerpot that the raccoon must've dropped sits on the floor. She bends down to grab the pieces with her bare hands.

Does she have a damn death wish?

"*Raelynn*," I walk to her and touch her shoulder, but I say it too late. The piece she picks up slips from her grasp, cutting her palm just as I hoped it wouldn't. She hisses, curses, and clamps her other hand around the wound. I watch the blood seep down her wrist, and I huff.

"How do you manage to keep yourself alive, love? I've been around you for an hour today, and you've nearly had a raccoon kill you, and then you slice your hand open."

I grab a rag from one of the benches and walk to her pained face as she sits on the floor. With her good hand, she brushes several curls out of her face and behind her ear, then shakes her head.

"It's just a little scratch, it's nothing," she lies as a drop of blood falls to the floor.

I hold her hurt hand, cupping it in mine and lowering it, walking her along to the bench where I tell her to sit. She does so, surprisingly.

I plop down on the floor in front of her, and her eyes widen, staring at my trousers. "Your clothes—"

"I don't care about my clothes. I think your bleeding is more important than the material getting dirty. Don't you think?" Why does she worry about my clothes so much? "Besides, my trousers are black."

She laughs as I dab the cloth on her wound, soaking up the blood, making sure she doesn't flinch. "Trousers?"

"What? They're called that, aren't they?" I glance up at her smile. It brightens up her face, the first smile I've seen from her.

When she speaks, I also notice the piercing on her tongue shimmer. It catches my gaze occasionally, like a star hidden in her mouth, calling for my attention. The small metal ball towards the tip of her tongue glistens under the hanging light above. I find myself wondering how it feels for it to be in your mouth. What does the metal feel like against your teeth? Is it cold?

"And it's— Are you listening to me?"

Shit, she was speaking.

I raise my eyebrows, looking back at her eyes. "I blanked out. What did you say?"

She huffs. "I said trousers is a funny word. Why don't you say pants?"

"*Pants*," I snort. "It's such a strange word for trousers."

She chuckles with one small huff as I continue cleaning her hand of the blood. A smile grows on my face at my success in making her laugh.

"*You're* strange, Milo," is all she says.

I furrow my brows, pausing my hand to stare up at her. "Is that a good thing or a bad thing?"

She pauses. Her throat bobs as she swallows, and her eyes rake me up and down to hold my eye contact when she eventually answers, "I don't know yet."

A moment of silence passes, and then she breaks our gaze and takes her hand back hastily, standing up. My smile drops, and so does a little something in me when I see her visibly close off from me. And there it is—that wall she holds so high, now stronger than ever. The wall that was beginning to sway was now finding its balance. The long book of Raelynn Garcia shuts closed, yet so many chapters are left to read.

She clears her throat and walks outside the greenhouse.

I huff, get to my feet, and follow her out.

I might as well skip gym days and spend them with her from now on. I'll burn the same number of calories from how much walking she does.

Outside, the sun is on the verge of setting, an orange tint dressing the sky. Soft, warm breezes travel through the leaves and grass of the small land. Various flowers scatter the outside garden, ranging from tulips to roses and many other flowers I don't know the name of. She spends her free time here—getting dirty and caring for plants. In a city where people are always on the go, with no time to spare or care to give. A city where looking your best is ideal, and anything less drags you down the social ladder. It's safe to say she's a breath of fresh air. I spot a squirrel running down a tree, and then I spot Raelynn wrapping a bandage around her hand. She stands beside a table, and I start towards her.

She eyes me and grabs her purse, hanging it off her shoulder.

"You're leaving?" I question.

"Yes, because I came here to occupy myself *without* distraction, and I'm not getting that. I might as well go home."

She grabs my coat, and I take it from her, sliding it over my shirt, spotted with soil. It's the dirtiest I've been in a while.

"If you wanted me to leave, you could've just—"

"Raelynn!" A woman's voice breaks my sentence. It's higher in pitch than Raelynn and more annoying, making my face askew.

I turn my head to the voice just as Raelynn shuts her eyes. "Fuck me," she whispers.

Okay— no. Fuck off, brain.

I look at the woman standing beside the front gate; she's tanned-skinned, with braids in her hair, and a man stands at her side. The woman grins widely and waves at me.

"Are you Milo?" She shouts.

I go to speak just when Raelynn steps in front of me, lifting onto her toes and wrapping her arms around my neck. I jerk down at her action, and my eyes widen as she presses her body against mine. I'm starting to question if something might be wrong with her, but no. She's here draping over me, so close, purposefully. My lips part, eyes darting between both of hers. Brown. There's so much of her beautiful brown right in my grasp. My hands shake as I rest them on the curve of her waist.

Oh, fuck.

She holds a hand full of my hair at the top of my head and lowers me just an inch away from hers. I grip her hips to balance. I'm afraid my knees might buckle below me if I don't.

"What are you doing?" I whisper.

She presses her lips together, swallowing. "Just... go with it." She lifts her head and kisses me.

My breath cuts off at the feeling of her lips against mine, soft and plump. Nothing today could have prepared me for this. I am unsure what I'd done that might've made me deserving of her lips. If electricity could shoot from her mouth and down every nook and cranny of my body, this is exactly how I imagine it feels. I stiffen and squeeze her hips in my hand, pressing myself harder against her.

I forget there are people around us, the sidewalk is visible, and anyone can walk past and see us. I forget about the woman and man standing meters away and that I only met Raelynn a few days ago.

The only thing that stays on my mind is keeping her here, against my mouth. She parts her lips slightly, allowing my tongue to break through the barrier her lips made to collide with her own. We explore each other, her soft breath brushing against my top lip as she exhales deeply. The piercing I'd admired minutes ago now grazes my tongue, the metal smooth, addictive, and cool, just like I imagined it would be. I suck on her bottom lip as she does so on my top, and right now, I want nothing more than to have her in my apartment, in my office, and on my desk—

My body burns, and my hand lowers down to her bare thigh just as she breaks away from the kiss.

I'm left panting, flustered, and a fucking mess that solely she has created.

She curls her lips into her teeth and darts her eyes low between us, clearing her throat.

I breathe. "What was..."

"Don't let it go to your head," she warns. "That was for her." She dips her head to the side at the woman I now remember is watching us.

Right, of course, it was. Why would it be for anything else?

"So, you're going along with my idea, hm?"

She breathes, whispering, "Only because I have no other choice. *Thanks to you*."

"Helloooo," the woman drags. "Amazing show, but I'd like to meet the cast!"

If she only knew of the act that we're pulling off right now.

Raelynn rolls her eyes. "She's my sister," she quickly informs. Then, she switches her face to a smile, a fake one. "Gia!" She names the woman. "Why didn't you tell me you were coming?"

She grabs my hand and threads my fingers into hers. I stare at them. Her chilling rings against my skin send a shiver up my spine. *Fucking hell.*

What did I get myself into?

Raelynn opens the gate, and on the other end is her sister, Gia, with a man holding her hand, who I'm assuming is the fiancé. He's shorter than me, which most people are. Not everyone's blessed with six and a half inches of height.

There's a wedding in a few months, I remember her mother saying. It must be theirs.

"I wanted to surprise you at your new apartment, but you weren't there, so I came here; it's the only other place you go around here," Gia answers, looking around at Raelynn's Garden. "This place always amazes me. How in the world have you kept up with all of this?"

The sisters hugged, and I turned to the man. He grins, and I extend my hand. He grabs it and pulls me towards him. I'm surprised momentarily, then quickly recover, giving him some pats on the back. "Nice to meet you. Milo, right?" He says as we part. I nod, and he tells me his name—Dallas.

But I find it hard to concentrate on what Dallas is fucking saying to me when Raelynn is at my side *caressing* my arm. I'm not sure if it's an anxiety thing or a part of her act, but her fingertips glide from my bicep to my wrist as she speaks to her sister. With her hand in mine, her body pressing into my arm, practically hugging it. She leans her head against my shoulder, and I slip my free hand into my khaki pockets, attempting to hide the visible bulge between my legs. I stay like that for the majority of the conversation.

"So, the wedding," Gia says to us both. "Inspired by my amazing sister, it's florist-themed. Don't forget, you know the date, be there!" She walks backward with Dallas towards their car.

Raelynn nods and waves her goodbye. "We heard you the last *four* times, Gia." But it's not loud enough for anyone but me to hear. The sister and fiancé get in the car and drive off.

As if the curtains closed and the audience isn't in view anymore, Raelynn turns to me, her smile drops, and her hand leaves mine. Instead, they get buried deep into the roots of her curly head of hair as she lets out a stress-filled sigh. She pulls on the strands so hard I nearly tell her to stop.

"I can't tell them yet," she says, releasing her grip and throwing her hands in the air. "About this not being real, about *you* not being real."

I raise an eyebrow. "So, what am I? Fake?"

She looks up at me with a dead expression. "You know what I mean. U*s* in this lie. God, I'm so sick of lies."

We start walking down the street that leads to our building, several minutes away. "We can always keep acting," I suggest. "You get to keep your charade for your family and me..."

She looks up at me. "You what? What would you gain from this other than having to '*be*' with someone you don't want to be with."

I look away from her. I don't think she could be any more wrong. I wanted nothing but to talk to her the second I stepped into the elevator. The desire to speak to her ate away at me, teaching me what it means to starve for someone. And here I thought being a teacher meant I knew it all. Though she's made it clear, she has no thought of us ever being something more than an illusion to her family. So, the thought exits my mind, and I find an answer to her question.

"My ex-girlfriend," I say. "We dated for a while; she quickly became a part of the family; my father loves her and wants me to marry the woman."

"What's the problem there...?"

"The problem is she's my ex for a reason. She's not exactly the most sane person, and getting rid of her is like getting rid of *mold*. She keeps coming back. I need to prove to her I've moved on, and—" I gasp for dramatic effect, looking down at Raelynn. "Here's my fake girlfriend to do just that."

I wrap an arm around her shoulders, and she rolls her eyes. If she keeps doing that, they'll get stuck that way, I swear it.

Raelynn huffs out a laugh through her nose. "So, you want me to run your ex-girlfriend away because.... what? She's too... obsessed with you?"

I pause. "Yes."

"Do you know how full of yourself you sound?"

"Love–"

"*Raelynn.*"

"Raelynn, when she realized I didn't want her anymore, she poked *holes* in our condoms with needles. If I hadn't caught her in the act, I'd be stuck with a baby from that woman. I'd rather live life in a cardboard box."

Raelynn's jaw drops. "Oh my God."

I nod. "The woman is fucking crazy, I'm telling you."

She hums. "Okay, fine. I run your ex-girlfriend away, and you help me convince my family I have my shit together." I nod in response. "But," she starts, "no touching me when you don't have to." She glances at my arm around her shoulders, and I take it off her, nodding. "No kissing when we don't necessarily have to, and *absolutely* no..." she pauses. "No... you know…"

I draw my eyebrows together at her loss of words. "No, what? *Sex*?" I fight the urge to smirk when her eyes dart away. "There, of course, won't be any sex, *Raelynn*." I laugh now, ignoring the fullness that still stretches out the material of my trousers.

Hopefully, Raelynn doesn't notice; she has a reputation for staring at my dick. She hugs herself with her hands as if suddenly becoming embarrassed. "Yeah, no sex."

I nod. "Deal." My hand slips from my pocket, and I hold it before her.

She takes it, her chilled rings rubbing against my skin as she shakes my hand. "Deal."

5

RAELYNN

I remember it so clearly. That day was two years ago.

At least I remember half of it clearly. The rest is all a blur.

That day was responsible for the change in me. The Raelynn that my mother once hated had died. It made me hide behind the leaves of plants, the smell of nature, and the distraction that planting and gardening gives. Because after that damn day, the simple touch of a man had made me hurl.

Not that I remember the exact moment when he took advantage of me, but cold, chilling water pools down my face from the shower head as I remember being drunk. I remember hanging out with him. I remember a cup getting handed to me. I remember him leading me to a bedroom before I blacked out. Then, the worst of it all—I remember waking up clothes-less, cold, and crying the next morning.

Only I knew how the pregnancy that followed weeks later had occurred. They thought I was being careless and sleeping around. And for the most part, before that day, I *had* been, but it was far from that. Mom made me get an abortion. It's all she ever made of the situation other than to remind me of how much of an embarrassment I was.

I didn't tell a soul what happened. Not my mother, sister, or best friends at the time. I never trusted anyone enough—never wanted anyone's pity.

He was popular, well-known, and liked. And I was known for being careless and wild, the Raelynn everyone was familiar with. Who would've believed a word I said? I didn't see it happen; I couldn't give any details. I missed the opportunity to go to the hospital. The blackout spared me the sight of the wicked act but also had rid me of my surety. To the point where even I questioned what I knew were facts. Nowadays, a woman needs *proof* for these sorts of things. Are the scars from his nails and scratches on my thighs not enough proof for them?

He's the reason for my sleepless nights.

Jaden Caddel.

I knew him for no more than an hour, but I guess an hour is all it takes for someone to decide your worth to them.

I sniffle, tears running down my face along with the shower's chilly water. God, can I get one day that I don't think about this shit? At least one restful night of sleep, so I don't look like the raccoon in my greenhouse the other day.

I turn the shower off, wrap my towel around my body, and catch a glance at the mirror. I pause to gaze at the reflection staring back at me.

Wet curls that end down the middle of my back drip water on the floor. My septum piercing glistens under the light, and the small ball of metal pierced into my tongue rubs against the room of my mouth. I got these piercings in high school and had to hide them from my mom for a few months. She still disapproves, but I'll never take them out; they're the part of me I sometimes miss, the Raelynn that didn't care so much. Along with the snake tattoo trailing up my thigh and disappearing under the towel.

My eyebrows jump as I dismiss myself from the shit show thoughts down memory lane. Then, I walk to my room.

I look at the clock perched on my brown dresser. Five in the morning. Wonderful.

I don't mean to be up this early. I just can't seem to sleep through the night. And I still have to open the new flower shop in just a few hours. I could try to fall asleep now, but I'll spare myself the hassle of staring at my ceiling.

The thought of Milo seeps into my thoughts as I rummage through my closet for clothes.

Besides my claustrophobia, being stuck with a man in an elevator increased my panic that day. I've gotten better at being around men; the closeness no longer turns me away or scares me. But I'll always keep my distance from them every chance I get. But Milo, I can't seem to understand why I don't distance myself from him. I tried, but he implanted himself into my life like a nail in a plank. And now I've agreed to fake this stupid relationship, and for some weird reason, the idea does not entirely repulse me.

A soft laugh leaves me, and I shake my head at the wildness of it all, pulling out fluffy pajama pants with pandas.

I willingly kissed him in my garden.

I can't help but feel proud of myself. I haven't kissed a man in two years. It's a step in the right direction, and Milo helped me without knowing it.

I pull off my towel and slip on my pants and one of my bleach-stained T-shirts. These kinds of shirts are the best; there's nothing better than wearing an old, worn-out shirt to bed. If only clothes came this way at the store—

A knocking startles me.

My chest tightens. There's no one around. I live alone, which in and of itself makes me paranoid. My eyes close, and a long breath leaves me, a weak attempt to calm my jumpiness.

I walk out to the front door and look through the peephole to see not a soul there.

My better judgment tells me not to open the door and check. I won't be one of those people in horror movies who die because of curiosity and cluelessness.

Instead, I lock my door and return to my room.

Another knock fills the silence.

I paused in my tracks. It's not coming from my front door. Looking at where the sound came from, I swallow hard as I stare at my fire escape window. The curtain covers it.

Maybe it's a bird or hail—No, not hail, it's the middle of April.

I pad my way to my closet and grab the bat inside it. Then, I walk towards my window, whipping the curtain open.

I scream.

He screams.

Milo sits on my fire escape behind my closed window in his most casual outfit yet, and his wide-opened eyes are on my bat.

His scream had muffled through the glass window. So do his words. I can't hear a thing he's saying.

I lower my bat, walking closer to the window. What the hell is he doing on my *fire escape*?

He raises his eyebrows, a hand gripping the center of his chest. Why is he acting like *I'm* the one who scared *him*? He's the one creeping on my fire escape.

His hair messily covers his forehead, but I know it's intentional. He wears a white shirt with gray sweatpants. Like I said, casual, yet unusual for him. That's especially true when I notice he's in socks.

Can this man get any crazier?

I attempt to read his lips.

Bat...

Sorry...

Scare you...

I shake my head as I follow his finger to the bottom of the window. He wants me to open it.

"No." I mouth. Absolutely *not*.

His head tilts slightly, mouthing the word, *why*.

My jaw could drop. What does he mean why? *Because you're a man on my fucking fire escape, and I don't know if I should trust you enough to let you in my apartment.* Duh.

I cross my arms around my visible breast under the material of my shirt to cover them from him, but he doesn't seem to be looking either way.

He nods after sitting for a minute. He mouths something, then gets up, starting down the stairs where his window is below mine. I inhale, leaning in and pulling the gate open, then the window, high enough for my body to stick out.

"Hey!" I shout, causing Milo to halt. He's just a few steps from his window, but I see him below through the rusted, chipped black painted metal bars. He looks up and beams that stupid smile at me.

"I thought you were dead," he says, walking back up. "It worried me."

I furrow my brows. "Why would I be dead?"

"You didn't answer your front door." I must've been in the shower when he knocked.

"What if I just... wasn't home?" I reason as he crouches in front of me, half my body till hanging out the window. I make it a mission not to let my eyes wander to anywhere other than his gray eyes.

"This early in the morning?"

I nod. "Some people work that early."

"Well, you clearly don't, since you're still here," his eyes trail down my half-visible body. I force myself not to shy away. "Cute PJs."

I huff. "Why are you on my fire escape? What do you want?"

"Do you have milk?"

"*Milk*?"

"Yes, milk," he grins. "You know that white substance. You swallow it, and it comes out of cows. It reminds me of—"

I close my eyes, raising my hand to stop that sentence before it ruins milk for me entirely. "*Don't*—"

"Vanilla. It reminds me of vanilla ice cream."

I roll my eyes. "And you couldn't just... go to the *store*?"

He shrugs. "And miss my chance at bonding with my fake girlfriend? Why would I do that?"

I slip back into my room. "You're ridiculous."

"I like your bottoms." I turn halfway to see him still outside, his eyes on my legs, or more so, my ass. I feel my face burn, whether from blush or insecurities, I don't know. "Pandas look good on you, Love. It's adorable."

I struggle to hold eye contact with him; eye contact comes naturally to him, it seems.

Love. I wonder if he calls everyone that.

"Stop staring at my ass," I say with a slight curve to my lip.

He only smirks.

I start to walk out of my room towards the kitchen when I pause and turn back to Milo, still sitting outside the window on the metal of the fire escape. I would've expected him to make his way in by now. But he only scales my room with his gaze.

"If you want..." I debate my next words for several seconds. He patiently waits for me to finish. "You can come in," I say.

He looks at me. "Yeah?"

I nod. "For your milk."

I watch him move to enter, but I walk up with a smirk, grab the gate, and shut it.

"Change of plans?" he says.

"Come in, but through the front door."

I watch his broad figure take the stairs to his window, his sweatpants riding low on his waist. I swallow. I can't deny it. He's an unbelievably gorgeous man.

Before completely disappearing, he glances up at my window, catching me gaping at him. Oh, for fucks sake.

He raises an eyebrow, and I roll my eyes, walking to my kitchen before he can torture me about my wandering eyes some more. I flick the lights on, leaving my front door open for Milo, and return to my kitchen. Flowers in flowerpots decorate the majority of it. It's a small kitchen, clean and stocked because I have no one but me to feed. Which isn't always a bad thing. Sometimes, I wish there were someone around to spend time with. I shake the thought of my loneliness out and open my fridge, grabbing the skinny milk jug.

I walk to the living room to see Milo sitting on my couch, his legs crossed, his feet on the coffee table, and arm under his head, watching the TV.

Who does this man think he is?

I roughly set the milk on the table, pressing my hand on my hip. "Get up. Now."

He darts his eye from the TV to me, then to the TV again. Then, to the posters hanging on my living room wall. *Spider-Man* posters.

"I didn't know you were a *spider-Man* fan," he says, ignoring me.

"Maybe that's because you know nothing about me," I walk in front of the TV that's playing the first *Spider-Man* movie. Then, I shove his feet off my coffee table, thanking God that they don't stink.

"Milo, I have a shift in a few hours. Here's your milk. Now leave," I demand.

He sits up getting off the couch. "Where do you work?"

I think over my words. If he had ill intentions, I would know by now, right? It's not like he means anything to me, nor do I want him to. Like he said, we're neighbors, acquaintances. Practically business partners at this point. And there's just something about him that I find unthreatening. If I'm being honest, nothing about this man is even threatening. The only thing he's successfully been is a pain in my ass.

"Flower shop a few blocks away." The words burst out of me. I take the milk back off the table just to have something to keep my hands busy with. I haven't had anyone else to share this exciting news with, and it feels good to spill this thing to someone I've been planning for over a year. "It's opening for the first time today, and I own it."

His brows raise like he just heard the most impressive thing. He walks around the coffee table, and I have to crank my neck as he gets closer. I take a step backward out of habit, but he doesn't notice.

My heart races as his eyes dart across my face, lips, and the milk in my hand. He slithers his long, soft fingers around my hands before reaching the container handle. I swallow.

"Congratulations, Raelynn. I'll see you in a few hours then."

"What? No—"

"Can you, by any chance, take me to your fire escape?"

"My window…?"

He nods.

Why on Earth does he want to see my window? I pivot one-eighty degrees, amazed at how strange this guy is, and walk to my room, where I raise my arm to show him the famous window, but he's already walking towards it. He slips his way in and on my fire escape, milk in hand. Is he allergic to front doors? He gives me one glance and a crooked smile as he makes his way down the stairs to his apartment fire escape.

I blink, jaw hanging wide, and burst into uncontrollable laughter, with snorts and a cackle I haven't heard in years escaping me.

Poor guy.

He must think he's Spiderman.

6

RAELYNN

"Dad, it's been three hours since the shop opened," I say, attempting not to cry. "Just give it time."

"And what if it doesn't work out? Then you've spent so much money on this flower shop that doesn't give any profit. I'm just saying, maybe you should reconsider working—"

I cut him off, "No, I'm not working at the *repair* shop."

His obsession with cars has been nonstop; working at his car repair shop several miles away is a generational thing. His father worked in the repair shop, and his *father's* father did, too, and so on. My dad's been trying to get me to work with him on cars for as long as I can remember. I'm probably more educated on the matter than a fucking mechanic, but it's never been something I wanted to do. Sometimes, I wonder if he wished he had a son instead of two daughters.

"It was just a suggestion," he sighs, and I hear metal rattling in the back.

A ringing cuts the silence as I water one of the flowerpots on my desk. I look at the landline sitting at the front desk, which brings in orders. I bounce in excitement.

"Gotta go, Dad, someone's calling," before he can say anything, I hang up and immediately pick up the shop phone.

"Rae's Flowers, Raelynn speaking. How can I help you?" My words are a little too high-pitched.

"I can practically see the grin on your face, love."

I immediately recognize the British male voice, and my smile drops to a scowl. I sit down in my desk chair and contemplate hanging up the phone. "What do you want? And if you're thinking about buying flowers, don't bother."

"Who said anything about buying flowers? I was checking how the shop's been doing so far." Milo says.

"Didn't you say you'd be here to see for yourself?"

He hesitates on his next words, "Do you miss me already?" His voice lowers to a low and rough tone, seductive even. A shiver trickles down my spine, and I swallow, shifting my executive chair from side to side.

"No, I'm glad you're not here, actually," I say spitefully. Whether that's true or false, I'm choosing to leave unanswered.

"Who said I wasn't there?" A soft laugh floats through the phone.

My eyes widen as I shoot my head up at the front door. It's shut now; people walk past the glass, but there is no sign of Milo anywhere.

"Don't look too excited to see me. You might break your neck." He jokes, somehow seeing my reaction from somewhere outside.

I stand up, embarrassed. He knows how terrible the shop has been doing if he's here. Not that I should care what he thinks, but I do.

"Please leave, Milo," I say, disappointed in myself.

"What's the matter?" He must've heard the tone of my voice drop, the assertion and confidence stripped like a bare bone. My throat tightens, tears threatening to break through.

I shake my head, whispering, "It's not going well." Sniffling, I walk towards one of my roses and fix how it sits in its boutique despite not needing fixing. "The shop, I mean."

He's briefly silent, and I look through the glass door, wondering where he is. Across the street? In a car? Possibly.

"How about you step outside," he says eventually.

"Unless you have pickles or something to give me, you won't be blessed with my presence."

"You like pickles?"

"Yes, but Kosher pickles are the only acceptable ones. And they have to be cut into, like, thin long slices, or else I'll struggle to eat it, and it gets messy quickly. Also, the blue top ones, Vlas—" Wait, why am I ranting to him about pickles?

"Go on," he says when he hears me cut myself off.

I shake my head, wiping away the trail of an earlier tear I'd let run down my cheek. "Never mind, it's not important."

"Says who?"

"Says..."

I hear him hum as if saying *I thought so.*

"Rae," he says. "I'd love to push you to continue this pickle conversation, but I think you'll feel better if you just step outside. You know how short New Yorkers' patience can be."

In the middle of pulling down my skirt that's ridden up from sitting, I freeze at his words. My heart begins to race.

"Milo..." I say for no reason as I practically run to the door and open it.

Stepping out, I stare at the line of people against my shop, taking up half the sidewalk. They talk amongst themselves, some laughing, others looking at the flowers out front. But all of them are waiting to be let in.

"That skirt is... a favorite of mine. The shirt, too." I nearly forgot he was on the phone.

I ignore him, looking at the woman first in line. She's fair-skinned, around my age, maybe younger, with long brunette hair. She wears a wide grin, and I notice the wedding or engagement ring on her hand.

"Hi, how long have you all been out here?" I ask her.

"Not long, really. Twenty or thirty minutes? We all assumed you were opening late since the sign on the door said *closed*. I'm back from college for spring break and decided to surprise my fiancé with some flowers!"

I gasp as I turn to look at the closed sign on the door. Then back at the woman. "I'm *so* sorry, we're open. I'm just stupid," I laugh and switch the sign, opening the door. Then I shout down the line of people, telling everyone that the shop is open. They all cheer softly. I beam at each of them as they file in, and then I stare at the nearby street, remembering Milo is still on the phone.

I bring the phone back to my ear. "Can you believe this?" I laugh into the phone.

A lady compliments my clothes, and I thank her.

Then I spot him. "Looks like you got some work to get to."

He's leaning against a car across the street, that black Tesla. He wears a black suit, one hand in his pants pocket with his feet crossed, staring right at me. He combs his hair back with his fingers, the warm wind causing a few strands to fall over his forehead, then lowers his head, looking at me through his deep-set eyes.

"I don't understand where they all came from," I say, looking into my store at the dozen people inside it, then at Milo. "You didn't have anything to do with it, did you?"

He shakes his head. "It was all you, love. I'm just here for moral support. Wipe your face. I can see your tears from here."

I breathe a laugh out. "Oh, shut up." But I wipe the tear lines off my face, then hang up the phone and give him one last look before he turns and opens his car door, getting in. A sense of sadness flashes over me as I watch him drive off. For a moment, a small part of me wanted him to stay and watch me work. I'm sure he's busy with his own life. The moment is gone as quickly as it came, and my smile grows. Turning around, I keep the shop door open and make my way to my customers.

"Hey!" The woman from the line says, stopping me with sunflowers in her hand. "These scream *sunshine*, right? Because my fiancé is a sunshine kind of guy," she says.

I nod with a smile. "Yeah, of course! I'll check them out for you over here."

I walk over to the cash register and spend the rest of the day keeping the shop clean and checking out boutiques of flowers while also answering questions and getting to know my hopefully casual customers. A restock is nearly needed, but by the end of the day, I'm fucking exhausted. I've been speaking about flowers for around eight hours with a grin on my face the entire time.

When I get to my building, the sun is beginning to set, casting an orange and yellow hue over downtown Manhattan, and the moon is almost up. My feet hurt. I don't think I sat down at all today; these stilettos might not have been the greatest idea. Despite it all, I'm still giddy with how great everything went. I have to make a mental note to call my dad and tell him I'm not a *complete* letdown like he might think I am. And to call Mom, even though she hasn't bothered checking in to hear about it at all.

Walking into the building, I look at Edna and wave. "Good evening, Edna!"

"Same to you. You're in a good mood, Ms. Garcia," she says, looking up from her crossword puzzle.

"It's a great day, is all."

I debated using the elevator or taking the stairs, remembering when I got stuck with Milo. It's a shame I live on the twenty-third floor. I walk towards the stairs despite the pain in the ball of my heels.

"Did you hear? They finally fixed the elevators. Mr. Evans brought in repairmen a few days ago."

I stop in my tracks and turn to Edna. "Mr. Evans... Milo, you mean?"

"Yes, the owner of this building, you were speaking with each other the other day. The elevator would break several times a week until he decided enough was enough a few days ago. Never seen him so eager to get something fixed so fast." The woman hums and resumes, looking back down at her crossword puzzle.

Mr. Evans? As in the man who teaches first graders and climbs up my fire escape, the Evans who's pretending to be my boyfriend, who got stuck in the elevator with me. The same Evans that I had kissed in my garden. Does he own this *fucking* building?

"Huh," I hum. "Is he home?" Edna keeps track of all the people in and out of this building. Especially people that don't live here. It's her job to know who's coming in and out and ensure no shady business is happening. It's one of the reasons I liked this building; the security is top-notch.

She shakes his head, laughing. "He came in an hour ago, then left. Not sure where to."

"What's funny?"

"Oh, nothing," she brushes me off with her hand.

The elevator in front of me opens, and a woman exits it with a kid of hers; I step in, saying my thanks and goodbye to Edna.

The elevator's empty, thankfully. My mind is racing still after all I've had to do today with the shop. I still have deliveries to pack and orders to process. I never thought things would go so well. My hand rubs over my now dirty skirt that's scrunched up too high on my thighs, and I pull it down. Milo had said he liked this outfit. I look down at my tight-cropped shirt, no bra on. I have a feeling on why he likes it, but instead of feeling gross to the bone after compliments, I smile as I replay his words in my head. I don't feel like crawling my body into a ball; I feel like flaunting myself. I shake my head and step out of the elevator, walking towards my door, where I see a small jar sitting on my welcome doormat. My head tilts as I step towards it, and the steady-paced clicks of my heels echo through the hallway. I bend to pick it up and turn it around. A jar of pickles. Kosher Vlasic pickles, with a red ribbon bow and a small square post-it note tied to it—my bottom lip curls between my teeth.

I flip over the note and read the nice handwriting on the other side:

Everything you say
will hold importance to me.
-Love, Milo.

Kayla Rose

7

Milo

"So, Milo, are you bringing the special lady to your father's celebration party?" My mother asks across the dinner table.

I swallow a sip of water, having my eyes rip away from the spec of rice falling on the tablecloth.

It's been three days since I dropped off those pickles for Raelynn. I wonder what she thought of them and my note, whether she ate or threw them away. What I wrote is true; I'm just hoping she believes it... platonically, at least.

I've been staying at my parent's house to look after my mother. She hasn't been well for a long time, not since her diagnosis with Leukemia cancer.

I shrug, having difficulty looking at her in the eyes knowing Raelynn and I are not an actual couple. Lying to her has always been difficult.

"Not sure if she'd want to go. She isn't used to this lifestyle." Neither does she know that my father is one of the wealthiest men in this city.

Morgan Evans. The Devil himself.

And I happen to be his son. Unfortunately, I wouldn't introduce my most hated enemy to that man if I had anything to do with it.

"Well, she is always welcome. I'd love to meet her," Mom says with a smile, followed by a series of whaling coughs that cause me to stand up from my chair at the dinner table. It screeches across the floor, and my heart nearly stops.

"*Mom*," I say, walking towards her.

From upstairs, I hear my sister's voice, "Milo! What's going on?" Her steps come racing downstairs, but my eyes are on Mom as she wheezes.

My breath shallows as I reach a shaking hand across the table for a glass of water and give it to her. "I'm calling 9-1-1."

She raises her hand, shaking her head. Her coughs have stopped, and she takes the cup of water from my hand and sips it.

"I'm fine, you guys. Just... got choked up on my rice, is all." She looks up, and I follow her gaze at the foot of the staircase across the house to Genesis.

Genesis stands tall, her eyes filled with tears and cheeks burning red. She's seventeen, my beautiful, kindhearted little sister. Jet black strands of hair fall over her face, sticking to her cheeks with the tears that have fallen them, her eyes trained on our sick mother.

"Gen, everything's fine—" I attempt to say, but she scoffs.

I press my lips together, knowing it wasn't just Mom choking on *rice*. She's sick, and she's been sick, and Genesis isn't stupid.

"What do you all think I am?" Genesis cries. "You can't just *lie* to me, all right? You can't just shut me out of what's happening with all of this. I hate it!"

I sigh, "How do you expect anyone to tell you anything if this is how you act? Like a *child*."

She steps closer to us, complicated steps, her hands in fists. "I'm not a *child*!" She snaps.

"Then stop *acting* like one!"

"You colossal *asshole*—"

"Enough!" Mom attempts to shout but strains her voice. "*Enough*. Milo, be kinder to your sister. She's trying her best. This is hard for all of us."

Genesis' eyebrows jump, "But not Dad." She says. I send her a glare, but she ignores it. "Where is he anyway? He's God knows where while his sick wife is at home?"

Mom stands up, and I help her out of her chair and follow her finger towards the living room couch.

"Morgan's at a meeting," Mom says, though she sounds like she believes that no more than any of us. Meaning, not at all. "He should be home soon."

I sit her down, ensuring she's comfortable and hydrated, before grabbing her pills from the bathroom to see Genesis gone, probably up in her room now. I know I should be easy on her, but being so dependent on mom her entire life, seeing mom so sick is hard. After I'm done, I make my way upstairs, mentally reminding myself to clean the dinner table.

Genesis door is cracked open slightly. I knock once and walk in to see her balled up on her bed, her back facing me. Her room is as decorated as the entire house is, to the T. A circle mirror sits above her bed, and picture frames of mom and her friends from a private school are on the side walls—a dresser on the opposite end.

"Get out," She mutters, not very convincingly.

"I'm sorry," I say, sitting beside her on the bed. "For keeping things about mom from you." I lean down on her pillows, and she slowly turns over, looking up at me with bloodshot eyes.

Her lip quivers as she speaks softly, "She's going to die, isn't she?"

I furrow my brows, shaking my head. "No, Gen, *no*. All right? She's fine, she's going to be fine." I take her head in my hand and bring her into a hug against my chest as she weeps, muffling her cries probably so Mom doesn't hear her.

It's been a year since the diagnosis, a long year of chemotherapy and doctor visits.

"She's going to be fine," I repeat once again, more for me than Genesis.

***

This morning, I woke up in Gen's room. Not that that's unusual; I've been forced to have sleepovers with her since she was around five years old and me thirteen. She never had other girls to play with; most of them were snobby bitches from a private school that I had to threaten a few times over the years.

If there's one thing to know about me, I'd go to *jail* for my sister.

"Milo, can you drop me off to track practice?" Genesis asks to enter my old room. It's been practically unused since I moved out and into the new apartment under Raelynn.

I shake my head, "I have to see someone today. Have you asked Morgan?"

"I'd rather *not* ask him." She enters my room and flops onto my bed like a starfish. I wrap my tie around my collar in the mirror and see her raise an eyebrow at me.

"Who're you seeing? You're new *girlfriend*?" She wiggles her eyebrows.

I bite back the urge to tell her to fuck off. " Mom wants her at that party tonight, so I'll have to ask her now or never."

She raises one brow. "You're seriously going?"

Halfway through the tie, I stopped my movements. "Not like I have a choice. Hey— do I look casual?"

I turn to face her. What better way to get women's advice than from another?

"Casual? Like normal New York citizen casual or a rich-ass-business-man casual?"

"The first one."

She shakes her head, gets up, and walks to my closet, which is still filled with old clothing. "You look like you're about to go to dinner with Elon Musk." Really?

She yanks out a few pieces and throws them on the bed: black slacks and a long-sleeve button-up.

"Wear that. It's the most casual set of clothes you have here. But don't girls like the rich-ass-business-man style?"

I take the clothes from the bed and sigh. "Not this one."

I dig in my pockets and throw her my car keys. She jumps and catches them and gasps.

"You're driving me?"

"You need to get your own damn driver's license already."

She squeals, running to hug me for two seconds before gagging at the hug and retracting herself from around me, running out of the room and probably straight to my car.

I shake my head, looking back at the clothes and thinking of Raelynn.

How long will she need me to fake this relationship for her? And when she doesn't need it anymore, what then? Do we stop speaking like nothing ever happened? Do we stay friends? For all it's worth, I'd rather not know the answer to that yet.

***

It's a little past noon when I drive up to Raelynn's garden right after dropping Genesis off at track practice.

It's the same garden she kissed me in. I honk to let her know I'm here by surprise. I need her number.

My mind goes back to that day, and I find my gut twisting at the thought of it. I close my eyes, leaning my head into my car seat. Her lips were so soft, so sweet against mine. Her slick, warm tongue glided with mine like butter, like they were meant to be together. I press a hand against the center of my slacks, against the bulge that's been created, and the pressure only turns me on more. I hiss, removing my hand and groaning, shifting in my seat. *Fuck me.*

"Milo?"

I jerk my body at the sound of my name. I put my arm on my bulge and look at Raelynn leaning on my window.

Her cleavage is on full display, and I feel like I might actually fucking pass out. They sit in a sports bra sort of top; overalls are the only thing covering her. But with her leaning over like this— *fuck.*

"My eyes are up here," she raises her brows, and I clear my throat.

"No— yeah, of course. I wasn't..." I feel my face burn, and I curse myself. And I curse Raelynn for being so... God damn sexy.

She bites her lip, and I have to look away at the road to contain myself. She's enjoying this too much for me.

"Right, well, if you're just sitting here to stare at my boobs, you can do that from afar while I plant," She says.

I almost take her up on her option. "Did you get the pickles?"

She nods, pushing a curl that falls over her face out of the way. "Yeah, thanks, by the way." Her voice softens.

I stare at her briefly before unlocking the doors, "Get in."

"Where to?"

"Just get in, and I'll show you."

She nips on her cheek from the inside as if nervous. "I'm dirty and wet, and I don't want to mess up your car."

"How wet?"

Stepping back, she shows me her soil-covered overalls that I've come to like—dark spots on the material shows where the water sits.

That's not what I meant.

But my eyes scale down her figure and I shrug. "My car will live." Reaching over the console, I push open the door.

Raelynn crosses her arms. "No, I'm not getting in there like this, Milo. I'm filthy. Wherever you're taking me, I need to change first.

I groan at her stubbornness and step out of my car, walking towards the trunk where I still have some clothes from the move. Opening it, I take out a white button-up shirt and sweatpants, shut the trunk, and walk around toward her.

"Here, wear these. We have an appointment to get to."

She grabs the clothes, and confusion crosses her face. "Appointment?"

"Mhm. Now go change, love." I walk away and around the front to get back into my car while Raelynn steps back into her garden to change.

She locks the front gate but doesn't go inside the greenhouse or little shed as I expected.

Instead, in full display to anyone walking past this street, she unbuttons her overall, letting them drop to her feet. She's left in her bra top and underwear, and I'm riled up more than I've been in a long time staring at the curves of her body.

Her bronze skin looks so soft, the round of her ass moving as she goes to step out of her overalls. Her locks of hair brushes against her shoulder blades, and my eyes scale up and down her body the entire time.

Slipping on my white button-up and going to button it over her breast, the end seam barely covers her ass.

She slips on my sweatpants, stringing them tight against her waist and tying it before turning to the gate and opening it back up.

She walks to me and steps into the car.

Her hands go up, she gathers her curls into a high ponytail, and I raise an eyebrow at her.

She glances at me, then grimaces, "*Gross*, don't even think about it. It's hot; I'm *hot*."

Yes, you are, darling.

"Think about what? I wasn't thinking about anything."

She rolls her eyes, the corner of her mouth rising, "*Right*."

She shuts the door and pulls her seatbelt down, and without a second to spare, I press down on the gas, driving into the street.

All while living through the pain that resides between my legs.

Love, Milo

8

MILO

"You're what?" she exclaims from the passenger seat as I drive.

"I'm taking you to buy a dress for my father's celebration party tonight," I repeat myself. "Believe it or not, we made a deal to fake a relationship."

I look away from the road to glance at her, arms folded over her chest, angry for some reason. Before I can ask her what's gotten her upset, she speaks.

"When were you planning to tell me you own that *building*?" She questions. "If you think I'm going to some preppy party filled with a bunch of old rich white men, you're wrong."

I stop the car, traffic holding up the cars, and turn to her. "I don't technically *own* the building; my father does. And I don't like the men at his parties either, but I have to go." Traffic clears up a bit, and I step on the gas.

"Fine," she says. "I'll go with you,"

I smirk. "Yeah?" That was easier than I thought—

"But you have to get me whatever I want today." She crosses her leg over another, and I notice the challenge on her face, the smug expression, knowing I can't say no.

"As if I could ever say no to that face," I mutter sarcastically.

She laughs excitedly and claps twice as we stop at the dress store. I park and unbuckle my seat belt, getting out of the car. Shutting the door and walking around to Raelynn's door, I see her struggling to unbuckle herself from the seat.

I pull the door open, and she huffs, looking at me, "It's stuck."

"Clearly," I smile, bending over and in the car. I place a hand on her shoulder to steady me while my other arm wraps around her waist to find the seatbelt lock. I feel her body flinch as my hand glides over her stomach.

I tug at the seatbelt, causing her to shift and bounce. A smirk rises as I look at her, purposefully taking longer than necessary to unbuckle her. Her breath fans against my chin, and I force myself not to groan.

We don't speak; I don't think either of us *can*. We only scale our gazes across each other's faces. I know she feels it, the electricity flowing between us. Leaning in and tilting my head, I close my eyes—

She clears her throat, licks her lips, and turns away. I press my forehead against her temple briefly and mentally curse myself.

Maybe she doesn't feel anything, and I imagine it all.

"Did you... uh, do it?" Her hips shift, and I clear my throat as well, freeing her from the seatbelt.

"Come."

She nods and steps out. I close the door behind her before walking into the dress stop.

Immediately, her face changes. Her eyes trail over the entire store and at all the dresses that hang around, a sparkle twinkling in each eye.

"What's my budget?" She asks me.

Budget? "Didn't you say I was supposed to get you whatever you want?"

"Yeah, well, I didn't think you'd take that *seriously*," she laughs briefly.

I shake my head, unbuttoning a button of my shirt, the heat getting the best of me in this place. "There's no budget, love." I find a seat and sit down, manspreading and leaning back against the wall. "You could buy the whole store. It wouldn't hurt my pockets."

She looks around once, then backs down at me. "Really?"

"Go at it, Rae."

She bites on her bottom lip, and then she's gone the next thing I know.

For the next two hours, I've been stuck in this hot fucking store, my eyes tracing Raelynn around, zigzagging through the dress racks. At some point, she pulls me up from the seat by my hand and makes me walk behind her around the store, asking me for my opinion on dresses. I told her yes to each one she asked me about. I didn't know women could talk for such a long time about clothing, but Raelynn did, and I listened to every word of it.

And when I thought we were done, she dragged me to the changing rooms—eight dresses in her hands.

"I'll be quick, I promise," she says. " I just have to try them all on first."

I sigh. "You said that three times already, an hour ago."

"*Yeah, yeah*," she brushes off.

I sit in front of her dressing room as she goes in and shuts the door.

Is this what it's like to have a regular girlfriend?

My phone in my pocket begins to ring, vibrating against my thigh. I slip it out of the pocket of my slacks. On the screen reads a name I hoped I wouldn't have to think about for another two hours.

I answer, bringing the phone to my ear "Father."

"Milo," Morgan greets, his voice low and intimidating to everyone but me. At least not anymore. "How was your mother while I was away last night?"

"You'd know if you were there *with* her. Where were you, dad?" I sit up, leaning my elbows on my knees.

"A meeting, not that that's any of your concern."

"Bull-fucking-*shit*. There aren't any meetings that last the entire fucking night, *Dad; where* the fuck were you?" I hush my voice so Raelynn doesn't hear.

"I think you're mistaken about who you're talking to, boy." He sharpens his tone but stays at a neutral volume. "I'm your father. I'm the source of your money. I'm the reason you're alive. You don't *fucking* question me, you hear me? I gave you all that you have, and I can take it away faster than you think. Do you understand me?"

I shake my head, dropping it between my shoulders, feeling my eyes burn.

"I asked you a question. Do you *understand* me?" His voice rises in volume.

"Yes, sir," I whisper.

He sighs. "Good. Then I'll see you tonight, and we can continue this conversation then." The line goes dead as soon as the words leave his mouth.

I watch my tears drop to the floor of the dressing room, and I sniffle, gripping the back of my head and pulling at a few strands of hair. My eyes shut as I pull harder until I yank out the strands. The sharp pain zips through my body. My hand comes down, and I look at the few dozen thin, long pieces of hair lying on my palm and then watch as they drift in the air and fall to the floor.

"Milo, look at this one—"

I look up at Raelynn exiting the dressing room in front of me. She's wearing a shiny red dress that reaches her ankles, thin straps, and a low neckline. It clings to her body and every curve and dip. But when my eyes reach her face, her smile drops at the sight of me. Fuck.

She furrows her brows in worry, walking towards me. "Milo? What's wrong?"

I shake my head, "Nothing."

"Yeah, nothing, my ass," she whispers, sitting on the floor in front of me, her knees down first and her bottom sitting on her feet.

I grip her arm. "Rae, please, get up off the floor."

She lifts a hand to my face, ignoring my words, and trains my face to look down at hers. And that's what I do.

I look at her. Every corner of her face, my eyes glide over. The septum piercing hanging from her sharp nose, the long natural lashes curled up from her eyelids, the way her brown eyes flick between mine like they're watching the most intriguing thing. The long curls fall over her shoulders and partially over her face. I look at her.

"What happened? I was in there for about five minutes. I come back, and you're a crying mess." Her soft hand and cool rings on my cheek are the only things I can think about now. But something clicks in me.

I put a hand over hers and slid it away from me. A frown appears on her face.

I shake my head, leaning in closer to her. "Don't pretend to give a shit. Caring wasn't in the deal."

"I'm not—"

I lean back. "Pick a dress, Raelynn. We don't have to bond, neither do we need to be friends. We don't have to do anything but *pretend* and follow your rules. Because that's what this is, right? Us pretending?"

Her lips part as she twists her jaw and scoffs, getting up. "This is what I get for trying to be nice to men like you."

"Men like me? And what's that supposed to mean." I stand up as well, following her. She doesn't answer.

I take hold of her hand and her hip, spinning her around.

But she snatches her hand out of mine. "Men who take things for granted because all they've ever wanted they could get with no problem."

"Don't *assume* my life was rainbows and butterflies. You know nothing about me or my life, darling."

"But I do know this. I will not be your pawn to abuse when you're having a little *bitch* fit, Milo. If that's what you see me as, then yes, this is nothing but a game of pretend."

A moment passes, her words lingering, scarring my chest, before she walks into the dressing room and shuts the door in my face.

I pace around, rubbing a hand down and over my chin, feeling the tiny hairs of my beard brush against my palm.

From the side, a worker asks, "Is everything all right?" She questions.

I turn to her, steam practically coming off me. "*Out*."

"Everything's fine!" Raelynn shouts with the friendliness from behind the door.

The woman's eyebrows jump, and she walks away.

Seconds later, Raelynn steps out in a black dress, short and long-sleeved and sculpted just for her, at least that's what it seems like. It covers her shoulders, but its neck is squared off, showing a large amount of cleavage. The bottom seam meets the start of her thighs. If she bends over, anyone behind her will see *everything*. And I have a feeling that's exactly what she was looking for. She holds the other dresses neatly folded in her hand along with the clothes of mine she wore and shoves them into my chest.

"I want *all* of them," She decides, walking away.

I watch the back of her figure, her high heels clicking on the tiled floor, the singular sound breaking the silence and joining the tension between us.

9

RAELYNN

I was trying to be nice.

My head rests on the window of Milo's car as he drives wherever this party is. We left the dress shop a few minutes ago after I stormed out. My dresses sit in the back seat. I should've gotten more. The buildings and streets illuminated by the orange sunset blur together as the car drives on.

My arms stay crossed, and I rub the goosebumps on my skin caused by the steady stream of cold air from the central console.

"Are you cold?" I hear Milo's question.

I don't answer him. No fucking shit, I'm cold; I'm not just hugging myself for no apparent reason.

He clicks the cold air off, reading my mind, turning on the warm air. Immediately, it satisfies my body, causing a sigh to seep out of my nose.

"Raelynn," he calls out softly. His voice scratches the back of my head, slipping down and through my body.

Why does my name on his tongue have to feel so damn good to hear?

His hand falls from the steering wheel, reaching over to rest on my thigh. I force myself not to flinch at the touch of his hand, but my body reacts in other ways.

His fingers stop against my inner thigh, a softness to his hand that makes places tingle that shouldn't be tingling. The flat of his thumb brushes against the side of my thigh, and he squeezes me.

I haven't been or let anyone touch me this way—in a place so intimate—in over two years. Then again, I haven't let anyone but Milo touch me at all, either…

"Rae, talk to me, please," He pleads. "Or else I might go crazy from your silent treatment."

I stare at his hand from hiding behind my hair. Veins travel around the back of his hand; my eyes trace them up his wrist, under the watch that probably cost more than my life expenses, and disappear under his sleeve. His fingers are so long and so well-kept.

My stomach twists at the movement of his hand. It's only a tiny movement, yet I'm going absolutely feral. I turn my head away, letting out a breath.

Control yourself, Raelynn.

"Do you want me to beg for forgiveness?" He asks. "Is that what you want?"

I shrug my shoulders, "Maybe." A blurry circle appears on the window caused by my breath hitting it.

He laughs briefly, nearly muttering, "You'd like that, wouldn't you?"

"Yes, and make sure you're down on your knees while you're at it," I say sardonically, rolling my eyes.

I glance at Milo, his jaw tense, and his hand on the steering wheel, turning it in a circle with one motion to turn a corner.

He clears his throat, squeezing my thigh before letting go, pulling at the center of his slacks, and shifting in his seat.

"You sure have a way with words," He whispers. My brows furrow, but I brush it off.

Silence falls upon us again for the remainder of the ride until he stops in front of a large complex building. He stops the car, parking as I stare at the surrounding area. Downtown Manhattan is surrounded by other expensive-looking cars parked at the sides of the streets. Standing in front of the building are people dressed like a million dollars.

He turns the car off. I look at him as he reaches into his back seat for a suit jacket. He slips it on himself, and I bite my lip nervously.

I've never been to anything like this before. What if I say something wrong? Or do something that's looked down upon?

Milo grabs his phone and slips it in his pocket, then turns to look at me, doing a double take. He stops his movement. "Just stay at my side and look pretty, love."

He pushes his door open and shuts it, walking around and opens my door. Without me saying anything, he unlocks the seatbelt from around me and takes my hand to help me out of the car. I roll my eyes, going along with his gentlemanly act.

I step out gracefully, and his eyes follow me with a smirk on their faces, shutting the door and locking it with a beep of the car keys.

"Is there anything I should know before we enter? About... Y'know, what to say?" My voice still holds annoyance from earlier. He throws his finger between mine, and we fall in line with each other steps. My heels click on the concrete below.

"I told you what all you needed to do several seconds ago." We make our way up the front stairs; several people wave at him and give me a curious glance.

"Just look pretty?" I repeat what he said quietly. That doesn't give me nearly enough reassurance.

"Mhm," He opens the door for me, and I walk into the lobby. He tugs at my hand and bends his head beside my ear, his other hand resting on the small of my back. A hot line of electricity travels down my spine.

"You're the prettiest woman here, Rae," He whispers against my neck. "You have nothing to worry about."

My cheeks burn, and goosebumps rise on my skin despite being warm.

He rises from beside my neck, his cheek brushing against my jaw; the roughness of his shallow stubble against me makes me shiver. He stops just far enough for us to look at each other. I watch his eyes trail down to my lips, his hand pressing into my back and closing the distance between our chests. My lips part, and I find it hard to breathe with him so close, my eyes heavy like two bricks sitting on them.

"Milo!" A female British voice breaks the dreadful tension between us, and his arms loosen from around me.

I bite my lip, looking away and down at the floor momentarily to regain the composure I lost moments ago.

A weight lifts off my chest, allowing me to breathe regularly again, and blood rushes back to my face.

Milo keeps a hand pressing into the small of my back as a petite, tall girl walks over to us. She holds her arms up with a wide grin at the sight of Milo. A long black dress hangs from her figure, a slit in the leg of it on the side. Looking around the lobby, I notice that neutral colors are the safe option for this party. Thank God I went for black and not the blue dress.

The girl hugs Milo, and he groans, "Genesis, you saw me not even twelve *hours* ago."

He lets go of the girl, and she pushes his shoulder. "Shut up. I was sick of being around people I hate, and it's only been an hour into the party."

An hour? Are we late?

The girl, who looks no more than eighteen, give or take an age, looks at me, and her eyes widen with a smile.

"Okay, holy shit, *woah*," She curses, her British accent dripping off her words just like Milo's. She looks at Milo, "You pulled *her*? How in the world—"

Milo shoves her shoulder with minimal force, "Gen, fuck off."

She giggles and extends her hand to me. "Hi, I'm Genesis, Milo's little sister."

I shake her hand. "I'm—"

"Raelynn Garcia, I know."

My mouth stays parted, and she laughs again, "Milo hasn't shut up about you."

I look up at a pink-faced Milo, his tongue poking at the inside of his cheek in frustration.

"Oh really?" I laugh briefly.

Milo grips my waist closer to him, bringing me along to an elevator he starts to walk towards. "Gen, why are you down here terrorizing me instead of being upstairs with Mom?"

"I saw your car from the roof and wanted to say hi to Raelynn, Mom with Dad."

The elevator door opens, and all three of us step in.

Milo sighs, keeping me planted at his side like his cane. Like I'm the only thing keeping him from collapsing.

Genesis starts to talk with Milo about a track team she's in and how well she did this morning. Milo congratulates her, and so do I. It's nice seeing their relationship. I wish I had a relationship like that with Gia.

The elevator door opens seconds later, noise oozing through the door, and my eyes widen instantly.

The party's on a *roof.*

Stepping out, I feel my body tense as I scan the several dozen people across the entire top of the roof. Soft music plays, and lightbulbs drape from poll to poll a few feet above our heads. A soft breeze brushes past us as we walk further in. My heart aches, and anxiety I wasn't ready for takes over.

I squeeze Milo's hand, the only thing keeping me sane.

He looks down at me. "You all right?"

I only nod.

Genesis, at some point, wanders off, and Milo walks around with me in his hand. Several people stop to greet him and talk about some position his fathers had gotten, congratulating him. They'll turn to me and wave and state their names, but I'd forget moments later. There are too many names and too many faces. I throw on a fake smile the whole time, keeping at Milo's side, with his hand being my only source of heat.

"Well," an older woman who's been talking with Milo says, looking at me. "Lovely dress."

I snap out of my thoughts and smile. "Thanks. You look... dashing." That's formal, I think. My eyes scale down her outfit, a dress that fits her... old age.

Milo lets go of my hand, and I look up at him. He places a hand on my shoulders. "I'll be back. I'll grab you something to drink."

Nodding okay, mentally preparing to be left alone, Milo lifts his finger under my chin and my head so I can look at him—and only him—directly.

His head bends, and he kisses the corner of my mouth. My heart jumps and sets off a minor explosion. I should pull away. But why? Isn't this us acting? It does mean anything, and it's a part of our deal.

Besides, no one said I couldn't *enjoy* it.

His kiss only lasts a moment, but the feeling in my chest stays much longer.

The reminder that this is all an act scratching at the back of my head.

I smile his way before he walks around me and into the crowd of black suits and fancy wine glasses. My smile drops, and I let out a long breath, leaning against the rooftop banister.

The woman, whom I nearly forgot was still beside me, laughs. I look at her and sip the wine in her glass.

"Sweetie," she chuckles. "I know we may look like we stepped out of a million-dollar family of an old black and white film, but no one uses the word *dashing*."

My eyes dart between her wrinkling green ones, "I..." I laugh, but it lacks humor. "I was just... being—" *Nice.*

"Oh, and I know this is your first Evans party, but next time maybe think of wearing something a little less... *slutty*. It isn't a good look on my grandson." She huffs a tired laugh.

"*Excuse* me?" My heart hammers at my chest; I can hear it thumping in my ears.

Grandson.

She waves a hand at me. "We all here know how little experience Milo has with women. He'll pick one out of a trash can and call her amazing if it wasn't for our insight." Her gaze travels from head to toe, and I'm lost for words.

Humiliation doesn't exactly describe how I feel. Nothing has made me want to shrivel up into a ball and get kicked off this roof more than this older woman's words about a relationship that isn't real.

The degrading words that remind me of my mothers.

My eyes sting, and I stare at her as she waves and walks away. Leaving me alone, shattered as one of the many wine glasses dropped on the floor.

I choke out a cry as I look down at my outfit. I thought I looked cute.

My face burns and boils scream boils at my core, but I swallow it. I swallow my cries and swallow my tears.

I shouldn't have come. Going home should've been my first thought when Milo stupidly commented about pretending. What was I thinking? Coming to this party filled with people I don't know in an unfamiliar community.

Not to mention Milo's Grandmother is a cruel *fucking* bitch.

I avoid eye contact with everyone as I attempt to approach the elevator we arrived on an hour and a half ago.

But someone rams into me, and I gasp as a sticky liquid of whatever they were drinking spills all over my chest and dress. The coolness of it uncomfortably runs down between my tits.

"Shit!" The man that rammed into me hisses. "Bubblegum, I'm so sorry—"

I don't even look at him, not that I'd be able to, with the tears blurring my vision.

I keep walking, tears streaming down my face now. Fuck this party, and fuck everyone here. Everyone including—

Gasps are heard from several people around me, and I turn around at the sound of glass shattering. In mid-action, I see Milo, his fist colliding with the man who had spilled me with his wine, the glass now shattered on the floor.

Several people shout at Milo to calm down. His sister, Genesis, holds a hand over her mouth, looking at her brother in shock.

"Milo, seriously?" Genesis shouts. But he steps right into the poor man's bruised face.

I'm close enough to hear exactly what he snarls. "Watch where the *fuck* you're going next time, Logan." His eyes were hard and gray, like a storm cloud at night.

The man—Logan—shoves Milo, and he barely moves a step back. Logan, who's just as broad, with his tie loosened, unbalanced on his feet, and clearly under the influence of alcohol, shoves Milo's chest.

"Fuck you, man! You wann— wanna act tough now that you have a girlfriend to show off? Hm?" He pushes Milo again, but Milo catches his wrist, lowers it, and grabs Logan—who he seems to know well—by the collar.

A circle has been created around them, women shouting and worried and the men afraid to intercept. My feet stay planted on the floor, unsure of what the hell to do.

"You're drunk, Logan. I don't want to hurt you."

Logan laughs, "A little fucking late for that, don't ya think?" His hand whips up and meets Milo's cheek with his knuckles, and I gasp, my hand coming over my mouth.

The brawl starts again, only to be halted by a loud shout from an older man.

"Boys!" The voice seems to shut everyone up, including Milo and Logan.

I see Milo glance at me once, not even a second long, but it still makes me feel all too responsible for all of this. He punched him because Logan bumped into *me*. Logan wouldn't have bumped into me if I had *stayed* where I was.

The older man walks between the two, facing Milo. "You know better than to embarrass me at my own party." Everyone stares, listening at who I soon realize is Milo's dad.

Yet, no British accent laces his voice, only an American one, just like his grandmother had.

His dad looks towards me. Despite me not meeting him the entire night, he seems to recognize and know who I am.

He points straight at me and looks at Milo. "Take her *home*. You've done enough damage because of her already." My face goes red; heat surrounds me like it would if I were floating above a volcano. Maybe I am—or maybe I'm standing on the top of a building from hell.

If steam could come out of humans, Milo would be fuming. His face read agitated, looking like he could punch the nearest person in his face—his dad.

But he doesn't; he steps aside, shoulder bumping into his father, and walks towards me.

I mash my lips together, curling them into my mouth, embarrassment flooding over me as eyes fall on us.

He grabs my hand just as I whisper to him. "Are you alright?" I look at his busted lips. "I'm so sor—"

I don't get to finish. Milo grips my hips, bringing me flush against his hard front, where he slams his lips into mine forcefully and with steadiness. My hand squeezes his bicep, my eyebrows jumping high.

Oh my *God*.

His hand travels to the back of my head, cupping it as he moves his mouth against mine. The metallic taste of blood seeps onto my tongue. Then he parts.

"Don't be sorry," he whispers before looking towards everyone watching, stunned at all that's just happened.

"If you haven't met her already, this is Raelynn Garcia," he says loud enough for the entire party to hear, wiping the flat of his thumb against the corner of his mouth. "My girlfriend. And if you have a problem with that…" he laughs bitterly, staring directly at his father. "by all means, let me be the first to know."

10

RAELYNN

The elevator door closes, and the silence falls heavy upon us.

I wipe my eyes with the back of my hand, replaying everything that just happened, just to make sure I didn't imagine it all.

Milo at my side sighs through his nose roughly, letting go of my hand and pressing his back against the elevator. His eyes stay closed, and his hand is bleeding I realize, the knuckles busted along with his lip.

I tuck a curl behind my ear and sniffle, "He did it by accident, Y'know." My voice is timid, rough from crying.

Milo raises his head and shakes it. "Logan does nothing by accident. I saw you walk away, and then I saw him walk directly in front of you. He spilled it deliberately."

I press my lips together. So much for *that*.

"Why did you run off anyway?" He questions.

I think about telling him what his grandmother said, the horrible things that came out of her mouth, but I think better of it, he's already had a hectic night, something tells me adding that to the pot will make him go back up there with no hesitation.

So, I shrug. "Nerves..."

The elevator dings, saving me from continuing this conversation. We walk out silently and make our way to his car out front. He opens my door, letting me in, and I buckle up as someone calls Milo's name.

He turns around from beside my door and I see Genesis and a woman. She's not very old, maybe late forties at most, but something about her appearance catches my eye instantly, and it's the fact that she's bald. She holds Genesis's arm and is smiling at Milo. By the way, her eyes are shaped, and her lips resemble that of both Genesis and Milo's; this is their mother. I'm sure of it.

Milo speaks, "Mom." *Bingo*. "What are you doing down here? Aren't you going home with Dad?"

The lady waves her hand. "I'm here to praise you. You're also riding your sister and me home. I've had enough of your father for one night." Her British accent is thicker than that of both her children. It makes sense now why Milo's accent isn't the strongest British accent ever and why he even has one to begin with.

"Praise me?" Milo opens the back door and helps his mother in.

Genesis waves at me from the side door, and I wave back. Her dark brunette waves brush against her shoulders.

"Of course, for sticking up for this darling before us. Were you not going to introduce me to her? Embarrassed of your dear old mum, hm?"

He stutters for a moment and scoffs annoyingly at her words. I turn around in my seat to face his mom as he speaks. "Don't say that. Mom, this is Raelynn. Raelynn... my mom."

I extend my hand and grin. "It's nice to meet you... Mrs. Evans."

She scoffs, shaking her hand. I don't miss the fact that her hands are jittery and cold to the touch. "Pfft. Call me Iris."

I nod. "Iris. Got it."

Milo sighs, shutting the door after Genesis gets in the back seat and then makes his way to the driver's seat.

Genesis starts to say how crazy the night has been; she also thanks me for being there and how Logan is a jerk. Just having the company of these two women makes me feel a whole lot better about the situation that happened. I let out a few laughs while Milo drives.

"Mom," Genesis says.

"Yes," Iris sighs. Yet, I can tell she enjoys her time with her daughter.

"What do you do to get a robot mad?"

"I don't know."

"You push all its buttons!" I watch Genesis in the back seat through the rearview mirror and begin to wheeze at her terrible joke, and it makes me giggle.

"You get it? Raelynn? Milo, you get it?" She leans forward between our two seats and looks at Milo's side profile.

Milo grumbles, "Yes, Genesis, we get it. You're beginning to push *my* buttons."

"Oh, shut up, your sense of humor is dryer than a burnt toast, you jackass—"

"*Language*," their mother intervenes.

Milo turns his head to say something, but I speak. "I have a joke for you, Genesis."

She grins. "Tell me."

"What do a tick and the Eiffel Tower have in common?"

She hums in question.

I giggle. "They're both *Paris sites*."

Genesis cackles, "Just like Milo!"

I laugh with her. My cackles and Genesis wheezes fill the car while Milo drives with low eyelids. Even Iris laughs silently as she stares out the window, shaking her head. For a moment, I forget about what happened; I forget the words that were said to me and the wine that dirties my skin. I spend the next few minutes in the car joking with Genesis.

"Hope you two are having fun," Milo mutters.

"I'm having the time of my life, you parasite," Genesis snickers.

Milo glances at me as he stops in front of a building, the headlights turning off. His face reads, *look what you've started.* I twist my face and shrug my shoulder as if saying, *oops*.

He reaches over to unbuckle my seatbelt, juggling it and me so it can come loose. However, he takes longer than usual, long enough for Iris and Genesis to get out behind us and shut the doors.

"Thank you," he says a second after their doors close.

I furrow my brows. "For what?" Making fun of him with his sister and mother for fifteen minutes straight?

"I haven't seen them smile and laugh like that in a long time. Especially my mother." His eyes dart between mine, the seatbelt coming undone between us. He slips it back to where it retracts from, his hand sliding across my body to do so.

"Oh..." I breathe in, looking down at your hand. A stutter breaks up my words, "of course."

"Milo!" Both of our heads turn to Genesis' frantic call for help from outside.

Milo darts out of the car, and so do I. Something's wrong. Milo runs beside his mother, who's bent over, coughing a strong and harsh cough.

"Mom! Mom, are you alright?" He holds her up, and Genesis lets go, backing up with a twisted face, eyes tearing.

I walk to her, not knowing what else to do, and take her hand in mine. She's not as tall as me, but she doesn't hesitate to bury her head into my shoulder, hugging me despite just meeting me. I let her body sink into mine, wishing I could make things better, but I don't have a clue what's even going on. I watch Milo and his mother; she coughs for several seconds before stopping and standing up straight. Milo goes through several questions with her to ensure she's alright enough to go upstairs. His face wears the most worry I've ever seen on him.

Genesis cries quietly in my arms, and I feel her shake. "She's fine, see?" I whisper.

Genesis shakes her head. "She's sick, Raelynn. Really sick. You wouldn't understand." I know she doesn't mean harm as her words fade with her sniffles, wiping her eyes dry. I don't respond because she's right. I don't understand. I've never wanted to understand something more. We follow Milo onto the elevator of this building that I've yet to recognize; it must be Iris's home. My deal with elevators I ignore for the time being. There are more important things to worry about, and there is not enough room in my head to think about the space I'm in. Once we get into the apartment, he tells me he's talking his mother to bed, then orders Genesis to show me the bathroom.

After he's out of sight, my eyes fall on the jaw-dropping sight of the house or the penthouse. It's large, with two floors and spacious windows overlooking New York City. The living room is gigantic, with a chandelier hanging from the high ceiling that illuminates the space just enough to see enough, to make the furniture glow dimly and faces show, but not bright enough to the point where it's overpowering.

I've always wanted ceiling-to-floor windows; it makes the rooms feel enormous, less like you're in a box and more like you are floating in the outside breeze. No matter how many flowers I sold, I couldn't afford a place like this.

It makes me wonder why Milo would live in the apartment under me when he could live *here*. Or why does he teach when it doesn't seem like he has to work a day in his life?

"Raelynn, come this way." Genesis snaps me out of my admiration of the house and guides me to the bathroom.

It's, of course, beautiful in here, just like the rest of the house. "You can strip in here and throw it in the laundry basket. I'd give you some of my clothes, but..." she looks at my body and sighs. "You seem a lot more developed than me."

I tilt my head, watching the red eyes she's gotten from crying. "That isn't always a good thing. It's a blessing and curse."

She shrugs. Then sadly mutters, "Yeah, but not to high school boys. They rarely see it that way." She shakes her head and tells me she's going to bed before I can say anything more.

I'm left alone in a large bathroom, a tub on one end and a shower on the other, with white and gray decorations. The floor below my feet is glossy with a pattern, unlike my tiled floor bathroom back at home.

An isolated burgundy bathtub is the only splash of color in this room. However, it suits the look. A bathroom for a queen, it seems like this was made for. I can't get over how polished everything is: the white marbled sink counters, the walk-in shower in the corner. Even the porcelain sink makes me feel too dirty to touch it. I walk towards the shower and turn it on.

I haven't showered in someone else's house in years, not after what happened.

But weighing my options of bath or shower, I make my way into the shower, trying my hardest to avoid that memory or *lack* of memory. The warm water runs down my chest, dripping down my neck and breast. I look down at my stomach and then my thighs, the white scars scaling around my area.

I was thankful my dress was long enough to cover them all, or else I wouldn't have worn it.

I close my eyes to make the thoughts disappear, but the images appear.

Images of me waking up, eyes blurry with sleep, my head pounding. Naked and scared, everything hurting—blood, *blood everywhere.* I gasp in a sharp, needed breath of air along with some streams of water, open my eyes, and slap a hand over my mouth to prevent myself from screaming. Coughs replace the urge to cry. My entire body trembles under the water, and I grip the bar connected to the wall, silently allowing myself to shed silent tears.

Wet curls fall over my face, and I sob, muffling cries against my palm so no one outside could hear.

I've once been told healing takes time, but it's been two fucking years, and yet it hurts every time I close my eyes. He probably doesn't think of it at all, let alone as much as I do.

"Rae," I hear Milo call from behind the bathroom door. "Gen said you needed clothes. I'm leaving my shirt and sweatpants on a hanger on the doorknob.

I clear my throat. "Thank you."

After several deep breaths, I shake away the thoughts and clean myself, braiding my hair into two rows down my head after realizing I don't have my products here.

I shut the water off and grab a clean towel under their sink.

Like Genesis said to do, I throw my dress in the laundry basket sitting in the corner and open the door just a bit, peaking out at the doorknob to see the clothes Milo said he left behind: black shirt and gray sweatpants.

I put them on over my underclothes and make my way out into the hallway.

Now, to find my way to Milo... not a problem, just walk around the million-dollar-looking apartment and hope not to get lost.

And getting lost is exactly what I do for at least five minutes before I come across an open door. I nearly walk past it until I see Milo sitting on the edge of the bed, his elbows digging into his thighs and his head low, hands connected at the back of his neck.

I step in slowly, knocking twice on the door to announce my presence. He turns his head so he's looking at me through one eye, one bloodshot wet eye.

The last time he was crying, he was rude. I won't make the mistake of attempting to comfort him again.

"If you want, I can... go home. I'll just use my GPS or something."

He shakes his head. "Why would I want you to go home?"

I jerk my eyebrows up, twisting the rings on my fingers. "When I found you crying earlier, things didn't go well. So..." my word trails off.

He nods, sniffling. I watch him stand up from the bed, tall.

So tall and broad, in a black shirt and sweats. Just like me.

We lock eyes as he makes his way over to me. He pushes his hair back, a few strands falling over his face. I notice he's cleaned his wounds as he stops an inch away from me.

Then, he drops to his knees.

I lower my chin, staring down at him, brows furrowing in confusion as I swap gazes from one eye to another.

"What are you doing?" I whisper.

"You said you wanted me on my knees, asking for forgiveness," he says, tears still residing in his eyes. "So here I am, on my knees, saying sorry."

He's serious, and that surprises me more than anything.

This man, who I've known for no more than a few weeks, is on his knees, saying sorry and hoping for *my* forgiveness.

This wasn't a part of the deal.

We didn't say we had to *like* each other to fake date. So why does he care if I am mad at him or not?

"Why?" I ask.

"Why what, love?"

"Why do you care whether I forgive you or not?"

"Because I'd rather be fake dating my friend than enemy, Raelynn. And right now, I really need you as my friend."

His face holds more sadness than puppy eyes. I slip my bottom lip between my teeth, hurting for him, looking down at him at my feet, wondering what the hell to do. We don't have to be friends. I don't think being his friend would be a good idea. Though staring at him right now... looking at the gray storm of his eyes, it's hard to turn down the chance. He's doing a lot for me by faking this relationship. The least I can do is be there when he needs someone.

"Then we're friends, Milo," I say after a moment.

He stands up from his knees and takes me into his arms tightly. They wrap completely around me, his head falling into my neck like a puzzle piece, weeping an unsteady cry. I'm stiff for what seems like forever before I relax in his hands.

And to my surprise, I'm not uncomfortable. I'm not itching to get away from his touch. I swallow the excitement down and turn my attention to the crying man in my arms.

I blink, blanking on what to do with this situation. I can't say I've done this before. It's not every day a gigantic man is crying into my shoulder.

I bring my hands to his back and rub them in circles, one hand traveling up to his neck. He holds me so tight that inhaling becomes a difficulty, but I don't move him or his hands that are wrapped around my torso.

"How is she?" I ask softly.

He shakes his head, sniffling against my ear. "Not good."

Sadness for him washes over me. His mother must have cancer; it's the only explanation for her absence of hair and the coughing spree in front of the building.

"How long has it been?"

"A year."

I rest my head on his shoulder. "And there'll be so many more to spend with her."

His fingers grip me, moving up to the back of my head, holding me like a piece of china. "I hope so, too."

Not saying another word, he loosens his hold on me and takes my hand in his. Turning his back to me and bringing me to the bed, sitting down.

"Would you like the bed? I'll take the floor or couch out in the living room."

I shake my head. "I can't take your bed," I laugh shortly. "That's not really fair."

"Well, you're out of your pretty mind if you think I'm letting you sleep on the floor or couch. My mother would kill me for listening to you and then kill you for not telling me to sleep on the floor."

I smile. "Fine. Then you sleep on that end." I point behind him to the empty side of the bed he isn't sitting on. "And I'll sleep here on this side."

He seems surprised that I even suggested we sleep in the same bed, which makes two of us.

He doesn't say another word, just nods in agreement.

Slipping his body under the covers, his face illuminated by the lamp on the nightstand, he opens the covers for me.

I stare at the space meant for me, then at him beside it.
I trust you.

Out of every man I've met in the past two years, I trust *him*. I don't know why, but I do.

So please, don't make me regret it, Milo.

He looks at me curiously, and I clear my throat, getting in and under the covers. He reaches over to his bedside table and shuts the lamp off, leaving us in the dark, the moonlight shining through the curtains on the wall beside us being the only light source.

"Goodnight, Love."

I turn to my side, my back facing him. My lip twitches at his last word.

"Night," I whisper, but my eyes stay open.

It's not like I'll be falling asleep anytime soon, anyway. I rarely do.

11

MILO

I don't know how long I've been staring at her sleep.

It's been quite a while. The sun is up now.

She twists at night, whimpers, and occasionally shuffles to cuddle next to me. She slept entirely on my chest for an hour or two. And that's when she stopped moving and making noise altogether when she was touching me in some way.

I fell asleep for a short while to wake up and now find her balled in a fetal position, my arm locked tightly against her body like a toddler with a stuffed animal.

When I say tightly, I mean the strength of an athlete on steroids. The circulation in my hand is practically cutting off.

But it makes my lip perk into a smile. Whatever she was dreaming about that caused those whimpers and worrisome twists and turns, I appeared inside of it and ridden the problem for her with the simple touch of my hand. It's a shame that it's nearly seven in the morning. I have to get ready for work, and I can smell the breakfast that either Genesis or our mother is making. I haven't had home-cooked food in a while, not since I moved out.

Wiggling my hand, I spend a minute freeing it from Raelynn's grip without waking her up before quietly and slowly getting out of bed to make my way to my private bathroom. I miss having a bathroom in my room, which the other apartment doesn't have. Though it's exactly like what I was looking for.

I shower, brush my teeth, and put on a change of clothes. My teacher's outfits weren't different from my usual ones other than me wearing more than black and white shirts.

Since today is an Easter celebration, I went for pink.

My students have been speaking about this week for days.

Some people would be surprised to know how much six and seven-year-olds actually chatter—most of the time about nothing at all.

Ruffling my hand in my damp hair, I leave the bathroom, my shirt not buttoned up entirely and my tie hanging around my neck undone.

I halt my stroll into my room when I see Raelynn sitting in my bed, wide awake and pale-faced.

"Rae?" She snaps her head to the side and looks at me as if frightened, and my brows furrow. "Are you alright? Did you sleep well?"

Stray strands of curly hair fall from her braids just past her shoulders. Her eyes are large and puffy with sleep. A morning Raelynn looks just as... appealing as any other Raelynn. How does she do it? Maybe it's her lack of flaws that attracts my eyes so strongly or how I pay so much attention to her that I notice things others wouldn't—how her jaw is naturally slanted ever so slightly, how she can't keep her lips from between her teeth, or how her smile isn't entirely symmetrical. I can't seem to tell.

She exhales through her mouth and then opens her eyes to look at me again.

"I slept?" She asks.

I blink. "Yeah, you slept." A breathy laugh leaves me following my '*obviously*' tone.

She smiles a small smile, showing her perfect teeth. "All the way through? Like, the whole night?"

I nod, stepping towards my desk mirror to fix my appearance. "I'm pretty sure that's how sleeping works, love. However, maybe look into that hand grip you got there. Ever thought about football because you nearly cut squeezed my damn hand into halves for—"

Raelynn squeals loudly and high-pitched like an out-of-tune piano, kicking her feet and slipping off the bed. I slowly face her as she runs around the bed and towards me, arms wide.

My eyes widen, and she collides with my body like a train, wrapping her legs around my torso. I'm thrown back a step or two, thankful my desk is behind us to help balance me.

"Thank you," she cries out. "Thank you so much. God, I can't thank you enough." She says, muffling her words against my neck.

"You're welcome," I stutter with a laugh, hugging her back tightly. "Though, I don't know what I did to deserve... *this*."

She squeals again, shuffling in my hands, and I squeeze her thighs against my sides to keep her glued to me. I try not to think about it much, her body glued to mine. The way her thighs sit in my grasp. The fact that her legs are willing wrapped around me followed by a smile plastered on her face. Her ass is just a foot away from my dick.

Whatever I did, I hope I do it again.

She grins and says, "Just know you've helped me." Her head rises, and she stares at me. A content smile sits on her pretty lips, and I stare at them for seconds too long, long enough for her to notice. Her brows drop in curiosity, and I dart my eyes to hers, but she's also staring at my mouth. I feel my body flush, igniting into flames. Her hand comes up to my face, and the simple touch of her thumb grazing over my lips makes me go internally insane.

"You have no idea what you've done," She whispers, her voice tickling every part of my brain.

I shake my head, panting. "Not a clue, but I'd do it a hundred times over if it makes you this happy with me."

I part my lips to speak again just as she leans in to kiss me. Softly and gentle, like she's afraid of what she's decided. It's so delicate that I'm hesitant to add more pressure despite my rapid heartbeat saying otherwise. Yet, her head tilts as she does it for me, squeezing her body against me by tightening her feet around my hips.

My face burns with arousal. With my hands on her thighs, I slide them up and under her shirt, feeling the soft skin of her defined lower back.

A soft whimper leaves her, opening her mouth for me to explore.

I take steps towards my bed, slipping my eager tongue into her mouth, finding her own to connect with. Her tongue piercing rubs against me. A rhythm between our mouths is found soon, and before I realize it, I have her under me, on my bed, her legs—covered in my sweatpants—spread apart, and my body snug between them.

Whatever has gotten into her this morning, I never want it to leave. I need it to stay forever.

The sounds of our deep kisses and her soft moans fill the air, and I back away for a moment to catch my breath.

I look at Raelynn, swollen-lipped from me sucking on them, her flushed face and bright with color, eyes low and a look in them that makes me nervous. I did it all.

The flat of my thumb pulls down her bottom lip just a bit. "*Fuck.*"

Her eyes dart between mine, a hand slipping into my hair, gripping it. She shifts us sideways, and I let her take control.

She moves me to my back and straddles me. My clothes cover her body, too much for my liking, but I don't attempt to take them off. If she wants them off, she'll do it herself.

Staying in this moment is my number one priority.

Her hips and sweet ass grind slightly against my bulge, and I whimper out a mess of a moan.

"So sexy," I whisper, and she takes in her bottom lip and smiles.

Lowering herself, she comes back down, kissing me again, filling my hunger for the addictive taste of her.

Her tongue explores my mouth, her kisses no longer soft and gentle but asserting and curious. Her fingers run down the shallow stubble on my cheeks, and a shiver travels down my spine, joining the blood gushing towards my growth under Raelynn's ass.

A doorknob twist makes us both gasp for a sharp breath of air. "Milo! Mom and I made you and Raelynn brea—" I snap my head to Genesis entering my room, holding a spatula in her hand.

Her jaw is practically on the floor, and her eyes shift between me pinned to the bed sheets and Raelynn being the reason for it.

"Um, first off, I'm disgusted," she announces, "and second, *lock your door* next time."

I glare at her. "How about you learn how to *knock*? You—" She shuts my door before I finish insulting her.

I close my eyes, finding that my heart still beats gf66 a thousand miles an hour, Raelynn's breath following the rhythm as well, I can hear it. I wonder if she's noticed mine, too.

She clears her throat and I look up at her. She darts her eyes away from me, something washing over her, and slips off my lap. I force myself not to groan and pull her back to the spot on my abs that's now cold.

But I sit beside her instead, Placing a hand on her knee.

"I shouldn't have..." she shakes her head, bringing her nails to her mouth as if to hide behind her hands and

I sigh, having no choice but to lift my hips and adjust my slacks. "Shouldn't have what exactly?"

A sorry isn't exactly what I expected to hear. In fact, it's the last words I expected to leave those lips.

"What, um, what I just did." Shyness falls over her, and she finds it hard to look me in the eye.

From what I know, she's not necessarily the shy type, yet she's all flustered because of me. I find it cuter than a fucking kitten.

"Kissing you," she clarifies after I stare at her for probably too long. "Sorry."

Her legs are crossed over one another; I wonder how bad the ache is between them or how much wetness resides on her underwear as she speaks to me.

I snap out of my filthy thoughts and lean back on the headboard, my hands behind my head.

"You're sorry for *kissing* me," I repeat slowly, looking at her.

She nods. "I mean, I should've asked... what if you didn't want to or didn't like it..." she stumbles over her words, but I chuckle.

"Raelynn, God, Raelynn," I recite her name quietly, groaning with a huffed laugh. She has no idea the pain I'm in. "Sweet, sweet, Raelynn." I shake my head, looking at the ceiling. "There's a reason I haven't moved from this spot on this bed yet."

Her head tilts. "What is it?"

I look back at her timid expression and then down at the tent my dick has created with my slacks. "I can't exactly walk out with a boner in front of my family."

I don't look at her, afraid she'll do something to make me grow instead of the opposite.

She's probably staring at it again—*Stop*.

Waffles. Yes, waffles sound interesting to think about right about now. Their fluffiness and sweet thick syrup... that drizzles over—

Fucking hell.

I sit up, stand without a word, and walk to the bathroom.

"Where're you going?" Raelynn asks from behind.

I look at her over my shoulder as I open my bathroom door. "I need to take care of what you started, love."

"*Seriously?*" She huffs a laugh and shakes her head in disapproval.

I raise an eyebrow. "Meaning a cold shower. Your head's still in the gutter, hm?"

"That's—" she halts. "That's what I was talking about. A shower, yeah." She smiles to play off her awful lie.

I step into the bathroom. "Right."

I close the door behind me, stripping immediately. Naked, I walk towards the shower and turn on the cool water. My second shower today.

Looking down at myself, large and at its fullness, I wrap my hand around my throbbing self, squeezing hard and tightly. A soundless moan leaves me as I throw my head back, the streams of water sliding down my chest and abs, drenching me in the wetness I imagine as her. But it isn't helping; nothing will help me besides myself or Raelynn, and right now, I only have one option.

I slide my hand down myself, sighing in relief from the pressure against my base.

I think of her, Raelynn dressed in my clothes. Soft, needy moans that left her throat filled my mouth—the way her body grounded perfectly against mine. My hand quickens.

My balance becomes unsteady.

I part my lips, circling my thumb against the sensitive spot on my tip. My lip pains from my teeth digging into it, cursing myself for how good it feels to think about her. How it feels to have tasted her mouth, to feel the addictive touch of her tongue piercing slipping around in my mouth, exploring its new home. I imagine it against my head, her kneeling over me while I lay down—her naked and enjoying the taste of me.

The thought of the cool metal on her tongue makes my body shake and shiver. She'd find herself over my face, her heat hovering just above my lips, my mouth watering for the taste of her breath brushing against her. She'd lower herself on my face, and I'd extend my tongue and press it against her soaked—

My eyes squeeze close as I'm pulled back into reality by the core of my stomach hurdling and twisting. My jaw hangs wide open, and my eyes roll to the back of my head as I squeeze myself at my base, letting loose onto the shower floor.

A long, tired groan escapes me, and Raelynn's name falls from my lips.

I'm left panting, rinsing myself off once and then twice with cold water to shake out the thoughts and images I've concocted in my head about my freshly made *friend*.

Turning off the shower, I step out dripping wet. I grab a towel from the holder and bring it to my face, sighing.

I freeze my movement when I hear the door to my room close shut after all this time.

12

Milo

With my hands in my pockets and a pang of embarrassment in my chest, I step ten minutes later into the kitchen to see Genesis, Raelynn, and Mom talking amongst themselves.

Raelynn, bronze skin glowing under the kitchen light, holds a bright grin on her face, laughing at something Genesis said. Mom stirs a pan filled with whatever she's cooking. Neither of them seems to notice me yet.

"Pass me the syrup behind you, please," Gen tells Raelynn.

I watch intensively as Raelynn turns to face my direction and freezes with her hand around the syrup.

My lips part and I try to find it in her face that shows she heard what I think she heard. Any sort of hint that she had been *listening* to me in the shower.

But she grins. "Milo, what took you so long? Your food is almost cold."

I squint at her, confused by her question. Could it mean something, or maybe nothing at all? My head drops, clearing my throat to speak as the others turn around at her words to look at me.

"Lost track of time in the shower," I resort to saying. "But I can't eat now. I'm late for work."

I walk towards the couch where my trench coat draped over the back from last night sits and throw it on. Raelynn gives Genesis the syrup bottle.

"Are you ready, my love?" I catch her eyes. My mom beside her smiles at my *supposed* affectionate words towards my *supposed* girlfriend. She looks better than she did yesterday after her episode. Her smile brings me joy.

She's the real reason for this thing with Raelynn, despite me telling Raelynn some other shit excuse at the time.

Technically, I hadn't lied, I do have an ex, her name I try never to think about. But she's no longer around, and I hope Raelynn never notices that.

Raelynn smiles a bit, and it catches my attention. "Ready for what?" She asks me.

"To meet my children."

She drops the metal spoon in her hand, and it falls to the tiled floor, clanking and rattling. Genesis and Mom turn to stare at her as she looks at me.

"Your *children*?"

Gen laughs. "His students, he means. Milo takes his job a little too seriously; those kids are practically his."

Raelynn's body relaxes. "Oh... yeah, right, teacher," she reminds herself briefly.

***

It's been a silent ride to the elementary school I work at. Raelynn sits in the passenger seat at my side, and I've been aching to speak about this morning. Her kisses, her on top of me, the way it had nothing to do with our charade.

"Spit it out," I say. She hasn't said a word to me the entire ride.

She turns her head to me, her hair in two braids still. It makes her look almost innocent, yet I feel she's far from it. Nothing about her grinding on me said innocence.

She turns her gaze from the window to me. "What are you talking about?"

"What's on your mind? You're quiet."

She shrugs. "Nothing."

I breathe deeply. Why can't women just say what's on their mind? There's something wrong yet finding it out is always a guessing game.

"I'm going to ask you again; this time, don't talk out of your ass—"

"This morning meant nothing," she admits quickly, staring at the side of my face as I drive. "The make-out session, I mean."

I'm struck in the heart momentarily, not expecting her words. Though, I should've.

Looking at her is impossible, afraid my eyes will give away my true feelings. True feelings that I'd rather just leave unknown and left in the far corner of my heart.

"What were you dreaming about?"

"What?"

I repeat myself, adding, "Whatever you were dreaming had to be why you kissed me. What was it?"

She is silent before I see her shrug in my peripheral vision.

"I can't remember anymore. And there wasn't a reason... it just happened, and it shouldn't have." She twists to look at me in her seat.

Her voice turns raspy, with a shake to it nearly, "What happened was a mistake. The other day in the store, you were telling the truth; we don't have to do anything but pretend. Kissing you was wrong. I don't want to..." she trails off.

My chest hurts, and breathing becomes a difficult task. I hide it well from her, thankful I don't have to look at her right now. "To what?"

"I don't want to..." she loses her words again.

"To string me along?" I glance at her, and she nods.

I nod, understanding exactly what she means. Whatever I thought she was beginning to feel for me was an illusion. This morning was an illusion, a lie, and I shouldn't be surprised, but I am. It's not every day a woman turns away from having me. Usually, I'm being thrown flirtatious smiles and smirks from women everywhere I go. Yet, this one, this woman who loves pickles, fights off raccoons and adores flowers to the extent of obsession, wants nothing to do with me romantically.

"Yeah," she finally confesses.

I laugh, shaking my head and stopping the car in front of the entrance of my school. Leaning over to unbuckle her broken seatbelt, I lean into her. "Don't get too cocky, darling. It wasn't serious to me either. Any woman can kiss me and rile me up it had nothing to do with you. Being more than friends has never crossed my mind."

The seatbelt unlocks with a tug, and her body shifts; I glance down at her breast through the black shirt she wears with a wide neckline. We stopped at our apartment so she could get a change of clothes, this shirt and a pair of black trousers.

She looks like she might be a part of some sort of badass crime organization with all this black. The thought of her holding a knife to my throat appears and disappears in the blink of an eye.

"Okay, *good*," she says. "Being more than friends with you hasn't crossed my mind either."

"Good."

She opens the door and steps out of the car; I go to do the same until I hear her voice.

"Do you know another Raelynn by any chance?" she asks, bending over to look at me.

"No?"

Her eyebrows jump, and her mouth twists. Behind her is the school entrance, with several dozen students finding their way inside and making noise.

"Well," she says quietly. "Next time you're in the shower, try to think about these words of yours and keep me out of your fantasies."

My heart stops.

She heard me, after all.

Heat crawls up my neck, seeping out my cheeks, and my throat burns from a tang of embarrassment.

"*What*?" I fumble.

She smiles, tilting her head. "You're five minutes late, and the kids are probably waiting on you." The doors shut, and I watch her figure, shirt tucked in the waist of her trousers, carving out her curves.

Why does her disinterest in me make her more intriguing? It should stop me from wanting her like I know I shouldn't. It's like the more she turns me down, the more I want to win her over.

Similar to a game, she's the objective.

It is a game that I have to play cautiously because, in the end, I either win her over or lose her entirely. And I have a feeling there are no due overs, no restates, or no hints to it at all.

If the slow game is what she wants, then fine, the slow game is what she'll get.

Raelynn waves to a few children, and I sigh, getting out of the car.

***

I clap three times at the class filled with six and seven-year-olds.

"Alright," I say loudly; getting their attention isn't so easy sometimes. The basket of eggs filled with candy in my hand helps instantly, however.

A dozen pairs of wide eyes of excitement, along with Raelynn at my side, stare at me as I speak. "Some of you may notice a new face." I walk towards Raelynn, and she grins. Since the moment she saw them, her smile hasn't faltered.

"Is that your wife!" One of my students blurts.

I stutter. "Um, No—"

A young boy, Robbin, raises his hand but speaks without permission anyway. "Mrs. Evans, do you two *hold hands?*" He says it as if it's the most obscure thing.

"Ewwwww!" Haven cringes, a little girl with two puffs of curly hair on each side of her parted head. "I heard— I heard boys are sick. *Cooties*! Don't touch hands!" She shakes her finger from side n to side.

"*Hey*! I don't have cooties," Robbin exclaims, his eyes glistening with tears.

I sigh, redirecting the conversation. "No, we don't hold hands, and no, this isn't my wife. This is..." My eyes lock with Raelynn, "My friend. She's here to help you all."

Raelynn waves and says hi to them, and they all seem to like her off the bat. *Surprising.* Who wouldn't?

For the next hour and a half, Raelynn and I are busy painting eggs with terrible paintings and kids that have dirtied my shirt and marked my face. Raelynn sits on the carpet surrounded by several kids crisscrossed with aprons on; painting boiled eggs still. She's just as dirty as me, and yet she doesn't seem to mind it. Her hair is in a large bun at the back of her head, and a few curls and strands fall around her face. She giggles as Haven pokes her septum piercing and says she wants the same one when she's older.

I listen to her conversation with Haven from the tables I wipe down.

"Do do— do you have a uh... children with Mr. Evans, Mrs. Evans?" Haven, with her high-pitched voice, asks a very personal, inappropriate question.

She's smart for her age, extremely. She's a grade or two above what she's supposed to be at. Whatever her parents were doing, they did it well. Must've been teaching her since birth.

I look over to see Raelynn's smile fall. "No, I don't. And you can call me Raelynn; Milo isn't my husband."

"Saying his first name is a bad word." She whispers, making it harder for me to hear her with all the chatter. I smile; I've told them all the same thing. Raelynn shakes her head. "No, the word fuck is a bad word. If you said I love these fucking eggs, then yeah. But I don't really know why anyone cares about cursing in the first place," Raelynn begins to ramble to herself more so. "If you're not using it to hurt anyone, then cursing is fine."

I need to stop this.

"So... cursing is good?" Haven asks.

Raelynn nods, "Not if you do it in front of adults—*but* you didn't hear it from me."

I straighten my back and wipe my hands on the rag going to end this incredibly ridiculous interaction just as Haven points to Raelynn's egg and smiles, "I like your fucking egg."

"*Don't* say that," I say loudly, making Haven jump. "Raelynn, what the f— *crap* do you have my kids saying?"

Raelynn laughs wickedly and covers her mouth. "Oh, come on, don't scare the girl. She was just listening to me. Sort of."

"That's exactly my point." I bend over and look at Haven. "Don't say that word, ever. It's bad."

Her big brown eyes stare back at me, nibbling on her finger. "Sorry."

I assure her she's okay, then send her off and turn to Raelynn. "Teaching them to curse. Really?" My words are stern and serious on the matter. "You're not the one who gets to hear the shit around here, so I'd rather you not."

She stands close, slips her hands in her back pocket, and nods. I watch her deep chocolate brown eyes, then trace the blue paint streak across her cheek.

"Got it," she says softly with a smile. "Won't happen again." She lifts her hand and makes an X across her chest where her heart is located, smirks, and then walks back to my students.

She claps once. "Who wants lunch? I'm *fucking* starving."

13

Raelynn

My back is pressed against the bathroom door as I listen in on Milo inside of it.

I can't believe him, and I can't believe it's me that's the cause of it.

Me. Of all other people, he might have to think about. He's doing this to the thought of me.

My body burns, and my center pulses painfully, wanting a release, anything to satisfy what kissing Milo has done to me.

His grunt comes through and meets my ear, along with the sound of water hitting the shower floor. I softly lean my head against the door as I stand and pull at the drawstrings of my sweatpants. My hand slips in and under my panties, and my jaw drops open.

The flat of my finger slides between my slit, rubbing my wetness into myself, feeling what Milo's easily done.

My back arches as a whimper of Milo leaves the bathroom, and I bite down on my bottom lip, rubbing my clit to the sound of him getting off.

This is insane, but I'm happy. Happy he's achieving in making me feel more than fear when it comes to being close to a man, let alone sexual activities.

Two fingers enter me with ease, and I swallow my cry as I curl them up, imagining Milo's fingers or tongue handling the job for me.

My stomach twists, and butterflies swarm every corner of it, my eyes watering as I slide down the door to sit.

Please, Milo...

He moans, cursing to himself, and my legs begin to shake as I quicken my fingers against my sweet spot.

I want to reach my end. I need to feel it just once again.

"Raelynn," *he cries out in between moans.*

The moan of my name, which should've ruined and caused me to melt like liquid on the floor from my climax, instead made my eyes shoot open.

Raelynn.

That same moan of my name, a memory I haven't had since now of that night—the night of the assult.

I close my eyes, and an image flashes over my lids. A body on top of mine, my name being moaned ever so slightly. No. The good feeling washes away immediately, and my heart races.

It always comes down to that day. My eyes swell with tears as I slip my hand out from inside my panties and cry against the door. I'll never be able to feel the same. There will always be that day there to take control of me forever. What was I thinking? That three weeks with this man might fix me. That maybe—just maybe—he'd make me forget about Jaden Caddel. When the truth is, nothing can.

I widen my face with my arm, but it's no use; the tears continue their pathetic stream down my cheek.

What makes me think anyone else can if I can't get myself off? If I continue this with Milo, I'll ruin it all.

So it's better I terminate... whatever we're becoming before it starts to form.

Suddenly, the sound of his shower stops, and I gasp soundlessly, getting up and running towards his door, opening it and closing it.

I press my back against it, sighing and taking deep breaths, completely wiping away the fact that I was crying.

A trick I've come to master.

***

"Are you tired? It's only the evening, and you're snoozing." I shoot my eyes open from the dreadful daydream, the sound of Milo's voice right next to me in his car.

I clear my throat, blinking away the reappearing tears, and shake my head. "No, just resting my eyes."

If only he knew what thoughts live inside my head. I continue pushing him away, hoping he'll just end up calling this fake dating thing off, but he doesn't seem to want to. Deep down, neither do I.

Not after meeting his family... the *nicer* people of his family. And declaring us friends when we aren't putting on a front.

Keeping away from him sexually is for his own good. I don't want to hurt him because of things that are shattered and twisted within me.

I'll just distance myself. I'll keep him out of my head. Forever.

I watch the road as Milo finally takes me to our building. A pang of disappointment rises in me, but I push it down. He stops the car and goes to unbuckle my seatbelt, but I put a hand up, not wanting to feel him so close.

"I got it," I say. He puts his hand up, watching me undo the lock.

After several attempts and smirks from a cocky Milo, I finally get it loose.

"See? I got it."

"I never said you didn't, Love." He gets out of his car and shuts the door. I'm left blowing a long, aggressive breath out from my mouth before stepping out of the car as well to meet him at the door.

"So, you think those kids learned some good things today?" I sarcastically question Milo as he opens the door for me.

A glare is sent my way. "If I hear even one parent complain about their child dropping the F-bomb, you're dead. Seriously, Rae, I'll come for you."

You already did, in the showe— No.

I shake my head and the thought away. Milo smirks at my side, but I choose to ignore him, and his mind seems to be on the same page as mine.

"Good evening, Mr. Evans," Edna greets from behind her desk, looking up from her glasses. I wonder why on Earth she's a security guard; she doesn't look a day under sixty.

"Edna," he shorty responds with a wave.

Her eyes dart to me. "Raelynn, hello." She smiles, looking between the two of us. "I see you two have found each other nicely."

I tilt my head, wondering what that actually means. However, I'm too tired to question her. Milo and I had stayed after school hours; I helped him clean and organize things and even talked about friend things like *Spider-Man*. Next thing you know it's nearly six at night when we headed home.

"Hope your day went well," Milo says, twisting the topic of conversation. "How is the elevator holding up? And the radio installment?" He calls the elevator down with the press of a button. I stand at his side.

"Good as new, thanks to you." He chuckles, wrinkles at the corner of her eyes. "That rhymed, didn't it?"

He smiles crookedly. "Yes, it did."

The elevator door opens and I step in first, Milo following, pressing my floor first. Twenty-three.

Just like he said seconds ago, a faint tune plays in the elevator, and I listen to it with my eyes closed, attempting to imagine I wasn't in a metal box.

"So you're family owns buildings?" I say, keeping my voice low and wanting him just to talk while the elevator climbs floors.

"Yes. I have access to my father's income, a large income, you might notice."

I glare up at him. "Don't show off, it's unattractive."

"I'm not showing off. In fact, I'd rather if I didn't have anything to do with my father if I'm being truthful. He's a man that doesn't deserve his wealth. If I could give it all to someone who does, I would, or at least try."

"What makes you hate him so much?"

"Too many things to list off." His voice turns shallow and weak, and I realize just how hard it is for him to speak about his dad. "I teach because I wanted a job of my own; regardless of how terrible the pay is, I wanted something not connected to *him*."

I nod, and the elevator door dings and opens. I let loose the tightness in my chest and step out first. "Why do you stick around him then."

Milo takes a moment to answer. "He'd cut us off."

I look up at him with pinched eyebrows. "What do you mean?"

"Genesis, me, my mother. He wants me to follow his footsteps, to be the obedient son he's always wanted me to be. If I don't listen to him, he'll take away everything from us. That house Mother and Gen live in? That's his. He pays Gen's private school tuition. The treatment for his sick wife, he's threatened to cut it all off, Rae."

My shoulders drop as I come to the end of the hallway where my door is located. I turn to look at Milo's face full of anger.

"Wow. I can't even believe that. It's... *heartless*," I whisper, feeling my chest tighten for him. How long has this been going on for? What else has his father done to him? What terrible lengths has he taken to make Milo so dependent on him?

My lips press into a thin line. "The most terrible people always seem to be the most fortunate." A soft, humorless laugh leaves me in replace of the frown that I want to show.

Milo glances down the hall and then back at me. "Well, enough about him. Keeping him out of my head for as long as needed is what brings me the most relief. I should get going."

I nod, understanding what he means. I would rather talk about anything than my parents.

Slipping off my keys from my pockets, I open my apartment door, revealing the erring quietness and dim lighting. The walls that hold memories of my nightmares and sleepless nights.

I clear my throat, turning around to look at Milo. My eyes trace his sharp jaw and perfect nose—the upward curls of his hair and the faint pink shade of his lips.

I shift my weight against the door. "I'll... see you." I nibble at my lip, turning my to glance at my apartment once again, then back at Milo.

He tilts his head and gives me one nod. "Goodnight, love."

My heart falls as he turns around and walks down the hall; I watch the distance between us increase for a second longer before I go to close my door. I shouldn't have expected him to want to spend more time with me, not after what I said to him in the car, about what happened between us. It would be better if we didn't spend more time than needed together.

Before my door closes completely I pause at the sound of my name. "Raelynn." I open the door too quickly, looking at him with raised brows.

"Yeah?"

He scratches the back of his head, stumbling on his words. "Do you, uh... want to— I'm making dinner." He blurts out. "Do you want some?"

I bite down on my bottom lip to prevent the massive grin that I want to show. Nodding, I step back out my door and shut it. "Yeah, sounds good."

Dinner won't hurt anyone. And I would rather not be by myself right now.

Following Milo down one flight of stairs to the twenty-second floor to the apartment right under mine, I wait patiently behind him as he unlocks his door and opens it.

Immediately, a series of barks come through, and a brown and black adolescent German Shepard is revealed behind the door. It jumps and scratches at Milo, barking and hanging its tongue from its mouth. One ear hangs floppy while the other stands up straight, and it causes me to laugh. Milo drops his hand on the puppy's head and pets it.

"Alright, girl, calm down." Girl. She's only a few months old, tinnier than a usual adult German Shepard.

I grin widely as I step inside his apartment, getting a greeting from his dog as well. Her tails wag, and I bend down to give her more pets than Milo gave. She clearly wants more attention—poor thing.

"Hi, gorgeous! Aren't you adorable," I speak highly. The dog drops low and spins around to show her belly. "Belly rubs?" Her tongue hands out the side of her mouth, wide brown eyes staring back at me.

I giggle and rub her stomach, causing one of her legs to kick uncontrollably.

Milo hangs his keys on a hook beside the door and locks it, slipping off his coat and hanging it.

"That's poppy," he says. "I got her around six months ago when I moved out of my parent's house. She's quite the mess."

I look around the house. The rather amazingly decorated house. Despite not being nearly as high-end as the one he used to live in, he sure knows how to make it look like it.

My eyes wander to the living room at the broken vase on the carpet. Milo walks towards it, sighing. "A pain in my ass also." He grabs a dustpan and broom and begins cleaning the mess Poppy's made.

"She's innocent; it's not her fault," I say and bend down to puppy-talk the dog. "Isn't that right? You're a saint, hmm?" She licks my nose, and I grin, standing up from my crouch.

Milo throws the last piece of the broken vase in the garbage and steps in front of me. Beside us, Poppy jumps on the couches, flips down, and nibbles on a bone.

"I need to take a shower first. Get rid of all the paint and shit on me. Make yourself at home." He waves his hand at his apartment and then says.

I nod and smirk. "No fantasies this time."

He raises an eyebrow and smiles. "Don't listen in on me this time." He fires back as he turns away.

My cheek burns slightly and the interaction, but I brush it off as he walks down his hallway, out of sight. He was kidding, a joke.

Seconds later I hear the running of water start up and a door close.

I twist my lips and find myself walking around his house.

What if I was a thief and wanted to rob his ass. Then what?

He'd probably just walk upstairs and rob it back from me...

Down the hall, past the bathroom he showers in, I walk towards the single bedroom at the end. It's cracked open, so I press two fingers against the wood, opening it wider.

A large king-sized bed sits against the wall in the middle, made and color-themed gray and white. Gray comforter, gray walls, gray carpet, white sheets, white picture frames, and white pillows to contrast.

A small bookshelf sits at his bedside table, a lamp on it that illuminates the room. A small window shines the setting sun rays through it, tinting the room. I walk along the perimeter, dragging my hand along the desk, when a door catches my eye. It's not normal for rooms in this apartment to have other doors like this one. I walk towards it, twisting the knob.

Peering inside, I scan the office-like room.

A faint red light shows along the top perimeter of the room, turning the entirety of it red. It must change to other colors too, I'm pretty sure they're called LED lights.

But I like the red. It fits with the secret room energy this place gives off.

An L-shaped black desk sits in the corner, a monitor on it and a few books and stacks of papers, along with a long couch against the wall.

I walk inside, eyes wide as I stare at the several bookshelves along the walls, books filling every one of them.

I knew he was a teacher, but holy hell, I didn't think he read *this* much.

Is this considered intrusive? He did say to make myself home; I'd rather see what this place includes before I do that.

Sitting in his chair, I cross my legs, feeling like a badass businesswoman of some sort. A laptop lay in front of me, and I chose to leave that alone. I'd rather not pry in his personal belongings.

But hypocritically, I open a few drawers, finding watches that are too big for me, rings that are too big for me, and other random things.

Getting to the bottom drawers, I open it to find *handcuffs*.

My brows pinch together, and I tilt my head when I see the rope and several other items along with it. A small *knife* is included. My eyes widen.

What the *fuck*?

I gasp, just as the door to the room opened wider. A gush of fear rushes through my body, goosebumps rising on my arms. My breath lodges in my throat and clears it, closing the dresser.

Milo stands in the entrance, fresh clothes on, his wet face paling, and his panicked eyes on me.

I stand up, side-stepping the dresser, and point to the last drawer with a shaking finger. "Milo..."

He puts up his hand. "Please, don't freak out."

14

RAELYNN

He's some sort of psychopath, isn't he? A murder? Criminal? *Both*?

It's now that I realize there's not much I know about the man standing before me. One question arises, one I should've wondered from the start. Who the hell is Milo Evans?

He steps closer, and I take a step back, eyes on him. Breathing is difficult; my lips part to attempt to breathe through my mouth.

"Who *are* you?" I ask him, my throat running dry. "Why— *why* is all of that in there, Milo?"

Oh God, what if he tries to hurt me?

"Raelynn, listen to me, please. It's not what it looks like." He steps closer, and my back hits the wall. I'm cornered, sandwiched between him and it.

I shake my head. "I want to go." I want to go *and report you*.

He reaches out for my hand, but I snatch it away, attempting to run around him.

He catches me by my waist, wrapping his hard arm around me and bringing me back in front of him.

I yelp, kicking and screaming at him to let go as he pins me against the wall by my shoulders.

"Please, calm down," His voice shaky, nervous almost. Nervous because he hurts people with those *tools*. "

Warm tears stream down my face as he pins my arms to the wall.

I was panting, tired and scared. I stop moving and just stare at him.

"Are you going to hurt me?" I ask He pinches his eyebrows together. "Raelynn, do you think I'm *insane*? You know I'd never hurt you, all right? Not even a single hair on your pretty head."

"I *don't* know you."

"You know me enough to know I wouldn't hurt you." He says as if offended. I even thought he would.

"Then why do you have those things? Knifes, ropes..." A singular tear falls from me, hating the way he's pinning me against the wall. The air in the room feels nonexistent. I can't breathe, and he's too close; I want to move my body, but he's preventing me, causing my throat to shut and my mind to panic.

I look at his hands on my shoulders, and he looks at them as well, immediately lifting his hands off me as if realizing I'm uncomfortable.

My eyes shut, relieved.

He turns around and closes the door, not fully, but nearly. I stand hugging my torso, telling myself to hear him out, praying that what I think isn't what is true. His hand runs through his wet head of hair, water dripping onto his black shirt every few seconds.

"When I said make yourself at home, I didn't mean go through my things, *Raelynn*."

An octave or two higher, and he'd be shouting, but I can hear the way he's limiting himself, the strain of his words.

"How was I supposed to know I was going to find your fucking *torture* kit!"

"It's not a fucking *torture kit*, don't be dense. You know exactly what they're for." He's looking at me now, across the room, his back against the wall and his hands in his sweatpants pockets.

I shake my head. "No, Milo, I don't know, so how about—"

"Pleasure," He whispers, cutting me off.

I stay silent, waiting for him to continue. *Pleasure.*

He walks towards the light switch and turns off the red glow, switching on a dull white regular light instead. The distinct pink shade of his cheeks shows as he walks towards the desk and pulls open the drawer, grabbing the handcuffs out.

I swallow, beginning to realize exactly what he means by pleasure.

I look at the metal item in his hand, then up at Milo as he walks towards me. The fear inside begins to diminish.

"You like... to use those on people?" I ask timidly, brushing a curl behind my ear.

He shakes his head no, stopping close to me. "I like it when they're used on *me*."

My throat runs dry, and a tingle travels down my spine. The blush and embarrassment on his face make my chest soften. It looks like he might cry. He presses his lips together, looking at me in the eyes; it seems grey clouds float in them. Dark towards the outside, lighter around the center. They dart from my left to right eye, desperately awaiting my response.

"Please, say something, or I might go mad. I don't want you to think I'm some sort of... danger. It's been years since I used any of these things, and I wasn't planning on getting you to use them, or even *find* them for that matter—"

"I'm sorry," It comes out coarse, apologetic. His eyes are red, and I feel bad for exposing such a personal thing to him. "I shouldn't have gone through your stuff. Or accused you of... doing bad things."

He shakes his head. "These *are* bad," he moves them around in his hands. "Just for all the right reasons. Not *your* reasons."

I swallow, curious nonetheless. Feeling myself relax more with him. My tears are gone, but my breath still struggles to regulate, though I think that has nothing to do with fear anymore.

Raising my hand slowly towards his, pressing a finger against the cold handcuffs, I drag it along the smooth metal.

My eyes flutter close as goosebumps surround my entire body.

Milo breathes out a deep breath, licking his lips, and lowers the cuffs; they clank against each other.

"I think it's best if you just go, Raelynn. I'll see you some other time whenever you need me." He swallows hard and walks towards the door, but I don't move.

Why can't I move? I should listen to him, leave his home, and leave him be. It's what I said I wanted for us to be nothing. I've been invited in, then snooped through his things only to accuse him of being a complete psychopath just after he's trusted me with personal information about his psychopathic father. He keeps the door open, revealing his bedroom, and looks back at me—confusion written on his forehead as to why I'm still here.

I hold my arms around myself, feeling a bit embarrassed that the feeling is back—the feeling from this morning. I crave the feeling and don't want to go away this time.

Please don't go away.

"Can you. . . show me?"

His brow rises slowly as he processes my words. I can practically see his tail wag.

He lets go of the door and walks to me. "What?"

I point to his hand, holding the handcuffs. "Show me. I want to know how to use them. The things you like, I mean."

Milo's hand rises to my chin and neck, holding me with a gentleness that makes my heart skip a beat. Lowering his head, eyes staring at me from under his lashes, he draws his bottom lip between his teeth and groans softly. He steps closer so that his chest is flush against my front. His head drops beside my ear, brushing his lips against my skin. I gasp soundlessly at the touch of him.

"Raelynn, you have no idea what you're doing." He whispers against me. "You can't say those things unless you're one *hundred* percent sure you mean it."

My clit pulses between my legs, his breath fanning against my ear, making my eyes flutter shut from the tingles running down to my stomach.

I swallow as he presses my body against the wall with his hard one. His palm digs into the wall beside my head.

I'm scared. Not of Milo anymore, but of me. I'm scared that I might push myself too much towards limits I can't reach.

I catch his eyes as he lifts his head back up. "I mean it," I challenge myself.

Looking between our bodies, I rub on the handcuffs along with his hand holding them. Curiosity is a son of a bitch. I had a great sex life before what happened, but I never involved tools like these.

Below our hand, his gray sweatpants sit tented by his boner. My lips part and I look up at him.

He turns his head to catch my lips, kissing me and lifting my head to give him more access and igniting me, surprising me with the pressure of his soft yet hard lips against mine—a real kiss, one more real than the last.

With my back glued to the wall by his body, my neck cranks upwards to meet his mouth easily.

The sound of the handcuffs hitting the carpet fills the room, and his hands gravitate to the sides of my neck, keeping my head in place as our lips move in sync. He feels incredible, and the soreness between my legs agrees.

I ache for him and only him, and I can't deny it, no matter how much I wish I could.

My hands glide up his hard body, up his abs that are definitely part of more than a six, and towards his back, where I slightly dig my fingers into his shirt.

He whines into my mouth and breaks away. I see his eyes roll back for a second, but they align quickly, more deadly now. I stare at him, panting and out of breath from our kiss.

He drops his hand and grips my hips. "Do you know what you're capable of doing to me?" He murmurs as he lifts me with ease.

My arms wrap around his neck, and my legs at the side of his hips. I shake my head.

He looks up at me now while he walks towards the door. I attempt to find words to speak. "Where are we going?" I breathe against his wet lips. I look at the handcuffs on the floor as he carries me out of the room and into his dimly lit bedroom. "I thought you were going to show me how to use..." my words trail off.

He shuts the door to his office while he holds me up with one hand, the hand gripping my ass.

"That comes later, love. Much later." He explains, gently digging his knee into his mattress and laying me down. "I want to make you feel good first. You come first. Always, all right?"

I nod, running my hands through his hanging mess of damp hair to see him better. He leans down and crashes his lips against mine again, gliding his hands along my body while he confidently squeezes my mouth. His tongue slides along my bottom lip, and he takes it between his teeth, sucking, nibbling, and popping it out before humming like I'm the best thing he's ever tasted.

I might as well be a puddle of water beneath him, pained and sore, wanting his mouth to return to mine.

But it doesn't; he kisses my nose instead, my cheek, my chin, my jaw, my neck, in between my collarbones. His body travels down mine, and so do his kisses, each one erupting an explosive within me.

I suck in my stomach, and I inhale, my shirt being slid up. He looks at me, his hands on both my hip as he lowers his head and sucks on the lower skin of my stomach, right above my center.

I throw my head back, moaning and reaching for his hair.

His voice raspy, rough and music to my ears, he speaks, "I want to taste you, Rae. May I?"

With my mouth hanging open with my pants, I stare at him for a moment, between my legs, the muscles in his arms flexing as he holds himself up.

I nod and swallow, hiding the fact that I'm afraid of the result. Afraid I won't be able to do what other women are capable of.

"*Yes,*" I answer.

He grins, showing his pearly whites, and unbuttons my pants. The pressure of his hands against my area and anticipation as he unzips me makes me squirm against his bed sheets.

I think of the scars on my thighs and stomach, but I push them away, praying it's too dark for him to notice anything at all.

"Milo..." I moan out for no reason at all, nibbling on my bottom lip.

"Yes, love?" He slips one hand under my back, lifting my hips up so he can pull my pants down my thighs.

I'm left in my flower underwear, embarrassed, to say the least. He runs his hand across the lace, creating butterflies within me.

"I didn't know anyone would... actually see them," I explain.

He shakes his head. "They're cute, pretty," He says. "But prettier when they're at your ankles."

My brows raise when he presses his lips against the fabric, right on my swelled clit underneath it.

I cry out from the overwhelming pleasure, feeling a burst of nerves swarm my body as he extends his tongue and licks over the fabric.

My lip pains from biting down on it, aching for the thin material that's between his lips and my clit to be removed. I can't remember the last time I wanted something this badly.

He looks up at me, and a knot in my stomach forms from just that simple glance. How is he this perfect looking?

"You smell so nice," He mutters before sucking on me. "I can see how much you want me through your poor panties."

He hooks his fingers around the thin sides of my underwear and pulls them down slowly. A deep groan falls from his lips while admiring my center. I watch his eyes twinkle like he's staring at a pot of gold that he can't believe is in front of him.

He rubs the side of my thighs and pulls the underwear down to my ankles, the place he thinks they look their best.

He lifts my legs to the sides of his head, kissing the sides of my thighs as he glances up at me, barely getting by.

"You doing okay?" He says as he lowers himself and licks my clit, giving me no time to respond. I ignore the cockiness in his tone.

Leaning on my elbows, I let my head hang back, the feeling of his warm tongue against me making it impossible to talk. I've missed this and feeling like I'm on top of the world. I miss being taken care of like this.

He surrounds my clit with his lips, circling his tongue around and over it with a quickness that makes my eyes roll to the back of my head.

I grip tightly on his hair, my other hand at the side of his head, feeling the overpowering pleasure he's bringing me.

Crying out inside my closed mouth, he presses the tip of his tongue inside of my warmth, curing his tongue against the rough wall of my pussy. His nose against my clit as he gets dirty with me. And he doesn't seem to care one bit.

"*Milo*," My voice shakes, and I push at his head, the ache and pleasure getting too much for me to handle, but he raises his hand and grabs mine to slide it away, continuing.

He mutters his words against me. "Cum on my tongue, princess. You can do it," Heat fanning against me, the name causing a twitch of my clit.

I want to. Gosh, I want to give him this more than anything in the world right now.

Focusing on his movement; the long strokes from the flat of his tongue collected my wetness. The way his hands stroke the sides of my thighs. The flushed cheeks and aroused expression on his face. Wetness dresses his lips, *my* wetness, and he enjoys every second I allow him to please me.

But no matter how good his tongue is against me, reaching my climax feels impossible.

It's nowhere in sight, and it never will be.

As I come to this inevitable conclusion, I feel it slip more and more away, my body becoming numb once again.

And just like that, it's all gone in a matter of seconds. The buildup, the butterflies, the overwhelming feeling. It's gone, and I miss it already.

I look at the ceiling, my eyes flooded with tears. My arm comes up to my mouth to attempt to hide my cries, but it's no use.

Milo stops immediately, but I'm not sure how he noticed something was wrong so quickly.

"*Raelynn*, what's wrong?" He says panicky. "Did I do something? I'm sorry, whatever I did, I didn't—"

I shake my head, sitting up. Tears fall from my eyes, wetting my lashes.

My arousal has disappeared; that's what's wrong.

"It's not your fault. I'm sorry," I croak. "I'm s-so sorry,"

His brows arch upward in worry. "Raelynn, you're scaring the fuck out of me. Why?" He crawls from between my legs and sits beside me, wrapping an arm around my shoulders and bringing me into his chest.

I fall into his hold, kicking my underwear away from my ankles. They're no longer pretty or cute. They're evidence of my failure now.

Crying against his shirt, I gripped the material, weeping and humiliated.

What will he say when he finds out I can't reach my end? Who wants a woman who can't reach her climax? No one at all.

Milo hugs me tightly against him. Clueless, yet caring with little knowledge of what's going on.

One arm wrapped around my waist, the other cupping my head against his chest, my curls tied into a bun at the top.

My breath hitches, my throat burning from wails, but Milo stays silent for most of it other than a few moments of assuring me that he's here for me, that I'm not alone.

I tighten my hold on him, grateful I'm stuck in this moment with him. Grateful that he holds his questions. Grateful for his comfort.

"You're all right, Love," he whispers as I sniffle, stroking the tears away on the side of my face. "You're okay."

15

MILO

I'm worried for her. Raelynn lays against my chest still, silently crying for the past hour.

Getting out of the shower, I hadn't expected to find her in my office. I had been going to lock the door so she wouldn't find the room, but in a way, I'm glad she did.

She's opened up a little, allowed me to see within her shell and through the strong wall she keeps up, but then locked me out completely. She says it isn't my fault. Though, I can't help but feel like I've done something to make her uncomfortable.

I stare at the ticking clock across the room, the only steady noise as I stroke her cheek.

Two in the morning, it reads. She might be sleeping. I don't dare move to check.

"Milo?" Her voice breaks the silence minutes later, confirming she's awake for me.

"Yes?"

"I need to tell you something," she whispers, sniffling, not lifting her head from my chest.

"What is it?" The flat of my thumb against her cheek.

"Two years ago," she starts, now lifting her head to look at me. She grabs my blanket draped over us and hugs it close to herself, around her shoulders. Her hair that she released a few minutes ago lay past her shoulders, one side tucked behind her ear. She takes a deep breath, looking out the fire escape to the side.

"Two years ago in college, at a frat party, I was assaulted by a g— by a guy I had only known for an hour." Her voice cracks, and I stare wide-eyed as her tears appear instantly.

I repeat her words in my head, my body stiffening as I process them.

I sit up as she continues, picking at her fingers. A tear drops from her eye. "I don't remember the moment he did it. I was drugged; *he* drugged me," she laughs, but it lacks any humor at all. "Sometimes when I close my eyes, I get new images of that night, quick second or two pictures of his body or the sound of him..."—she swallows—"him grunting my *name*."

My heart hurts as her words reach my ears. "*Rae*," I say softly, hiding the anger that's boiling in me, thinking of someone laying a finger on this woman's body.

She doesn't look at me, her face morphed by quiet sobs that she's trying to hold back.

I listen. "It's just I haven't *slept* in *forever*. My head consistently hurts from it. I'm tired—*all* of the time, Milo. Every time I close my eyes, I see him, I feel him, I *hear* his voice. And it—" she cracks, looking at me. "It's draining. To the point where he's completely ruined me."

I shake my head, swallowing the lump in my throat. "That isn't true."

She nods, eyes bloodshot and swollen. "Yes, it is. I can't... I can't get to places I should when it comes to sex. It doesn't work anymore. Nothing helps. Not you, not even myself."

I shake my head, hurting to see her in so much pain. I would've never thought she was going through it all. She always seemed so strong in the month I've known her. And now I know she's even stronger than I thought.

"It all takes time, Raelynn." An hour ago, when I was looking at her legs, I noticed the scars on her stomach and thighs. Though it was dark, I felt them, but I'm not one to point out things like that.

None of it matters. I wouldn't want it done to my scars.

"How much time? I don't think I can wait anymore. I want to be *normal*," Her cries break her words up, fast sobs shaking her body while tears flood down her face.

Lifting my hand, I motion for her to come to me. Her frown digs deep into her face, wet cheeks, and puffy eyes.

She looks younger, helpless, and scared.

She sits in my cross lap, our bodies as close as possible, arms wrapped around my chest and legs around my waist.

Her head falls sideways against my shoulder, digging into my neck with a steady, silent cry.

"What's his name?" I ask, wrapping my arms around her body.

A second passes, "Jaden Caddel." The name falls like a weight on her tongue.

I nod. Jaden Caddel. I write it into my memory, saving the name for future purposes.

I lean back against the headboard with Raelynn clinging onto me. "You're safe with me, love. I won't let anything happen to you. You know that, right? Not a thing?"

She responds with a nod and a whimper of a cry.

I shuffle my shoulder, causing her head to rise. My hand comes up between us, and I brush tears from her cheeks. "Stop crying, darling. He doesn't deserve them. He deserves a list of things much worse, but none includes your tears."

She holds a hand against the back of mine on her face, "I haven't slept through the night since I slept beside you. Just this night... if it's okay..."

I furrow my brows until I realize what she's asking. "You can sleep here for as long as you like, Rae. You could never leave my sight; I'd be more than okay with that. As long as you feel safe."

Her lip twitches and turns up for a moment. "I feel safe with you," she whispers.

I sigh in relief hearing those words. Proud that I've earned the trust of a woman who must trust no one.

I lower her head with mine and bring her down to kiss her forehead. "Then that's all that matters."

Her head falls back on my shoulders, and I lay on my back, pulling the covers over us. Her hands rest on my chest, bare legs at my sides.

Her rapid heartbeat slows as time passes. I can only stare at the ceiling, holding Raelynn in both arms as she falls asleep against me. My eyes twitch, thinking of what she's told me, finding it hard to process. The thought makes my stomach turn and twist in the most horrible ways. If I didn't have this girl in my hands, sleeping, I'd be finding more on the sick fuck that took it upon himself to do the things he did to her.

I need to know what ever happened to him. Is he in jail? Dead? Did she tell anyone other than me?

Two years is a long time, yet it affects her like yesterday. Her tears are new, her heart still hurts, her body still reacts and will never forget, and it pains me.

She thinks her body needs fixing. She couldn't be more wrong. All she needs is to be retaught. Starting from the very beginning, I'll be the one to teach her. Until she knows he holds nothing over her.

I need to find him. I have to. What I'll do when I find him is another matter.

And it's a good thing finding people comes easily when I have millions to spare.

***

The weight of Raelynn is no longer on my chest, making me lift my head, that's foggy with sleep.

"Raelynn?" I mutter sleepily, blinking awake.

I didn't go to sleep till nearly five at night. I'll have to call in a substitute today for my class. But looking at the time, I was supposed to be up three hours ago.

I slept in till *nine*. What the hell? I'm usually up at six. It's when I'm in a sitting position when I smell the scent of pancakes. I go to the bathroom first, brushing my mouth and flossing before following the scent towards the kitchen. The humming of Raelynn makes a smile rise on my lips.

I step silently in front of the kitchen entrance, her back facing me. She wiggles her shoulders to the music playing in headphones, muttering the words.

My long white socks reach to the top of her calves, and a long white button-up shirt of mine is on as well. She must've showered while I was asleep. Her hair is braided into two, the part split down the middle.

She shuffles her ass to whatever beat is in her ear as she flips a pancake and applauses herself for perfecting it.

Turning around, she reaches for the whipped cream sitting on the counter and then yelps out a scream when she sees me standing there.

She yanks her headphones out her ear, putting her phone on the counter.

"Milo!" She laughs. "You scared the crap out of me."

Jesus, I can't stop smiling at her happiness. Have I caused it?

Whatever wave of pain she faced before our sleep is gone. Or at least pushed away for the time being.

"What are you doing dirtying my kitchen?" I joke, looking around.

She grins, pushing my arm before walking closer and hugging me unexpectedly. Her slender arms wrap around my neck, bringing me down an inch or two.

I'm frozen for a moment. *I have to get used to this.*

She presses herself into my body, and I slip my hands around the small of her back, squeezing.

"You smell like blueberries," I mutter against her neck. She kisses my cheek, and I flush, feeling tingly.

Tingly? For fucks sake. How in the world has she made me feel *tingly* of all things?

"That's because I made us blueberry pancakes. I woke up an hour before you, so I decided this would be a good idea. That you might like it." She looks at me hopefully over her shoulder as she stands back in front of the frying pan—a bowl of pancake mix on the counter.

I step behind her, dipping my finger in the mix and having a taste.

"Hey!" Raelynn laughs, nudging me with her elbow.

"Mm," I hum. "Sweet." My head drops, and I whisper against her ear. "Just like you."

I watch her gasp a little, her eyes widening and shifting away with a smile on her face. She says nothing else of the matter, and I tell myself not to laugh at her flustered self.

"You've made only *two*?" I look at the two lonely things on the plate. "What have you been doing all this time?"

She whips a spatula toward me. I lean my head away from the weapon. "I wanted them to be perfect."

I take the spatula away from her grip with a quick yank. "Shouldn't I be the one cooking for you? I didn't get to make dinner last night..."

Raelynn, behind me, mutters her words, though I just barely make them out. "*I* was your dinner."

I turn to see her in the fridge, her eyes wide and a smirk playing on her lips.

"What was that, love?" I ask.

She shakes her head, pulling out the jar of pickles. Pickles in the morning? "I said nothing."

"Mhm," I smirk—such a terrible liar.

I walk towards her and hug her from behind, kissing her neck. "You're right. You were a *fantastic* dinner."

She snickers, wiggling out of my hands, and attempts to hide the large smile on her face by turning her head away from me.

If I'm not wrong, she hasn't had someone be intimate with her for nearly two years. Neither have I in seven. For several reasons, I chose to avoid getting close to women.

Raelynn, however, has caught my eye ever since she stepped into that elevator.

I grab the pancake mix and pour two small circles on the pan. "I need to call out of work—"

"Oh, I did it for you," she says, hopping you into the counter beside me.

"You did?"

She nods and dips her finger in the pancake mix, just as she scolded me for doing a few minutes ago. "Yeah, I said you were really sick and couldn't make it. I hope that's fine..."

I nod. "And how are you holding up?" Humor leaves my tone for this question.

Her face drops and I nearly regret bringing anything from last night up. She shrugs, "I'm alright."

I nod again, wanting to change the subject for her. Dipping my finger in the pancake mix, I smudge a bit on the tip of her nose.

She gasps and drops down from the counter, gathering mix for herself and throwing it at me. It lands on my cheek, a lot of it.

"You little shit," I curse, wiping it and licking it off my fingers.

"You *gigantic* shit," She smiles challengingly.

I launch myself at her as she tries to flee the small kitchen. Her figure nearly gets past, but I catch her with both hands on her waist, pulling and pinning her against the counter. My shirt sits unbuttoned on her, showing the sports bra she wears and sink pajama shorts. My eyes fail to leave her body.

She's a laughing mess. I press my hands dirty with pancake mix on her cheeks and bend my head down to kiss her on her lips.

Her hands fall on my chest as I savor the kiss for as long as possible, nerves bursting in my mouth.

Breaking away, I stare at her mesmerizing brown eyes before turning to flip my pancakes.

Raelynn clears her throat behind me, and I feel her arms wrap around my body from behind as I cook. She squeezes me tightly as if saying thank you. For what particular, I'm not too sure of.

"This lady had come into my store the first day it opened. I remember her saying her fiancé was a sunshine guy." She mutters against my shoulder blades. "It makes me think."

"Think of what?" I scoop the pancakes onto the plate, washing my hands with Raelynn still clinging to my back.

After last night, it doesn't seem she wants to stop touching me. She's opening up, and quickly.

I never want her to close again.

"I think you're a tulip," she says. "Red tulips."

"Why a tulip?"

She shrugs at me. "No reason."

Raelynn and I sat in the living room alongside Poppy for the next few hours, eating our Pancakes and watching mainly whatever she wished.

Her head rested on my shoulder, her smile not faltering for a moment other than when she cried because we finished a sad movie. She had snuggled close to me, urging me to cry with her, but I could only stare at her and smile.

She stayed at my house the entire week, sleeping on my chest, eating the pickles from my fridge, and reorganizing my bathroom to fit her hair products.

I never thought women needed so many things for their hair. Especially Raelynn.

What on earth is a hair mask?

She introduced me to a bonnet, the long silky purple material she puts her hair in for hair protection.

"I wear it so that my hair doesn't break off. You see how it's long and curly?" She said, touching her curls.

I nodded. "Very pretty."

She flushed, rolling her eyes. My smile rose as she continued. "I use this at night. It doesn't dry out my hair like pillowcases do." She stood on her toes and wrapped it around my head. "Like that."

Driving in my car, thinking back at that memory, I smile at no one other than myself.

While Raelynn works at the shop, I make my way home to check on Mom and Gen. Getting up the building, unlocking the door.

I step inside the house, expecting to see Genesis doing homework and Mom walking around when she should be in bed.

Instead, I hear a voice that's all too familiar to my ears, a voice I would much rather not be hearing.

"Do you have his number? I think the fucker blocked me." I hear Logan say from the kitchen as I enter the house.

What the hell is he doing here?

"No, Logan, I'm not giving you Milo's number," Gen says. "You aren't even supposed to be in here. You're lucky mom in the hospital; she'd probably have the cops on you by now— Actually, no, she'd feed you food, then call Milo, and then *he'd* call the cops."

Moms in the hospital?

"At least tell me where he is. I've come around three times this week."

I make myself known with my steps. "What do you want."

Logan turns to me, his dirt blonde hair is messy on the top of his head. And so does Genesis, freezing as she stops with a plate in her hand.

"Milo," she greets. "Awesome, now this one can leave me alone."

"Why are you opening the door for people that aren't family?" I ask her.

She looks at Logan, her face dropping. "He was family once." She stops unloading the dishwasher, leaving us, but not before muttering in French, "Avant le premier combat, au moins."

Before the first fight, at least.

We rarely use our native tongue; when we do, it's mainly to hide what we're saying from others. I chose to ignore her words.

I turn to Logan. His eye still has the faint outline of where I hit him when he knocked into Raelynn last week. Not a shred of sorrow sits within me.

I've known Logan Ledger since we were teens. He was a boy snooping through the trash around my dad's neighborhood.

When I found him, he said a rich person's trash is a poor person's treasure.

I took him to my house that day where mom—who wasn't sick then—and dad, who wasn't the worst, had cooked him dinner and treated him as she would me. I wasn't a kid who made many friends, so Logan and I becoming close was a big deal. Genesis was much younger then, though, over the years he became a second brother to her as well.

He was with me through thick and thin, and me with him. Through his alcohol problem, the problems with his toxic household. The person he called when he needed a roof over his head. I was there.

Until he threw me under a bridge. Multiple times.

"I'm sorry, man," he says. "About the party and your girl."

"I don't want to hear it, get out." My fist clenches at my side.

"I mean it. It was a dick move. I was trying to make you mad after you cut me off. It's been forever. Seven years, dude."

"I don't give a shit. You *slept* with two of my girlfriends," I exclaim. "Fucking yeah, I'd cut you off."

"Come on, you mean that crazy chick you didn't even fucking like? I was doing you the favor! And the other one, the one your dad made you date? You didn't like her either, dude, you were fucking miserable with her."

"That's beside the point." He's pissing me off. "You don't go and screw my girlfriends because you think I'm better off! Are you fucking mad?"

My breath quickens with anger as I think of him trying something on Raelynn. Despite her not being my true girlfriend...

I continue, "And the money? You stole half a *million* out of my dad's account. Who did he blame? *Me*."

He stares at me—no words to back him up on this one.

I walk close to him, locked with his gaze. "You knew my father. You *knew* how he'd react and who he would blame, and you still did it."

He drops his head and shakes it. "I'm sorry, man," the words rough.

"I don't think you are, Logan." I push him, and he stumbles back, knocking over a stray spoon and huffing from his nose. My fists are now aching for a punch to his jaw. "You're still best buddies with my father; you're the son he wishes he had. Go back to him then."

"I don't want to fight you, Milo. I didn't come here for that."

"He nearly *KILLED* me!" I shout in his face, the words straining my throat. "I couldn't go to school for two weeks after what you did because of the swelling in my face caused by his hands. I couldn't lay down for months after the many hits to my back with his fucking belt!"

I push his chest again. "Do you know what leather feels like ripping into your skin over and over again? Because I do." I wrap a hand around the collar of my shirt, my blood boiling and my head hammering at my chest. "Do you know what it feels like never to want to take your shirt off? To never want eyes on you? Because I fucking *do*."

"Milo, stop it!" Genesis shouts from behind me.

I let go of Logan, turning to see my crying sister, a hand over her mouth. "Genesis, go to your room if it doesn't concern you."

"Yeah, like hell I will," she pulls out her phone and dials a number. "I'm calling the police."

I almost reach for the phone, but she taps her finger against my chin. Twice.

A code we created when we were little. It meant 'play along.' We used it so we wouldn't blow up each other lies in front of people.

I take a long breath in my hand as Logan begins to panic. "You're just gonna let her call the police on me?"

I stare at him, leaning back against the island counter.

His jaw tenses, and he shakes his head, scoffing. "Fuck you, Milo." He looks at Genesis, holding the phone to her ear, but does nothing but shake his head. The only think he *can* do.

I watch as he stomps away and out of the house, opening the front door and slamming it shut.

My gaze lingers on it, wondering how we got to this point after being so close.

I look at Genesis, and she gives me a pitiful smile. "You're welcome."

Pushing off the counter, I walk towards her, ruffling her hair. "You said mom was in the hospital. Why?"

"Her checkup. Dad took her there an hour or two ago." Surprising.

"Is she alright?"

"They haven't finished running the test, should know by tomorrow."

I sigh, stress leaving my body by the second, just as my phone dings. I pull it out, reading a text from Raelynn.

Rae: My moms at my apartment and looking for my boyfriend of two years, who's my date for my sister's wedding.

Rae: It's in a month, don't forget.

I smirk at the message and go to type back.

Me: I haven't forgotten. I'm on my way; tell her about how much you adore me to pass the time.

She sends back an emoji, rolling her eyes, and I close my own, imagining her doing just that, rolling her eyes. A chill runs down my spine.

God, how I want to make her do that every chance I get. But instead of attitude, she'd be doing it because she can't stop coming. I'd be achieving something for her she desperately wants. And I will, with time.

"Oh lord, is that Raelynn you're texting?" Genesis, who I forgot was in the room, speaks from the couch across the room. Fucking hell.

"Yes, how could you even tell?"

Her face is full of disgust, "because... your *face*. It's all gushy and lovey-dovey looking. It's actually beginning to creep me out."

"You're a liar," I press, embarrassed.

"Nope. Your cheeks get all red. It's gross. My big brother is finally a sucker for someone. Took you long enough," She snorts.

I walk towards the couch near me and grab a throw pillow, putting the name to use and flinging it at Genesis.

16

MILO

"So, Milo," Ruth, Raelynn's mother, starts, and she lowers her fork onto her plate. "When do you plan on proposing?"

I nearly choke on the rice, traveling halfway down my throat. Raelynn holds her mouth shut beside me to prevent spitting water out.

Propose? We aren't even together.

Giving a quick clear to my throat before speaking, "If I tell you, it won't be a surprise," I laugh heartedly, hiding my shock.

Raelynn, behind me, sets her glass of water down on her dinner table. "Don't you think it's a little too early for marriage, mom?"

I look around the table at the faces. Ruth, Gia, and David—Her dad—all look around knowingly. I can't help but feel like I'm intruding on this family dinner. Raelynn and her mom have been throwing one another daggers with their gazes. Gia has spoken about her wedding numerous times, and David hasn't really spoken at all other than an attempt to scare me with passive-aggressive threats.

"*Early?*" Ruth exclaims. "It's been two years, hasn't it?" *Zero years, actually.* "Gia got engaged six months after Dallas, and she got together."

Gia nods her head in confirmation.

Raelynn huffs impatiently at my side, sliding her fork around her plate. She hasn't really eaten a full bite since we sat down thirty minutes ago.

"Well, it's a good thing not everyone wants to be Gia, mom. I get it, she's *perfect.* Isn't that right, Gia?" her voice rises. The tension spewing off of her runs a chill down my spine. I hate seeing her so agitated.

From beneath the table, I slide a hand on her thigh to feel it shaking rapidly. My thumb rubs against the side, her simple spring dress allowing me to do so.

"Don't bring me into this," says Gia, raising her hands. "I'm a bystander."

"You're already in it. You've been in it since I was born, since all I've ever been compared to is my *amazing* older sister." The sarcasm drips off her words. She scoffs. "I mean, God forbid anyone fucks before they're married—"

"Raelynn!" Ruth shouts.

"Oh, sorry, Mom. Did you not like hearing your own fucking words? Don't pretend you're some kind Christian mother because Milo's in front of you because I promise you, he will hear every crappy thing you've ever done to me."

Ruth's jaw locks as she stares intently at Raelynn, her grip on her fork concerningly tight.

"Well, I'm sorry I tried to discipline you! You were careless, and you're lucky any man wants what's left of you, let alone this one." She points to me, and the brewing anger is now rising.

It pisses me off the way she speaks to Raelynn. The same way my father's words had. I grind my teeth, sitting back in my chair, my hand still set on Raelynn's leg, the only thing stopping me from setting off.

Raelynn stands, and my hand slips to the back of her knee. "I know this is shocking, but I don't *need* a man. I have one because I chose to. He's here because I *allowed* him to be."

"Does he know about your past?"

"My past is no one's concern but my own!" Her voice is nearly at shouting level, shaky and uneven.

"Does he know you were with a different boy each night? How I'd be so afraid something happened to you only to find out my daughter was just screwing any boy that looked in her direction!" She laughs menacingly, shaking her head.

I stand up with Raelynn, attempting to end this, but she puts a hand on my chest before I can speak. "You know what?" Raelynn scoffs, shaking her head and holding a finger to her mother.

Raelynn eyes turn glossy. "Yeah, I had sex, Mom. That's what teenagers do; they have SEX!"

Ruth stands, slamming her hand on the table. "You ruined this family's name!"

"All you ever care about is your *fucking* reputation," her voice cracks. "You couldn't brag about having a virgin daughter. Well, too fucking bad."

Ruth laughs. "Never mind you being a virgin. That was out the window a long time ago. It was the fact you were careless. A baby and abortion at nineteen? You hadn't even gotten your first job. You lived with me, and you—"

"Was *raped*!" The two words spewed from Raelynn echo through the house, bouncing off the walls surrounding us and hushing the room. "I was raped, mom."

Emotion leaves with her words like her soul was used to create them, hitting me square in the heart despite me knowing already.

Gasps follow from Gia, a hand falling over her mouth and a pained look on her face. The father looks at Raelynn, confused.

Had they not known? *None* of them?

Tears stream down Raelynn's face and her body shakes. I slide a hand onto the small of her back, but she hits my hand responsively.

"*Stop*!" she shouts at me, turning. The anger in her eyes dissipates when she looks at me as if she wants to apologize but just shakes her head. "Please, just... don't." She whispers, whipping her tears from her cheeks.

"Raelynn," Gia says. "What are you talking about? When did this happen?"

Raelynn rolls her eyes. "I think this is over. Everyone should get going." She grabs her plate, but her hand wobbles too much to pick it up.

I reach forward and take the plate from her. "I'll get it later, love," I say softly.

Her bloodshot eyes blink, tears falling as she hugs herself. She's scared, like a kid lost in a mall. She stands with the announcement of her rape floating in the air.

"Raelynn," her mother walks around the table, her voice low. "Why didn't you tell me?"

She swallows. "I tried. I tried, Mom, and you didn't *listen* to me." Her voice strains. "The only thing you heard was the word *pregnant*; the next thing I know, I was off at the abortion center. Several awful words followed."

My chest twists, my heart aching with the words I'm hearing. That bastard needs to rot for what he's down to her. The pain he's caused her. And so does her mother.

"I didn't know," Ruth shakes her. She reaches for her daughter's arm, but Raelynn yanks it back.

"I said to get out. All of you."

Gia stands up, nodding and crying, giving me one goodbye glance and a sad smile before going to find her things in the front. David also looks pained, though not a word to show his sympathy, as he leaves the dining room hastily.

Ruth stands before us, and Raelynn backs away behind my arm.

Ruth speaks, "Raelynn—"

"She said to leave," I interrupt, my voice low and asserting.

"I'm speaking to my daughter. I like you, don't make me change that."

I step forward, looking down at her, Raelynn standing quietly behind me. "It seems my kindness was given too loosely, hm? I don't care if you like me or not; once you disrespected Raelynn, you became unimportant to me, and neither am I here for you to 'like me.' I know you know nothing about me, but I'll make sure you see what I'm capable of if you don't leave this apartment in the next ten seconds."

A scoff leaves her lips, and her nose flairs as if offended. Good, be offended. It's probably not even a quarter of the pain I know Raelynn has been through.

I feel Raelynn latch on to my arm, hugging it close to her body for comfort.

"What are you inciting? That you'll hit an old woman? What does that say about you then?" Ruth crosses her arms across her chest.

I clap my hands behind my back. "Hit you?" I shake my head. "I don't need to hit anyone to ruin their lives. I can call a publisher, and in about twenty minutes, they can, and will, concoct and publish just about any story I want into the local newspapers. Now, if you want to keep your job and your *sacred family name*, you now have *three* seconds to get the hell out of our faces." My face stays flat, drowning my anger for Raelynn's sake.

Ruth shakes her head, turning around and waving me off while mumbling to herself. I watch her grab her bag, and her thing's angrily, following the other family members who've already made their way out the door.

The door shuts with a slam, the sound leaving static behind.

I close my eyes immediately to cool myself for the precious woman behind me, turning to Raelynn, who unlatches my arm and begins sobbing.

The muffled wails fill the room, and my eyes drop in sadness. She turns to the dining table and starts to clean it as tears fall from the dirty plates.

"Raelynn," I call out of her. "Raelynn, look at me."

She shakes her head, her cry hitching, shaking her chest rapidly as she inhales. "No, Milo, just go home." She grabs the stacked plates and carries them to the sink, dropping them in and turning on the water.

"Please, love, talk to me."

"I just want to be happy! I want to have a family—someone who cares. Dad didn't even *look* at me after I said what happened. How do you hear your daughter's been raped and not say a *word*? I just, I can't breathe, Milo."

She grips the edge of the sink, and I walk up behind her, long sobs falling from her lips.

I slip my hands around her waist and stomach, the back of my eyes burning for her as she lets me touch her. I shut the water off and turned her around, bringing her into my arms. She clings to me as her life depends on it.

"I care," I tell her, kissing the side of her head. "So much more than you may know." She sniffles with cries against my chest, and her heart beats rapidly. I repeat the words, kissing her head again.

My head falls to her ear. "Meeting you was by far the best thing to happen to me in the last seven years, Raelynn."

She tightens her grip on me, her arms wrapped around my chest. Her cries soften, growing quiet with my words of comfort, leaning back against the kitchen counter.

I stand here with her for several minutes, stroking her back and kissing her head now and again as she digs her head into my chest.

I wish I could cheer her up; I *want* to cheer her up. I want nothing more than to see a smile on her face right now, and I think I know somewhere and something that'll do just that.

"Come on," I say.

She lifts her head from my cheek, her eyes puffy and red and her nose glowing a shade brighter. I wipe a tear away with my thumb and slide it down to take her hand in mine.

"Where?"

I bring her hand up to my lips and kiss her knuckles. "Somewhere you can breathe, darling."

***

Driving in the USA will always confuse me, especially when I come home from visiting my mom's side of the family in London.
With the whole wheel on the other side, deal. But I adjust quickly, just like I do with many things, just like I did with Raelynn.

My hand sits on her thigh. Her dress has ridden up a bit, showing a tattoo I haven't noticed before on the upper thigh. A snake twirls in an S shape.

I slide my finger against it and look back at the road.

"Nice tattoo," I say, breaking the silence.

"Thanks." She whispers. "I got it to cover some of my scars."

My lips turn down. I know the feeling. For the first time, I want to tell someone about mine. The long white scars run in all directions across my back. The scars that engrained into my flesh the permanent evidence of how cruel my father can be. I want to show Raelynn. Show her she isn't alone in that aspect, just like she taught me without even realizing it.

"You're beautiful," I say, glancing at her. "All of you." Her head drops a little, hair falling over her face as she flushes. She doesn't need to say thank you; that reaction will be enough for me every single time.

I stop my car in front of our designation and unbuckle my seatbelt.

Raelynn leans in her chair and looks in front of us. "The Brooklyn Bridge?" She questions curiously.

I nod, unbuckling her even though she knows how to do it herself. In the small compartment of my car, I open it and pull out two of the three locks in there. Genesis usually forgets her locks for her track lockers at home, so I keep spares in here.

Holding it up, I show her the lock and smirk.

"What are you up to?" She laughs softly, and it makes my heartbeat quicken.

"Stay here."

I exit the car and walk around to her side, opening the door and offering my hand.

She giggles. "Being a gentleman, hm?" She takes my hand and steps out.

I close the door. "My mother raised me to treat the women I adore with high respect."

She's looking at me with soft, large eyes, like she was questioning whether my words were real or not. I lock her hand in mine and begin walking along the famous bridge.

The sky above displays the full moon. No clouds fog the sight either; only the glow of the many sky-scraping buildings behind us illuminates the otherwise night. The wooden floor of the bridge beneath us slows a breeze from the East River below to seep through. Raelynn looks at the water, fascinated and intrigued by the waves and the singular speed boat shooting past.

She looks up at the structure of the brown bridge, her mouth parted slightly and her eyes wide with excitement.

"Have you never been to the Brooklyn Bridge before?" I ask her.

She looks at me and shakes her head. "No, I never had a reason to."

A smile grows on my face. I'm her reason now.

When I get to the section of the bridge I want, I stop her stride and turn her to the patterned metal fence of the bridge where hundreds and maybe even thousands of locks sit hanging.

Her jaw drops as she looks at them all. "Oh my God," she whispers, grinning. "There're so many!" She drags her hand across some of the locks. "I knew people did this. I never actually thought there was—awe. This one says, *my dog and I forever*," She pokes her bottom lip out, looks at me with the lock connected to the metal in her hand, and then drops it.

"I heard this is a tradition in New York. It signifies a bond and relationship that won't break. I wanted us to join it." I had the lock with my pointer finger. She looks at it, walking closer to me.

"Really?" She looks at me with hope and then back at the lock.

I nod, "Yes, darling."

Slipping out the sharpie and uncapping it, I write on the lock a small note on the front, and then on the back, I write the date at the bottom:

I adore you, Raelynn Garcia
—Love, Milo
March '21

I show her the lock, and she gasps softly.

"I love it," her eyes twinkle with tears as she slowly takes it from my hand. She grins, and I smile at her so hard my cheeks hurt.

She takes the Sharpie from my hand. flips the lock and begins to write. A moment later, she lowers it and hands it to me. "I think it's done now," she says.

I take the lock and read the other side:

I admire you, Milo Evans
—Love, Rae ♡

My stomach twists with a weird flutter, and my cheeks burn fiercely.

Without a second to spare, I grip her waist and pull her flat against my body, dropping my forehead against hers and kissing her. Hard.

She grips my shoulders, and I swallow her giggles, leaning her backward into the kiss, not feeling close enough, but can't possibly get any closer.

I keep the kiss slow, cautious of how fast my mouth is moving, cautious of the placement of my hands, keeping them just above her tailbone.

She grabs my face between her hands, rubbing her thumbs against the rubble on my cheeks and squeezing, puckering my lips. She looks at me.

"Meeting you is the best thing to happen to me, too, Milo." She pecks me once on my puckered lips and lets go.

"So much for pretending," I say before letting go of her and locking the lock around one of the flat metal lines of the fence. It sits with the others, labeling this very day.

I look back at Raelynn, and she's biting her lip with a smile.

I tilt my head. "Did this cheer you up well, love?"

She nods. "Yes, but I want to go to your apartment now."

I take her hand in mine and walk alongside her, making way for a biker to ride past. "Tired already? It's only ten."

She shakes her head and raises herself on her tiptoes so people walking past can't hear the words she whispers in my ear.

"No, I want to try your tongue again."

Kayla Rose

17

RAELYNN

I've never wanted something— *someone* so badly.

That they've completely overtaken my body, heart, soul, and whatever sentimental pieces of me are left to confiscate, because the truth is, I don't even feel like myself with his lips on my neck and his hands running down my body, like I'm the hottest woman he's ever encountered. If he's not touching me for more than a hot second, I'd materialize and dissipate just like I do in his fantasies, just like he does in *mine*.

Milo locks the front door behind us without looking, the click followed by our kisses filling the living room.

"Raelynn," His lips brush against mine as he pants. I open my eyes, wanting his lips back, wanting the feeling— one that feels so foreign now— back instantly.

I raise my toes to try to reach his lips, but his height fights against me. He takes my jaw in his hand, clicking his tongue so that a soft sound seeps out his mouth. My swollen lips squish together with his gentle pinch.

He smirks and I stare at the curve of his mouth. "Eager, hm?"

I nod, and his hand drops from my cheeks, down my neck, and softly wraps around the base of my neck as his forehead dips down and presses against mine.

A rush of heat falls over me, my body being pinned to the front door. His lips touch my ear.

"You never leave my mind. You know that, right, princess?" The British seductive accent that might never stop turning me on drips off of that damn nickname, slithering its way between my legs.

Nodding, I squeeze my thighs together to find relief, but the softness of his fingers finds the back of my left thigh, raising it high beside his hips as he presses his hardness against the thin material of my dress.

"Speak, Raelynn. I need to know you want me as badly as I want you right now. I need to know you're *okay*."

He kisses my neck. I melt, the only thing holding me up being his hands around my body and the spaghetti legs under me.

Speak? I can't even *think* straight, let alone form words and pass them up my cardboard throat.

My eyes struggle to stay open as he sucks on my skin underneath my ear.

He isn't helping his cause; my back arches off the door and closes whatever space has resonated between Milo and my body, leaving only the thin material of our clothes keeping us apart.

I nod, and he shakes his head, laughing. "*Words*, darling. I want to hear your pretty voice." He leans his head up and cups my cheek, his other hand squeezing my bare thigh so close to the center of my legs that I nearly lose it.

I swallow, "I'm okay." I manage to let out. "I'm more than okay, Milo." A silence follows my words as I think of the next ones, hard and long. "I trust you." It's barely audible, the three words, but I know he's heard them. The way his eyes widen with a new desire proves it to me.

A new shade of gray covers his eyes, intoxicating me like staring into the sky right before a rainstorm. Intimidating, stern, but dangerously exciting, I can practically see myself running in the rain, soaked and high off euphoria.

"You do?" He questions with a crooked smile.

I answer him with a nod. "I do."

His hand on my face drops down to my other thigh, and he lifts it as well, sliding his arm around my waist and pulling me off the door.

I cling onto him, my arm around his neck as he carries me down his hallway.

My words meet his ear in a whisper, "I promise this time I'll work or at least I hope."

He opens his already cracked open room door with his foot. "You don't need to promise me anything." He lowers me to my feet, both palms rising to my cheeks, and he bends his neck to kiss me on my nose. My clit throbs below the wet cloth of my soaked underwear.

His lips travel from my nose to my forehead, placing a gentle kiss on it. "You work perfectly fine, Rae, perfectly fine."

"You think so?"

He smirks, "I guarantee it." My dress rises with his hands. Above my hips, up my waist, past my breasts. "Raise your arms, my love."

I raise them, and he pulls my dress over my head and drops it on the floor beside us, taking a long slow gaze at my body with parted lips and colored cheeks. His eyes run down at my snake tattoo on my thigh, to my feet, and all the way back up to meet my eyes again. A stare that makes me feel capable of anything in this disdainful world.

He steps closer, putting his hands on my hips and moving me along with him until the back of my knees hit the bed.

"Are you going to show me how to use your favorite things?" He helps me to the middle of the bed and kisses my collarbone.

"Tonight isn't about me," he says. "I want to discover everything that sets those eyes fluttering, Raelynn." Pecks of kisses travel down my stomach below my belly button, and I moan, grabbing his hair.

"I want to explore you," *Kiss*. "Find out exactly what it is that makes you scream," *kiss*, "and be the *only* one capable of making you come."

My underwear is ruined; he ruined them. The pulsing twitch underneath them, becoming nearly unbearable, painful even.

"I want to," I nearly whine, my breath shallow and pleading.

"I know you do." He kisses the lace of my panties. "I know."

He doesn't take off my underwear. Instead, he hooks a finger around the wet center and pulls it to the side, exposing me. A low groan escapes his throat, the dim light of his bedroom casting a shadow beneath his eyebrows as he looks down at me in awe.

I fight the small voice at the back of my head telling me to hide, to run away from his gaze. But I fight it.

I fight Jaden away,

He will not control me; I won't let him any longer.

Milo looks up at my face and pauses a bit; his mouth twists as if thoughts are running through his head. His brows furrowed cutely with a face that says a lot, yet nothing at all. What is on his mind?

"What is it?" I question.

"Take them off," He orders.

A second passes before I listen, raising my hips and slipping off my underwear till they're at my ankles and then on the bed sheets.

He only sticks his arm out, offering me his hand. "Get up."

I take his hand with no further thought and follow his movement curiously as he brings me up to my knees and takes over the spot, I once laid in seconds ago. He rubs the back of my hand with his thumb and gently pulls me closer to him, tugging my leg over his torso so that I'm straddling his lap.

I look down at him, the delighted smile on his face as the feeling of control immediately overtakes me. I like being up here.

He kisses my hand, "Use my face, princess."

He guides me to his head, and my chin lowers closer to my chest the more I inch my dripping wetness to his lips.

My breath shallows, quickening, his hands grabbing my ass from behind.

We hold eye contact as I lower myself slowly onto his mouth, feeling him kiss my clit.

My legs jerk at the amazing burst of nerves that flutters through me from one taste of satisfaction. My hands find his hair, and he lets me take my time, lowering myself back onto him.

This time he takes my clit between his lips, sucking me and slipping his tongue along the slick lips of my pussy.

I gasp for air, my chest deprived of breaths I'm forgetting to feed it. But I can't think of anything, anything other than his warm, long tongue dragging against me.

I lower myself more and let out a long sigh as I watch him enjoy the taste of me. My hips begin to rock, creating a rhythm between his tongue and mine.

"*Yes*, God, yes," I cry out as he quickly flicks the tip of his tongue against me.

My fingers grip tighter around the dark, straight hair strands on his head.

He hums, the vibration shooting through me. A gust of wind brushes past me from the cracked open fire escape window, adding to the goosebumps rising all over my skin.

I grind violently against Milo's tongue, making high-pitched noises that are probably being heard from somewhere next door, but I couldn't care less.

Milo wraps his hand around my thighs and inserts his tongue inside of me, thrusting it in and out at a speed I just can't fucking handle.

My breath completely halts, eyes rolling to the back of my eyes and my stomach sucking in. He shakes his head, rubbing his lips into me, inserting his tongue again, creating that amazing feeling consecutively until—

My legs begin to shake, and I squirm above him. "It's too..." My words drift off as I attempt to catch my bearings. "It's too much, Milo, I *can't*." I slow my hips, losing the energy to continue my movement.

"*Mm-nm,*" He hums in disapproval, raising both of us as he sits up, his mouth still attached to me.

He grabs my waist and drops me down hard on my back, pinning me against the bed and locking my legs over his shoulders.

My lower stomach begins to twist with something hot. I feel it; it's so close. *I'm so close.*

Milo's tongue runs dangerously steady at a speed not too fast or too slow, making sure to slip inside of me every few seconds. My back arches off the bed. "*Milo,*" I whimper. "I— fucking *yes,"* Long groans, leaving me. *"Please."*

My legs spazz, and my clit twitches against his tongue as a warm gush of me squirts into his mouth for the first time in two years. A squeaking scream of praises and cries ripples through me, representing every part of me that feels too good to express with words. My body shakes uncontrollably, and Milo cleans me, hums following. My mouth drops wide open, my eyelids failing to keep still as they flutter, trying to watch as Milo continues.

Continues? He's continuing.

My already soaked, sensitive clit jerks and jumps with every pass his tongue does over it. With no control over my strength, I begin to pull at Milos's hair, tears of pleasure and euphoria filling my eyes as he fills my cup and spills it over. He removes his lips from against me, giving me a second breather.

He licks his lips clean and praises me, "Look at you." I smile. "One more, baby. I know you got it." His words run a shiver up my spine.

I shake my head, unsure if I truly can.

He only smiles, showing his teeth, and lowers his pink, wet lips against my warmth again.

It doesn't take him long to prove me wrong; not even minutes later, I am shivering and squealing as I cum for the second time against his tongue. This time harder, stronger, and breathtaking, sucking the little air stored in my lungs out.

My head floats, or so it feels like it, up into the clouds, higher than the tallest buildings and the tallest mountains and above all else, because that's how Milo's achieved in making me feel.

Like I'm on top of this God damn world.

I pant as Milo rises, his hands digging into the bed at the sides of my head. He leans down and kisses me hard and quickly.

"I did it!" My voice cracks as my eyes fill with tears for surpassing an achievement I thought was impossible. Turns out nothing ever is. "*Twice.*"

I grin and giggle, kissing Milo as a thank you.

He smiles against my lips, "Good job, darling." His voice is so raspy and low I can feel it in my chest. "You did such a good job."

I wrap my hands around his neck to hug him before noticing his face, the painful look on it, and the redness across his nose and cheeks.

"Milo, are you alright?"

He brushes a curl away from my face and nods. "I'll be fine. I'm just glad. Glad I could help."

My eyes shift between his shiny ones. "*You* need help," I say to myself, mostly out of realization. "Don't you?"

He shakes his head and leans up, but I grab his hand in mine. He lets out a breathy laugh.

"You don't owe me anything, Raelynn, I can go to the bathroom—"

"Oh, shut up," I roll my eyes and plant my feet on the floor. He watches me, hard, confused as I get down on my knees, the carpet cushioning me.

I look up at him, his legs in front of me and the clear bulge that's probably the cause of his pained expression visible in his slacks.

"Are you sure?" He brings a hand to my chin and pulls it up a bit while he scoots closer to the edge of the bed.

I nod. "I want to do this for you." With all he's helped me with, with all he's done, this is the least I want to do to him. "You deserve to feel as good as you made me feel," I whisper.

He turns his head and closes his eyes, his jaw flexing as he bites down.

Turning his head back to me, he drops his hand and brings them up and around my curls, locking them in a gentle ponytail.

"Do what you want to me, darling."

18

Raelynn

There are not many people I can say I am attached to.

Not many things have my heart, if it doesn't include flowers and cold dirt that get stuck underneath my nails.

So, when I finally choose to give my heart out, I wear it on my sleeves, out and vulnerable to the poor soul who has to handle it carefully.

He sits in front of me, not knowing he has my heart in the palm of his hands, as he strokes the side of my jaw with his thumb.

Do what you want to me, Love. Words I've never heard said by a man. I've always been the pawn, the one being done, not the one doing. I never had power or control during sex. I never had this empowering feeling of what it's like to take control.

It's like my very own cocaine.

Milo watches me intently as I unzip his black slacks, the zipper slipping over the bump underneath caused by his boner. My face burns.

He lifts himself a bit, slipping down his pants and revealing his gray boxers underneath; a small damp spot in the center from his pre-cum wets the material, and the sight revives the pulsing heartbeat between my legs.

I look up at Milo, whose cheeks are beaming red, his pants at his ankles, and his eyes wide. The veins in his left arm pop out as he leans back on it, lifting his hips into a thrust a bit to adjust himself.

"You want to see?" He asks me breathlessly.

I nod at him, my hands lying flat on my thighs as he widens his knees further apart.

He grins at me, pulling his lips to one side of his face, and cocks his head to the side for a second. "Then what's the wait? Scared?"

I raise an eyebrow, catching the cockiness of his tone.

I suppress my smile, "Don't let my finish go to your head, or I might just let you sit in misery while I go and sleep."

His eyes lower as if he likes my threat to torture him. "Being the only guy to get you off " sounds like an accomplishment worth bragging about. Especially with how loud you got. I didn't think I'd love hearing someone scream my name so much until a few minutes ago—"

I stand up and clamp my hand over the embarrassing words leaving his mouth.

Laughs break through my lips as I climb on top of Milo, bringing him down to his back with his body between my legs.

He eyes my tits that bounce in his face like a dog looking at traffic.

I sit purposefully on his bulge. *Oh.*

His eyes close tightly, and he groans loud into my palm, thrusting his hips up against my pussy. Gasping sharply at the single harsh force, butterflies swarm up my stomach.

He feels giant underneath me, full and perfect, and I haven't even seen him yet. Just the pulsing heat of him below, separated by the single piece of gray material he wears, and his twitches are nearly enough to make me cum again.

I let go of his mouth and grind my hips into him, my jaw dropping and breath shallowing.

"Fuck me," He pleads out softly, his eyes dark and gleaming with arousal, and I rub myself against his hardness, trying to pull myself together just as much as him. "*Please.*"

"No," I say with a smirk.

Teasing him a bit won't hurt. It won't hurt at all.

My head drops beside his, and my lips brush his stubble on the way down. "Not until I think you've been a good boy."

My nails run through his hair, and I pull slightly, rocking my clit into him at a faster speed.

"*Raelynn*," a mess of a whimper leaves his throat; the sound of my name is barely distinguishable.

His hand rubs softly up and down my back as he mutters my name over and over again.

I press my palms into the shirt he still wears, too close to another climax to worry about taking it off of him.

My eyes fail to stay open as I rock my hips violently into him. Wetness dresses his boxers, drenching them along with the drips pre-cum that make their way out of him.

I feel it, myself flying alongside the clouds once again, the lightness of my head and the tightness of my stomach from my building orgasm. I bite down on my bottom lip and throw my head back, jaw-dropping and stomach-twisting.

God, oh my *fucking* God.

A third round of me drips onto Milo's boxers, sticking to his throbbing bulge that sits between my lips.

Everything in this room could evaporate, disappear, and I wouldn't notice. I grin and giggle with a moan as I ride out the feeling. This might become my new favorite thing. There's a reason I loved it so much two years ago, but this? This with Milo is different on so many levels. I never want to lose it. I need this forever. I need him forever.

I look down to see Milo staring at me in fascination, his jaw slanted and pupils dilated.

"You are incredible," he tells me. "I don't think I'll ever get tired of seeing you cum for me like that."

Many rings of curls cover my face, so I slide a hand under and flip them back, a few fall back in their previous place anyway.

I grin at Milo and lean down to peck his lips. "I hope you never do," I whisper. "It's fun."

When I go to pull back, he catches my head with hair in his hand, lifting a little to speak in my ear. "Have your fun, princess." The words sound more like a warning than sincere. "Turn around and have fun trying to fit me down that pretty throat of yours."

My eyes widen and he lets go, tapping my leg. Without another word, I rise and twist myself so my ass face Milo, my knees at his shoulders. His pants have fallen to the ground now, leaving him in just his boxers, practically dripping with my cum. I wrap my fingers around the waistband, dragging it along his waist, and bend myself over onto one elbow beside his hip just as he grabs my thighs from behind. He plants kisses on my inner thighs, near my scars, and over my ass, tracing his fingers over my tattoo.

I slip his boxers down slowly, watching as his dick makes itself known by falling hard against his stomach. Milo sighs against my skin.

With one hand on his hip, I hesitantly take hold of his base, wrapping my hands around him. Veins travel from his pink tip all the way down the length of him.

Knowingly, my thumb presses into the slit of his tip, and he groans, cursing while I rub in circles the sweet spot men love so much.

I stroke him as I do so, dropping my head to the side to drag my tongue up his base just as slowly.

From behind me, Milo's head lifts, and his lips lock around my clit, and I gasp when he spits on it, pressing the flat of his tongue out to stimulate me.

From the hour we've been in this room, he's discovered the perfect place to rub his tongue on me, making my eyes roll back uncontrollably.

Attempting to focus and do just as good as he, I hold Milo by his base, kissing and wrapping my lips around his tip.

His size is just as big as I expected. Maybe even more. My mouth stretches open as I slide him inside, letting my saliva soak him. His thighs tense, and he groans into my pussy.

I drag my lips down the side of him, then back up, encasing my mouth back around his thickness once again.

This time, I slide down, feeling him throb against my tongue as his tip travels to the back of my throat.

My breath stops, and I flex my throat against his tip, then quickly lift my head to gasp for air.

"Fuck yeah, Raelynn," he mutters, inserting his finger in me. "Take me deeper."

I stroke him in my hands a bit before repeating my steps. Quickly bobbing my head on him, his tip hits the back of my throat every time. I moan from his mouth also on me. and he helps by thrusting his hips up and toward my mouth.

Groans leave his mouth against me, and he squeezes my ass tight. Breathing becomes impossible as his tip bobs up and down my throat, and Milo's whimpers become louder until he stiffens under me just as my clit twitches in his mouth, getting me off on his tongue for the fourth time.

He lets loose in my throat, and I let him. When he's done, I swallow his release, leaving him twitching.

I turn around, and from under me, Milo is exhausted, it seems, his chest heaving and his jaw slanted open as he pants. All because of me.

He opens his eyes and grins. I grin at him, seeing him rise and close my face so he can kiss me. And he does, long and passionately, with his fingers buried in my hair. And for the first time in a long time, I feel safe in my own skin around a man my trust runs deeply with.

I part from Milo's lips and give him a small smile. "Thank you."

He kisses my cheek in response. "What do you want to eat? Pizza? Choose anything you want."

I laugh and stare at him, wondering why he hasn't tried having sex with me. He can, I would let him. I'd let him do a lot of things. But I let it go, wondering if I'm getting ahead of myself. I've done things today that I haven't done for years, and it was amazing. I don't want to ruin it by overthinking.

"Pizza," I answer with a smile.

He nods and gets off the bed with my hand in his, kissing me once again before bringing me along with him.

"It should be here when you get out of the shower," he says. "I'll give you a change of your clothes."

I put a hand on his shirt, "Can I wear your things?" I question. "I like them better."

We stop at the bathroom, and he smirks. "I like you better in them too, love." He opens the door to the bathroom and starts the shower. I watch him bend down, eyeing his shirt that he's yet to take off.

"Milo," I say. "You aren't getting in with me?"

He turns and takes a moment to answer. "No, I'll just take one after you."

I walk closer to him, placing my hand against his chest. It's hard underneath. I can feel every muscle tense under my touch. So, he can't possibly be insecure about himself. Right?

"Why?" I slip my hands under his shirt and glide them over his hard abs. God. Counting six... seven... eight?

But I notice his demeanor change, his eyes turning into worry and his jaw clenching as my hands explore what he hides under this shirt. He looks almost scared. Scared of what exactly I can't seem to pinpoint.

My hands reach his back and it's then when I gasp at the texture, a bumpy feeling my fingers drag over. Like trenches and welts in the ground of a warzone.

Milo backs away in panic, pulling my hands away and shaking his head. Turning around to face the sink. "No."

I stand behind him, confused and unsure what to make of what I just felt. Scars, I'm sure of it. I have them myself, the familiar roughness of the skin.

But he felt much more severe. No nails that had been dug into his back like my thighs, but something much more brutal, and my eyes began to sting just thinking of all the possibilities.

I press my lips together as I walk behind Milo, hearing him sniffle, his head drops between his shoulders.

My hand rises, and I lay it on his back over the shirt, feeling the damage. "Milo... what happened?" My voice cracks, tears full of hurt for him spilling from my eyes.

He shakes his head. "Nothing you need to worry about." He lifts his head, and I watch him in the mirror. His nose, cheeks, and eyes are red from the tears that shine under the light. My chest twisted at the sight of him crying.

I put both of my arms around him, hugging him from behind. My arms wrap around his chest, and I squeeze, feeling his body shake as he cries.

"I'm here for you, Milo. You don't have to hide from me." I whisper. "Whatever it is, it's okay."

I tilt my head to the side to watch him from the Mirror. His tears drop into the sink, and his jaw is tense. "I don't want to ruin our night with sad shit," he says.

I shake my head, rubbing his chest. "You won't, I promise."

I let go of him as he turns around and look at me, unfazed that I was watching his tears fall from his face. It strikes me.

He takes my hand in his and brings it up to his lips, where he kisses my knuckles. The water behind us slams against the shower floor, filling the otherwise silent bathroom.

Milo drops my hand, reaches over his shoulders to his shirt, and pulls it over his head in one motion.

He blocks my view of the mirror, blocking my view of his back. "I wanted to show you ever since I've seen your scars. But I just couldn't bring myself to show this part of me, even with someone I adore as much as you."

I run my nails down his chest, and I feel him shiver. My gaze returns to his, "You don't have to, Y'know, show me, I mean."

He shakes his head. "I do. You've shown me all of you, and you deserve to see the same from me." He turns around.

I'm speechless for a moment, my mouth parted, and my eyes continue filling with tears as my gaze scales every lined scar across his back. They're white like it's been a long time since they were made, long and risen a little from off his back. They resemble the branches of a tree; his branches travel from the small of his back to his shoulder blades in every direction imaginable. They ripple against the muscles of his back; I can only imagine the pain he endured for these to be so permanent.

Slowly, I raise my hands, dragging a finger along one of the scars, feeling Milo shiver underneath my touch.

"The first time was seven years ago." He croaks. "The first beating my father gave me. I was eighteen and dependent on him." My throat burns as he continues. "It went on till I was twenty-one. The first time I ever tried fighting back."

Milo turns around, faces me, and speaks. "I gave him a black eye that day. Since then, he stopped hitting me, but the scars stayed. You're the first to see them... in seven years. You can say I'm pathetic for letting him go on for so long at such an age, you can get dress and leave me right now and I won't blame you one bit because even I am ashamed of myself—" His voice collapses.

"Milo, *no*," I grab his face, and he breaks into audible sobs, his forehead dropping to mine.

"I'm not going anywhere, don't be crazy. I'm right here." I rub away his tears with my thumb and kiss the side of his lips. He grips my waist before wrapping his arms tightly around me. Engulfed in his arms, I feel at home almost more than the home that sits right above our heads. I can't even remember the last time those walls left remotely as safe as these two large arms around me.

I hug him, rubbing my hands along the skin of his back.

He picks me up and sits me on the sink, dropping his head into my neck. "I want to be with you, Raelynn."

"What?"

"I want to be yours. I don't want the rules we fail even to follow. I don't want a fake relationship. I want a real one. I want to be with you."

He holds the back of my head, raising his to look at me. "I know it might be a lot for you, and if you need to think about it first, I'll understand, but I haven't been this happy in years." He pauses. "You make me happy."

God, why does he have to be such a sweetheart? His words massage my thawing heart and revive it back to warmth. A relationship. A real, true one. I've never had one before, not something so serious.

After a few seconds of silence, he brushes a curl away from my face. "What's going through your pretty mind?"

"I'm scared," I admit.

"Of what? *Me*?"

"No, of messing up. I've never committed to something like this before. I mean, what if I hurt you? I don't want to hurt you, Milo. I'm sure you know how to do boyfriend things, but I have not a fucking clue how to be a good girlfriend. especially with your expectations I need to meet. And I just..." I huff, frustrated at myself and embarrassed. "I like you a lot. And I don't want to lose this."

He proudly smiles at me, surprisingly. "Cute," he says. "You're so God damn cute."

I squint my eyes, confused. "I'm *cute*. Is that all you have to say about that whole speech? It was really hard to tell you that, and you're just laughing at me."

He twists his mouth to try to hide his smile but fails. "I'm not laughing at you."

"Yes, you are. You're *smiling*," I glare at him and push his abdomen to attempt to get down, but he grips my waist, bringing me closer to his body wedged between my legs.

"I'm smiling because I can't believe I've gotten so lucky." He kisses my neck. "You won't hurt me, Raelynn. And if you somehow do, if you somehow break my heart or shatter my soul, I'd build it back together and hand it to you to break again."

He kisses my jaw as I sniffle. "You trusted me of all men after the terrible things that happened. Now it's time I trust you. And I do, heart and soul." his lips Brush against mine and presses down into a kiss.

"And who said anything about expectations? What expectations are you talking about?" He adds.

"I just assumed with how your family is, you'd want someone of your... status. Your grandmother doesn't even like me," I breathe out a laugh. "She *hates* me, actually."

His face runs seriously, and he looks between my eyes. "The party. Is she why you ran away like that, to begin with?"

I nod, pressing my lips together. "She said terrible things, and I just needed to get the hell out of there. Then I bumped into that Logan guy you beat up." I giggle, recalling the day a few weeks ago.

He twists his jaw, anger washing over his face, and I press my hand on his cheek. "It's over with already."

He shakes his head. "I'm sorry you had to go through that. You already have your own family to deal with. I don't want to add mine to your list of headaches. I will talk to her. Her and my father."

"You don't have to."

"I want to. They will respect the woman I call mine."

I grin against his lips and subtly glide my hands up and down his back. I can't believe this is my life, wrapped around the only man I can see myself with. Safe In his arms and far away from Jaden Caddel.

"I like how those sounds. Being called yours."

His scowl dissipates. "Yeah?"

I nod and lock my legs around his waist. "Yeah. What's the first thing we should do as boyfriend and girlfriend? True ones, that is." It feels weird saying that, declaring myself in a relationship but I wouldn't want to start this new chapter of my any differently. But aware of boldness and confidence breezes through me. I reached down between us and took him in my hand, "There is still so much of me you need to explore."

He shakes his head. "I don't want to fuck you."

I freeze when his words process, setting him free. My heart beats in my ears, and my cheeks burn with embarrassment. I push him away, and he stumbles back as I drop off the sink. My breath shallows. *What*? I walk into his bedroom and grab my dress, slipping it over me just as my hand catches into his, and he spins me around.

He shakes his head. "I— I meant I don't want to fuck you *yet*. It came out bad. I want you; trust me, I do so *fucking* bad, you have no idea. But I want to wait till things are right."

I tilt my head, still a pang of shame in my chest. "What isn't right? I don't understand."

Not even half an hour ago was he begging me to take him. What changed?

"Many things that you may not. . . get right now."

"Well, then try me."

He shakes his head. "You just have to trust me, all right?"

My brows furrow in confusion. "Milo, what the hell are you talking about? What do you *mean?*"

But he doesn't get to answer my questions; his phone sitting on the bedside table interrupts, and he walks towards it, picking it up and reading whatever text is on the screen. "Milo," I say. His face goes grave, and it scares me.

He walks quickly to gather fresh clothes, putting the layers on with speed, and I watch him, unsure of what to say or do. He tells me I'm his, sweet words following and kisses that melt my heart. Though he doesn't want me entirely and then gets up to leave? I don't understand it. Did I do something? Had I rushed him, and he didn't like it? I knew I'd mess up and it hadn't even been minutes.

Milo slips into his shoes and looks at me. "I have to go," he mutters.

"It's almost one in the morning; where do I possibly have to go this late?"

He throws his coat on and walks over to me, grabbing his hand. "I'm sorry, I am. But it's something important I have to handle." He lifts my hand and kisses my palm, inhaling my scent before squeezing my hand and letting go.

Before I know it, he's gone, and I'm left standing in the middle of his bedroom alone with thousands of questions swarming my head. One of them eating me alive from the inside out.

Had it been another woman who texted his phone? What had him running out of the door and away from me without thinking? My heart is telling me to trust him like I desperately do, but my mind wonders.

Leaving me wondering that maybe it might just be him who hurts me in the end instead.

I'm attached, yes, but is he?

19

MILO

My mind races at a thousand miles an hour as I pace my father's office.

I've been up here in one of his owned buildings for nearly half an hour, waiting for him to arrive after the bullshit text he threw at me when I was with Raelynn.

He knows what he's doing. Any slither of happiness that man sees in me; he goes out of his way to drain it completely. He's done it with every friend I've ever made. Even in elementary school, he'd scare them away. Any girlfriend he disapproved of had no chance of going anywhere with me. How much longer? How much longer will he control my life?

I could get past the other things he's done to me, but trying to get me to leave Raelynn? He's out of his Goddamn mind with this one.

I know I should've told her what was going on. Raelynn. My darling, Raelynn. there isn't any universe where she will ever understand it all.

It was so long ago when the deal was made, the deal I made with my father. I thought it was done for me, that I would never have to think about it again, but things beg to differ.

I'm a fool to think being engaged to another would be brushed under the rug so easily.

My heart pounds against my chest as I stare at my phone to re-read Morgan's text: *Need to speak with you ASAP. Jenna and her family have returned, and she wants her wedding. And husband.*

Gripping my phone, I groan in my palm, sitting on Morgan's desk as memories flood my brain.

Jenna. My ex. Jenna. Poking condoms. Jenna. *fucking crazy*. Jenna... my fiancé of seven years.

Seven years. It always seems to fall back to seven fucking years ago. Seven years since my first beating. Seven years since my friendship with Logan ended. Seven years since my dad forced me to get engaged to Jenna Briggs so her father could collaborate business deals with him. Eighteen and stupid I was. It's not like Jenna and I were ever in a serious relationship. She may have thought so, at least, with her desire to have children and get married. But after she slept with Logan, I was lucky enough to find out she was moving across the country, far away from me and from my life. But still connected by our engagement. My father hadn't cared to break it off. My sadness meant nothing as long as I faked my love for his friend's daughter and his business deals were still strong.

The door to his office opens, and I get on my feet, watching my father walk in quickly; I catch a glimpse behind him before the door shuts of Jenna, her father, and her mother talking amongst themselves.

"Son," Morgan says, sitting at his desk. "You got here quick."

"Quick?" I laugh humorlessly. "It's been thirty fucking minutes; I left my girlfriend—"

"That woman is not your girlfriend. The one standing outside that door is now. Your fiancé at that." He pulls out some papers and begins to scribble down on sheets. I stare at his graying head of hair and solid facial expression. "I have to admit, I hadn't expected them to return, but her father wants to work beside me. Do you know how good that will be for our company? Collaborating permanently?"

I walk towards him, slamming my hands on his desk, "I don't give a flying fuck about your companies. I will not marry that woman. I won't. I'm twenty-five. I'm not a child anymore that you can hit with your belt and expect to follow your orders like a dog."

Morgan lifts his head and hums. "I see she's getting to you?" He says, standing. His voice had always been something that intimidated me; chills would run down my spine and make me shiver. But I stand strong, remembering the touch of Raelynn's arms around me just an hour ago. "Is she who you can depend on?"

Before I can speak, he continues. "Can she provide for you if... let's say I cut you off, rid you of your money and pretty cars you drive her around with? Then what? Can you two raise children together, both poor?"

"I will go poor for her then. I will struggle *with* her. At the end of the day it will be *our* problem together. Take the money, see if I care."

He walks around the desk slowly, not a wrinkle in his suit or a fault in his posture. "Then what? What life will you live? How do you know she isn't with you for this money you care so little about, hm?"

"She isn't."

"How do you know?"

"I said she's *not*!"

He shakes his head, standing tall in front of me. I keep my chin high as he speaks. "Raise your voice again, boy. And I'll show you what a man truly is because clearly, you've forgotten." He pauses, and I'm silent. "Now, I've done some digging on that girl. Raelynn, her name is?"

I don't answer him, and he nods.

"Beautiful flower shop she owns. And garden as well, right in the perfect place of Manhattan, don't you think?" He grips my shoulder tightly. My throat swells as I realize where he's going with this. "It'd be a shame if someone ran her out of her property and ridden her hard work. I'd put good use to it all, maybe more offices for my men, new shops—"

"Leave her out of this," I plead. "She's done nothing wrong, leave her alone."

His eyebrows raise, "You're right, she's done nothing, son. It's really up to you to choose what you want to do. Keep dating her and explain to her why all her pretty flowers have to go, or end whatever you two have going on and let her live happily without any problems. Sure, a little heartbreak, but it's simpler this way; you're smart enough to understand that, Milo. At least I hope you are.

"I heard from Genesis about Iris in the hospital as well. Did you know about the surgeries she needs to do?" He slyly threatens. "Who do you expect to pay for them if not me? If you want to choose a woman you just met over your mother, then you deserve nothing at all."

"That's your *wife*."

"She's no more my wife than she is the mother of my children."

"Does it matter? You play with her life like she means nothing to you!"

"That isn't the point of all of this."

My eyes flick between his two gray ones. I hate sharing so much with him: our dark hair, gray eyes, and broad frame. Genesis is lucky to have been blessed with their mother's brown eyes and hair. I stare at him, wishing I could burn with my gaze, but I can only tear up. I hate crying in front of him. I hate showing that he's getting to me. That he's winning. Again.

"Why?" I break. "Why do you take every chance you get to ruin my life?"

He smiles and shakes his head. "Your life is just beginning, boy. Don't be so dramatic." He points to the door. "Now, go out there and say hello to your fiancé. I suggest you learn to get along with her; she'll be around for much longer this time." He chuckles and turns his back to me.

"A few days," I say. "Just give me a few days to break it."

He waves his hand in the air. "Just get it done."

I turn my head and wipe my eyes before opening the door to the office, not wanting to speak another word to the devil of a man behind me.

On the other side is Jenna, her eyes gleaming green with a tight black dress that matches the purse in her hand.

"Milo," she says with a smile. I only stare at her. "Long time no sees." Her hand rises to wave at me.

Her parents look my way, and her father walks towards me with a handout. "Milo! Buddy, good to see you. Morgan told me how much you've been missing Jenna." He hugs me, and I clear my throat, willing myself not to say anything. If I say something to them other than excuse myself, I might blow it all, hurting Raelynn in the end.

"Yeah," I whisper, glancing over the family. "Will you all excuse me? I have to go. It's very late." I don't wait for them to say goodbyes before ushering myself towards the staircase and down to my car.

Breathing becomes nearly impossible as I open my car door and get in, slamming it shut. I strip my coat off, pulling my sleeves up and unbuttoning a shirt button. I can't breathe. God, why can't I breathe?

"Raelynn," I whisper, now sobbing to myself. "I'm so sorry."

My hand approaches the steering wheel, and I slam my palm into it repeatedly until a sting pain resides up my arm.

If it were just me, he was threatening, I'd be okay. I'd be more than okay because he's done much more to me than sending a few threats. But when he targeted Mom, Raelynn, her shop, and her garden, my heart dropped, and it still lies on the floor, ready for him to step on it.

I've known this woman for a month and some, and she already has my heart in the palm of her hands. When you spend every waking moment, especially for a month, thinking about a single person, spending your days with them, they tend to play a big role in your life. I've never needed someone as much as I need Raelynn.

But I see no other way around what my father has put me in the middle of so abruptly.

One moment, I'm having the time of my life, giving Raelynn the time of hers. Next, I'm thinking of ways to break up the relationship I just asked to create with her.

It's all my fault, really. I knew I was engaged; I knew it, and I thought it meant nothing since it's been so long.

I even stopped Raelynn and me from going any further because I wanted to make sure I had broken off this bullshit engagement all those years ago.

I couldn't let her think I was entirely hers when I had another thinking the same. I couldn't. I can't, and I won't. Raelynn deserves more. She deserves much better than that.

My phone rings in my coat pocket, and I reach for it, reading Raelynn's name and staring at her contact picture. It's her eating a pickle. I took it randomly the first week she stayed at my home. She looks so beautiful, round cheeks and brown eyes, a beaming smile I'd die for.

I answer the phone, and Raelynn gasps softly. "Baby?" She says in a sleepy voice. My chest tightens at the little nickname. I want to hear it again. "I've been calling you; where did you go?"

Painful tears fill my eyes, and I drop my head, squeezing the steering wheel. "I had to make an errand," I whisper.

"It's really late. I can't fall asleep without you... I don't want... any more memories," she mutters her words, fighting her sleep.

I nod, assuming she means nightmares. Clearing my throat, I speak. "I'll be there in a few minutes, my love."

"Okay," she mutters. "Are you mad at me?"

I furrow my brows. "Why would I ever be mad at you?"

She hums something that sounds like she doesn't know, "You seemed off when you left."

I shake my head even though she can't see me. *I'm getting married to another.* But I don't say that. Not now, not yet. Just a little bit longer, can I live in a life where things are perfect?

"You've done nothing wrong. You never have. I'll be there in a little." We say our goodbyes, and I find myself on the road again, back to Raelynn with a throbbing headache and an aching heart.

Getting to our apartment building, up the stairs and inside doesn't take long.

It's dark, with a few lamps paving my way after I slip my shoes off and go to the bedroom.

And in my bed lays Raelynn, hugging one of my pillows tightly against her as she whimpers a cry.

My eyes soften in worry, and I quickly slip off my coat and throw it over my desk chair, taking off onto the bed without another thought and making my way towards her.

Digging my knee into the bed, I nudge her hips softly, "Rae?"

She continues to cry and rock, and I'm positive she has no clue she's dreaming about whatever it is that she's seeing.

"Raelynn, darling, wake up." I sit down and take her arm, rocking her a bit, and she jerks awake with a yelp, frantic and in a panic. "*Hey*, hey, It's me. It's Milo," I assure her.

She breathes roughly, and her face is drenched with tears and maybe sweat as she stares at me in confusion. Then her eyes soften, and she sighs and drops her head into me.

"I hate sleeping," She weeps. "I *hate* it. He haunts every one of them." Her arms wrap around me, and I tightly hold her head against my chest. She continues. "Make him go away, Milo. You s-scare him away," her words blur together with her sobs, and I cry as I listen to her, stroking her hair and keeping her locked against me.

"He's gone," I kiss her temple, and she sniffles, digging her face into my neck. "He won't ever hurt you again, my love."

It is me who will.

20

MILO

Five days have gone by since I found out Jenna's in town.

Each day that passed inches buried me deeper and deeper in my guilt; my mind raced while I worked in the mornings. It raced while I sat beside my sick mother; she knew something was wrong, and she always did, but I couldn't tell her and give her more problems on top of her sickness. It wouldn't be fair to her. My mind raced as I held Raelynn close at night, crawling within her head and protecting her each time she closed her eyes. I close my own now. It's tiring; this brain carries the secrets that could take everything from me. It's tiring of racing.

"Milo," Logan says, sitting beside me as I gouge down my third shot of Whisky. "Why'd you call me here, man? You know I'm all for getting pissy drunk, but-" he laughs, "you're the last person I expected to call me."

Lowering the glass, the clank meets my ear. Why *did* I call him?

The last time I saw Logan was when I kicked him out of my mother's house. I haven't spoken to him since. Till the sting of this Whisky met my tongue and my tired brain fell out of my bloody head.

I shrug, raising a finger at the bartender, who looks over and nods, readying my fifth shot. "Maybe I wanted to rekindle our broken friendship."

Logan snorts. "Right, and I date Beyonce. You're drunk as shit, let's go." Standing up, he puts a hand on my shoulder, and I aggressively shrug him off me.

"Fuck off then. I'm not going anywhere."

A long breath leaves his nose, and he sits back down just as the bartender drops another shot before me. Logan grabs it and throws his head back, the liquid dripping down his throat. I glare at him after he swallows, and he raises his hand. "I'm broke. If you expect me to stay here and listen to your British ass have a bitch fit sober, you're so wrong, buddy."

"Go ask my dear dad for money," I mutter. "Better yet, steal it from him. I'm sure he won't mind."

Logan taps his tongue against the roof of his mouth. "It was *seven* years ago."

I turn to look at his slouched figure, and my jaw clenches. If he says that shit one more time, I might lose it.

"Seven years, and my dad's still blackmailing me. Seven years, yet I'm still paying for what you did." My voice stays low and calm. I've never been a terrible drunk; holding my liquor has never been a problem for me. I shake my head as the bartender lowers a replacement of the last shot before me. This time I scoop it up and drink it before Logan can.

"Blackmailing you? What the hell are you talking about?" He pushes his hair out of his eyes. "Don't you have a girlfriend somewhere or maybe... I don't know, *children* to teach. It's-" He checks his phone. "-*ten* in the *God damn* morning," he says as if just now realizing how early it is. "And you're here getting your ass wasted on a Friday. I thought something might happen to you when you called, but *nooo*."

"How do you know my job?" I called out sick today. What harm can be done? They're in first grade. They can go a day without painting their hands to put on paper.

"Why is *that* the only thing focused on out of all that?"

"Jenna's back in town," I drop, rubbing my finger over the rim of the shot glass. "That's why I'm here."

His silence and the soft music fill the bar. Not many people are in here at this time of day other than alcoholics and men drowning in guilt.

"Jenna," He repeats with an inhale. "Fuck."

I nod once. "Yes, the one you fucked. Glad you remember."

Logan points at me. "The one who poked your condoms.

I look at him, and he continues speaking, "That's right, I remember *everything* you tell me." He looks at me.

For several seconds, we stay challenging each other attention span, his blue eyes squinting, and the staring contest is broken with his blink and our soft chuckles.

"You're a son of a bitch," I shake my head.

He slaps my back. "Yeah, I am, actually. And you're a petty mother fucker with daddy issues."

I don't have the mental capacity to be angry at him right now. The alcohol flooding through my veins, slightly blurring my visions and making me concentrate on my words a little harder so I don't slur, takes over for the most part.

In all, though I'd never admit it to him, he's right, it *was* seven years ago, and no matter how much I want to blame him—anyone—for how shit my life is becoming at the moment, it doesn't change the fact that my father has always hated me. The stolen money was just a valid reason he found to hurt me.

Holding Jenna sleeping with my best friend over him for so long was just *my* way of getting even with Logan. I don't give a shit that he slept with her.

"I am," I admit.

He laughs shortly. "Two peas in a fucking pod. It's alright, bud. It's alright." The nickname goes way back. He always seemed to come up with the strangest ones. *Buddy* was one I despised, though. He said it solely to tick me off, but after a few years of hearing it constantly, it stuck.

The bartender, a woman that I haven't really taken a second look at, comes over with another shot, two.

"Life gettin' to you boys?" She grins widely, a southern accent lacing her words, sliding the glasses towards us.

Logan says, "Oh, you've got no idea."

He clicks his teeth, wraps his fingers around the glass, and holds out his other hand to introduce himself.

"Logan." She shakes her hand and voices her name, which I can't seem to care a bit about right now.

I wonder what Raelynn is up to, whether a raccoon is giving her trouble like the one those weeks ago. Or if business is going well for her shop today. I should stop by soon and surprise her with my kisses. What do you buy a woman who owns a flower shop? Surely, she doesn't want more flowers; she has them at her disposal.

Pickles... She loves those things. Love. What else does she love? *Who* else. The possibility of my Raelynn falling in love with me both turns me on and frightens me.

My eyes close, and I take a deep breath, gripping my hair and groaning internally. I need to tell her.

The fairly young woman behind the bar taps my hand, and I look up at her. She has red hair, curly and in a ponytail. "Did ya' hear me, cutie? I asked what's your name?"

I shake my head. "I have a girlfriend."

She grunts sadly. "The cute ones always do."

Logan throws his hands up in the air. "Hel-*fucking*-lo?!" He exclaims. "What's that supposed to mean, *Kristal-with-a-k?* Hmm? I'm cute *and* single."

She shrugs. "Sure."

He grabs his shirt as if offended. "Y'know someone once said Kristal sounds like pure class. Tell me, are your pure class, Kristal?"

"Excuse me?"

Kristal, as Logan called her, spoke for several minutes, Logan inevitably giving me secondhand embarrassment every time he opened his mouth. The conversation ends with a piece of paper with Logan's number in her bra. He turns to me with a smile filled with accomplishment even though I'm a hundred percent sure this woman isn't calling him back.

"So back to it," He drinks. "How's bubblegum?"

"Who?"

"Your girl. Bubblegum." Weird ass nicknames, as usual.

"It's Raelynn, and she's fine. The problem is with Jenna," I paused, sighing. "We're engaged."

"*What*?"

I tell Logan what's going on, under it all, thankful that I have someone to talk to about it, even if it is my ex-best friend. He listens, and that's all I need right now. For someone to listen.

"Shit, you need to tell her," he says, "Like ASAP, or this is gonna end in a shit show of screams and sad words, I'm telling you." He warns me with more concern than I thought he would have, stealing my drink again. "I didn't know your dad was still fucking you over this much, man."

He shakes his head, continuing, "I stopped speaking with him, Y'know. After the party where you punched the shit out of me? Yeah, I felt like shit."

I ignore his comment about my father, not wanting to speak about him. "How do I tell her something like that? That I'm engaged, and I have been for this long. That I'm set to get married."

Logan shrugs and hums an 'I don't know' so much for his help. Getting off the stool, feeling myself sway a bit, I decide it's best to get the hell out and on my way. Whatever I do, I need to do it soon. Morgan is running out of patience, and I'd never forgive myself if he messes with my mother's surgeries or touches Raelyn's things. Never.

My phone on the bar counter dings as I dig in my wallet to pull out money for the onslaught of drinks I must pay for.

"Hey, uh, Bud," Logan clears his throat.

"*What*?" I mutter, looking down at my wallet.

"I think you got much bigger problems ahead of you..."

I look up from my wallet. "What are you talking about?"

Dropping a hundred-dollar bill on the counter and putting a glass over it, I look at Logan holding my phone. Before I can shout at him for reading my messages, he turns the phone to me and my body freezes.

On the screen is a picture of Raelynn; she holds flowers in her hand, her hair in braids that end at her hip, and a large grin on her face. but what makes my blood run cold and my heart twist is the woman beside her.

Jenna. A grin just as wide on her face.

I snatch the phone from Logan.

He whistles and says, "You're in deep fucking shit."

I read the message from Raelynn below the picture with my girlfriend and my alleged 'fiancée':

Rae: Guess what!

Rae: I've hired a new employee today at work. Her name's Jenna. Super sweet, too. I think I just made my first REAL friend. Anyway, how's work going?

21

Raelynn

I hand the older lady a boutique of roses. "That'll be thirteen dollars."

She hands me the money and I turn to Jenna, my new employee, with a smile, putting the money in the cash register and shutting it. "See? Just like that."

Jenna came in this morning, looking for a job, with a hopeful smile on her face. So, I gave her one. We quickly clicked, and I think that's rare when it comes to me and other people.

"Got it," Jenna says as the old lady leaves the shop, making it empty. "How long have you had the shop?"

I think back to when the shop first opened, Milo on my fire escape, the milk. I smile and answer with, "Almost two months ago."

Blonde hair falls over, and behind her shoulders, a red pigmented lipstick that matches the roses I just gave my previous customer. Sharp jaw and cheekbones contour her face.

She's pretty; I wouldn't be surprised if she had guys at her heels wherever she walked.

"That's incredible, the progress." She walks around the store, sniffing and brushing her hands over my flowers.

My phone dings, and I sit in my chair, looking down at Milo's text.

Milo: When you close the shop, meet me at my apartment. We need to talk.

My brows pinch together. He didn't even acknowledge the picture I sent him with Jenna. Talk? Talk about *what*?

Me: What is it?

I twist my lip, biting down on my bottom one nervously. Scared and anxious that it's *me* he wants to talk about. *Us*. In our new relationship, he's become very distant recently. His smile has been strained. I don't think he knows that I notice, but I do. He has barely even touched me since last time...

"Everything okay?" Jenna's voice breaks my thoughts.

I shoot my head up, clearing my throat and blinking my eyes to get rid of the appearing tears. "Yeah, just... boyfriend problems."

My phone buzzes, and I read the text.

Milo: I'll tell you when I see you.

I shut the screen off with frustration and sigh. Jenna walks slowly towards the front desk that I sit behind.

"He's acting weird," I say out loud, begging to talk to someone about this, and right now, Jenna's ears have to suffer through my rant.

"We've gotten together just last week, and things were... *amazing* before. But now it's just... not the same. I've never felt this way about a man before, so attached... and now I'm scared that he's just—that *I've* done something to make him not want to be with me."

What if I'm too clingy? Or do I talk too much? Or annoy him so much he's rethinking ever moving things further. My mind races with possibilities, and they all end in heartbreak.

Jenna looks at me with a weary expression that makes me think I have something in my teeth.

"Look," she says softly. "God, I thought I could do this." The words are practically said to herself. "I thought—" She grabs her hair at the roots, shakes her head, and looks at me. "It's not *you* that's the problem."

I tilt my head at her, standing up. "What? What do you mean?" The expression on her face scares me, eyes red like she might cry.

"I didn't come here to find a job," she sighs.

I stand still, not sure what to think or do. My hands raise, and I grab my newly installed box braids, stroking them nervously. "Oh... well, why are you here for then?"

"I was sent to meet you. To get you to break up with Milo."

"*Wha*—"

"Before you speak, please hear me out!" She pleads before I can interject. My heart pounds in my chest. Does she know Milo? How? Who the fuck is she?

My brows rise. "You have five seconds to explain what the hell you're talking about."

She speaks quickly. "Milo and I are engaged— I know this might sound crazy, okay. But you have to understand—"

I turn my back towards her, and my eyes widen with disbelief and confusion at her words, a coldness shooting through my chest. This must be a dream, a funny joke being played on me. This doesn't happen in real life. Women don't just show up and declare themselves engaged to your boyfriend. It doesn't happen. It can't, and I won't believe it.

I spin. "I don't believe you." But she knew his name. How did she know his name? I never *told* her his name.

She raises her hand and shows me the large ring on her finger. An engagement ring sits dazzling on it. I step forward slowly, feeling my head begin to pound, tilting with realization.

"You are the ex..." I whisper, looking up at her. "You poked his condoms. The crazy one." I laugh humorlessly. "Why should I believe *anything* you tell me?"

Her lips press together, and her brows jump. "The crazy one. Wow. So that's how he describes me—not surprised. I poked his condoms, yes, but I purposefully made sure he found them poked so he could try to get his father to break out arrangements. I *wanted* him to think I was crazy. I never wanted Milo. He never wanted me," she laughs. "I even slept with his friend, for fucks sake."

I stare at her, my eye twitching. "I don't understand," I shake my head. "You and Milo are...*married*? Why wouldn't he tell me something like that? Why—"

"No, we're just engaged. Not that that makes things better, but it was seven years ago when his dad made him propose," she explains. "I wasn't forced to accept it, but I did for the sake of my dad's company—"

Someone steps into the store, and I look at the random person. "Store is *closed* for the day," I say a little harshly. Walking over as they slip back out, I grab the open sign and turn it closed, lowering the blinds.

My head goes light, and I sit in one of the chairs off against the walls before I fucking faint.

"You're engaged to my *boyfriend*," I say to myself mostly, soaking in the reality of the words, hurt and every other emotion making my heart numb of feeling.

Like my body is hollow, I should've expected that he was too good to be true. There are too few flaws. There had to be *something*.

Jenna sits next to me, and I hold back the urge to get mad, scream, kick, and yell at her because if it weren't for her, I wouldn't even know. She's told me before he has. He decided to date, kiss, and explore me while another had him. Real or not, it hurts.

I blink, and a tear spills from my eyes. The back of my hand comes up and wipes it away.

"I'm sorry," Jenna whispers. "If it makes you feel any better, there was never anything romantic between us. We never even... Y'know, slept together. If I remember correctly, he didn't even sleep with anyone before we met," she laughs, rambling, and my gaze turns to her. "It's one of the reasons I never wanted to have sex with him. He deserved someone he cared about to take that away from him. That's when the whole poking condoms thing came up. I have to say, not the best solution I've come up with."

"Wait," I say. "You and Milo never had... sex?"

She shakes her head. "We were eighteen, a virgin, and *not* what I was looking for. But our fathers had other plans for us *clearly*. Luckily, my family moved away for a few years after deals were set in stone."

A virgin. Milo? Is that why he didn't want to go further with me? Or is it because he knew he was engaged? What about his... *toys*? It was seven years ago; he's probably had it taken away by now, right?

Too many questions flood my brain with not enough answers.

"But you're back here," I say.

"*Yeah*, with a boyfriend of my own back home," She laughs. "I understand what Milo is probably feeling right now. I'm in the same situation. I'm here to end this crap agreement our fathers have going on. It's not fair, not me, him, or *you*."

I sit up, sniffling, shuffling my body towards her. "How will you do that? End it, I mean. Milo's dad is..."

"A *dick*, I know," She rolls her eyes. "His threats are the reason I'm here. I have an idea, but I'm sure Milo wouldn't even be willing to head me out. Both of you would have to... give up so much." She looks around the shop.

I blink at her, biting my lips, willing for her to continue.

"Move away," she elaborates. "Move out of the state, both of you. Don't tell a soul, just... move. Of course, I'll do my business with my boyfriend back home, and you two would go about yours. We have to get away one way or another, and trying to persuade those men isn't going to get us anywhere."

"Move..." I repeat, sitting back in my chair. "Like leave everything behind?" This can't be my life right now. How has it changed so quickly?

Jenna nods. "I know it's a big deal. But it's the only way I see things going. If I leave on my own, and if I do, I'm worried it'll lead them to think Milo is at fault. They'll take it out on both him *and* you."

I shake my head, the image of Milo's back flashing over my eyelids. "Don't!" I breath, touching her arm. "Don't leave."

She smiles sadly. "I won't. In the meantime," she raises her ring off and hands it to me, "I don't need this. But it's worth a fucking shit ton, keep it, just in case."

I nod once, slowly, staring at the beautiful ring.

Jenna's phone rings, and she stands up, declining it. "I have to go," she hands me her phone with her number on it. "Put it in your phone." I take her number down, and she gives me a small smile, and my head races at a thousand miles an hour. "Don't let it weigh too much on yourself; I'm sure he's puking his guts knowing what he thinks you don't."

I swallow, looking away, and she exits the shop. Tears still spill every few seconds from my eyes as I stare at the engagement ring.

Unable to speak. Unable to do anything really but think.

Think about what I'm getting myself into. What am I willing to sacrifice for him? Milo Evans. He is a man I met not long ago, but he feels like I've known him for much longer.

When I look at him, my heart flips. When I'm wrapped around his arms, it gets hard to *breathe.*

And when he kisses me— God, those lips—my lungs collapse like a balloon losing its helium.

Am I willing to give all of that up, or willing to lose everything for it?

***

I decided to open the shop back again for the entirely of my shift. Maybe to get my mind off things, but it didn't work.

I'm pretty sure I gave a lady too much change back once.

Now, walking through the building door, I spot Edna at the desk on the side, and she waves at me.

"Evening, Ms. Garcia. How's your day going?" she asks me, pulling her reading glasses to the tip of her nose.

I push the up button on the elevator and inhale deeply. "Um... it's been unexpected."

He chuckles. "Not good then, huh? It seems you have that in common with Mr. Evans today," she grins and chuckles, and I only smile softly as the elevator door opens.

I step in and press twenty-two. The door shuts and I close my eyes, listening to the music Milo installed. Images of a large flower field play in my mind.

I'm not in a confined elevator. I'm not closed off. I'm not in a metal square; I chant to myself. I'm with flowers and—

The door pings and opens. I let go of the breath within me, stepping out and congratulating myself like every time I took that elevator. At least I'm not balled up on the floor this time.

With each step towards Milo's door, my knees grow weaker. I haven't told him about what Jenna told me. I can only pray this night goes well.

Knocking on his door, a bark echoes through from behind. Poppy. The German Shepard is usually about her own business most of the time, playing with her toys or sleeping, bouncing around the living room, if not the other two options.

The door opens shortly after, and behind it, Milo is revealed. "Quiet, girl," he softly orders Poppy, and she listens.

My heart speeds up at just the sight of him. The sound of his raspy voice was like he had just woken up. It ripples through my body.

But with one glance at his face, I can tell he's been going through every emotion in the book.

His eyes are swollen and red. His hair is now fluffed in all directions, and the unbuttoned dress shirt he wears is wrinkled, untucked from his dress pants, a tie loosely hanging from around his neck. He looks like he caught a cold or has been crying his eyes out—one of the two.

"You look like shit," I say with raised eyebrows.

He steps sideways and opens the door. "And you look as beautiful as always."

My lips press together as my cheeks blush, stepping into his dim apartment, feeling his gaze on me when I pass him.

I turn. "What is it you wanted to talk about?"

He shuts the door and locks it, stepping forward and looking down at me with sad eyes. He reaches for me, and once our hands touch, he pulls me into him before completely collapsing onto my body.

I stumble back as I wrap my arms around him, his head burring into my neck and his arms tightly pinning my hips to his.

He begins to cry. Well, that's an understatement.

Weeping probably better describes the cracks of sobs leaving his throat.

His chest shakes, and his body shivers in my hold and with being so close, I can smell the scent of alcohol that's oozing off him.

He's drunk, crying, and an utter mess. But *my* mess.

I bring a hand to his hair and stroke his wild strands, feeling his tears wet my neck.

"I'm sorry," he cries. "I'm so sorry."

I let him speak, guiltily wanting to hear his suffering from keeping this from me. Maybe next time, he'll learn to speak and communicate his troubles.

"I- I can't lose you," He slurs. "I can't lose my heart." He lifts his head and presses his forehead against mine, taking my head between his palms.

I hold back the urge to laugh or cry, whichever tears swelling my eyes are for. "You're my heart, Raelynn. And I don't want to keep secrets anymore. Never again."

He's starting to squish my cheeks together, causing my lips to pucker. He kisses my nose, and my eyes flutter. Then, my cheek, forehead, and back to my nose.

Tears still stream down his face, bloodshot eyes making my heart swell.

"Don't get angry, please?" he says softly, pressing his forehead back onto mine. "I should've told you. I swear it means *nothing* to me, but still, I'm a fool for not telling you that I'm—"

"Engaged to Jenna?" I finish his sentence.

"No, that I'm—" pausing, his brows furrow. "Wait, *what*?"

22

RAELYNN

I like to think falling in love is no different than skydiving.

I've never gone skydiving before, nor have I fallen in love yet... I think. But I wonder, and I assume.

The fear in the mid of it all, the steps you take before plummeting out into the sky, should scare many away from the crazy ass activity but instead draws many in.

You jump out of that airplane willingly, knowing the risk, knowing that the parachute on your back literally has your life threaded in its strings and material that created the contraption.

Knowing that when you need it most, you can pull that latch, and your safety net can fail.

But it's a game of risk. A game of thrill. A game of *Trust*.

He's my risk, my thrill, and he holds my trust. Maybe too much of me he holds; sometimes I'm afraid he might hold enough to the point where there's nothing he can do to make me hate him. And it scares me, being so vulnerable so suddenly. Where did Raelynn two months ago go? I'm completely bare; my walls have been pealed and broken down by this tearing man in front of me.

What has Milo Evans done to me?

He looks at me in confusion. Eyes darting quickly from my left, then right, giving me a small shake of his head. "You- you *know*?"

My lips press together into a thin line as I nod. "Yes, Milo, I know. She told me—Jenna—she told me everything. Your dad, the arrangement, you both being forced. Everything."

Turning around, I walk towards the kitchen and out of his hold on my shoulders.

His footsteps are heard shortly after, silence following my words. Alcohol bottles two and three sit on the marble counter of his kitchen.

He was drinking for how long, I don't know, but the reason is pretty obvious.

He'd rather wallow in whisky than tell me the truth.

My lips twist as I grab their necks and walk to the trash can, stepping on the lever so the top pops open to throw the empty bottles in. Turning around, I lean against the counter and fold my arms as I look at Milo, his head inclined a bit as he looks at me from under his brow like a dog ready to be disciplined.

"Why didn't you tell me sooner?" It comes out in a whisper, disappointment dripping off my words. "I thought we were past the part where we kept secrets from each other, but clearly, I can't trust you as much as I thought I could."

He shakes his head. "Don't say that, you can trust me, Raelynn. If there's one person you trust, let it be me. I didn't know what to *do or* to think... to *say, I*—"

"I don't know, maybe you're *engaged* to someone?" Sarcasm laces my voice as I step toward Milo, pushing my body off the counter.

"And *then* what?" He strains in a hushed voice, taking slow steps towards me as well. "I tell you I'm engaged, and then what? You would've hated me, Rae. It would've been a shit show and you know it. Even now, with everything you know, you're upset with me."

I swallow the annoyance, the tone of my next words soaked with it, "I'm upset because you *kept* it from me!" We stand in front of each other now with an inch separating us as I stare up at his sorrowful face.

"I kept it from you because I didn't want to lose you!"

"That's what *talking* is for, Milo. Couples talk out their problems, and when they talk, they resolve things. I want and need you to *talk to me*," desperation wraps around my voice like a blanket, my eyes stinging. "How do I know you aren't keeping anything else a secret? I feel like I barely even know who you are sometimes," I laugh briefly. "I want to be a *part* of your life, not discover it from the sidelines like some side piece—"

"You aren't a *side piece*, Raelynn."

"Well, you sure as hell make me *feel* like I am."

Milo takes my left hand in his right, the mere size of his fingers encasing softly around mine, threading between them and squeezing. "I'm sorry I didn't tell you sooner," He utters softly, pressing a hooked finger under my chin. "I'm sorry I kept it from you. I'm sorry I made you feel less than the most important woman in my life." He tenderly rubs his thumb across my chin, and my eyes blur with tears as I lick my lips, sniffling. "You want to know me? Ask. Ask me anything, and the answer is yours. *I'm* yours."

A moment passes. "Did she ever mean anything to you?"

His hand drops to my braids, and he picks one up, sliding his hand down it before answering. "Yes. Long ago and briefly," He answers, my heart cracking and shifting in my chest.

A sharp pain is running right through it. Jenna told me they hadn't cared for each other; I dropped my head, ashamed of the tears falling from my eyes because I shouldn't care who he'd been with before me.

But with their agreement, my worry can't help but grow.

"*Hey*," he says, lifting my head with his fingers; I watch his eyes follow a tear down my cheek, and a pained expression falls on his face. "It was years ago, my love. A pinpoint amount of interest was formed for her, and it was gone before I realized it. As it did with others, but... *fucking hell,* Raelynn, no one's ever made me feel the way you do. Even when I'm not sober, you completely consume me."

His words wrap around my heart, sheltering it. I nod as he swipes one of my tears away.

I stare up at him, a small smile rising at the corner of my lips. "What's your favorite color?"

He blinks, confused, most likely unexpecting the basic questions.

Then he laughs, his chest deflates as he exhales a long sigh, laying his palm on my hip. "Brown."

I tilt my head. "Brown? I don't think I've ever seen you in anything brown before."

He smirks at me, lifting his hand to the side of my face, dragging his fingers along my skin, tracing my jaw, his thumb gliding over my bottom lip and pulling it down. "The things I could respond to that with."

My eyes immediately widen when I realize where his mind has gone. My cheeks were burning and flustered.

"But your eyes," he says. "Your skin, your hair. You're my favorite kind of brown." He lowers his face and breathes me in. "Hell, you smell like Heaven."

Milo slips his hand around my waist and slams me into his body, causing me to gasp softly, an ache pulsing between my legs.

His kiss falls on my neck and I put a hand on his face, pulling back a little. He looks at me with furrowed brows, and I smile. "You need a *cold* shower..." I say. "And some shampoo." I lift and hand, ruffling his messy hair as we share laughs.

In seconds, I'm hauled up in his arms, my legs wrapped around his waist, and I'm carried to the bathroom, where he lowers me to the floor and takes a step back, pulling off his loose tie.

It drops to the floor, and I watch with parted lips as he unbuttons his wrinkled white dress shirt and slides it off.

I may smell like Heaven, but he *is* Heaven.

How can a man's body be so well made? Every muscle is defined and previously hidden behind the material of clothes.

My breath picks up as he raises an eyebrow and points his chin at my body.

"Are you going to undress for me, or would you like if I peel your clothes off one by one?" He grabs his belt buckle, undoing it, his black slacks dropping to the floor.

He steps out of them, leaving him in just his boxers, walking past me to turn the shower on.

His back faces me while he bends over, scars on full display, and he doesn't seem to care one bit that I may be staring at them.

I swallow the lump he's created in my throat and shake my head, finding it hard to direct my eyes away from his chest when he turns around to face me.

"I have two hands. I can undress myself."

A crooked smile plays on his face, leaning against the sink with folded arms and staring at me. "Go on then."

A wave of embarrassment washes over me from his gaze dragging up and down my clothed body. A simple black blouse covers my top half, and blue mom jeans on the bottom.

I curl my fingers over the hem of my top, lifting it up and over my head, my braids falling down my back and shoulders. His eyes bore into me like a laser, I feel them on my breast, my stomach, my face, and it serves me.

Left in my bra, I sink my teeth into my bottom lip. "You're staring."

"I'm your boyfriend, Darling. Of course, I'm staring at you," He smirks. "Unless you want me to look away. Is that what you want?"

Is it?

Yes? *No*.

No, it's not.

I like his eyes on me. It gives an odd boost of confidence. Before Milo, men's eyes on me make me hide and shrivel into a dark corner. Before Milo, I hadn't wanted *any* eyes on my body for fear it would remind me of the eyes I just barely saw while—

I close my eyes, shaking my head at Milo and shutting out the image of the blue eyes. Unbuckling my jeans and then unzipping them.

"Raelynn, you don't have to, you know." Milo's voice makes me open my eyes. He stands in front of me now, a hand on mine, stopping it. "You can shower after me if you'd like that more."

"No, I'm alright," I say weakly, shuffling my jeans down my thighs and to the floor. Milo goes to open his mouth to say something else, but he seems to lose track of his words, stuttering as his gaze travels down my nearly bare body.

I turn my back to him, gathering my braids in my hands and around my shoulder. I look sideways at Milo. "Unclip me?"

He clears his throat and nods, stepping closer to me and wrapping his hands gently over the material of my bra. His fingers graze my skin and goosebumps scale my arms and legs, shivers and a chill making my eyes flutter. He affects me like no one else; his softest touch can make my center throb, and I don't know what to do about it all.

One moment I want to pounce at him; the next, I'm the old Raelynn, scared and afraid of intimacy.

I guess it's a good thing he's so patient with me.

Nothing but the water hitting the bottom of the tub like a rainstorm at night fills the silence of the bathroom.

Milo unclips me, his body flattening with mine from behind, pulling my bra off my shoulders for me and to the floor along with the other pieces of clothing. His bulge presses into my ass, and he cups my breast in his large hands... squeezing. *God.* My eyes close momentarily, attempting to control myself.

"You're the only one on my mind," He whispers in my ear. "Twenty-four seven, day and night. It's you. Not Jenna and not anyone else. *You.*"

His body drops, and he curls his fingers around my panties and slides them down to my ankles, where I step out of them, turning around to face him.

Lost in his cloudy eyes, I press a hand on his chest. This must be it, me jumping out of the airplane. My heart freefalls, plummeting out that Goddamn plane every time he speaks these words to me. Like I'm falling but never hitting the ground, or if I ever get to the end, Milo will catch me. Either way, I feel myself falling, and I've been slowly falling since I first met him.

I barely realize he's taken off his boxers, holding my waist close as I inhale.

"Milo," I say in almost a panic.

His brows form a V shape. "Yes?"

"I um... I think I might be falling in love with you," I admit hesitantly, scared.

His body goes rigid under my hand on his chest, his eyes glowing brighter by the second as my words swarm his head.

"I *am* falling in love with you," I correct myself, stumbling over my words like I'm the one who's been drinking. "This probably isn't the best night to tell you this, with the things that happened today, but if I didn't say it now, I don't think I could find another chance to tell you. If you don't feel the same way, that... *okay*. I just *really* needed to tell you it. That I'm falling in love with you."

I sound terrible; my words are too unsteady; I shouldn't have told him. What if this makes him distant? What if he hasn't been falling in love, too? I said it was okay, but is it really? He's staring at me, expressionless, and the fact that I can't tell what he's thinking makes my mind run wild with possibilities.

I lick my lips, close my eyes, stepping back, his hands slipping from my waist before tightening again.

"Where are you going?" he asks almost sadly.

"I..." *have no idea.* But I lose the ability to fucking form the words. "You're silent."

"Sorry," he says with a grin. I grin so large I can practically see every perfect tooth in his mouth. "I had to make sure I wasn't making this up. That I wasn't dreaming."

I give him a small smile and shake my head. "Nope. Not dreaming." I poke his nose with my pointer finger, and he blinks. "I'm all real."

He cups my face in his hand and hums. "Then, in that case, I'm falling in love with you too, Raelynn." His lips graze mine as he speaks, so close, so warm, the shower's steam filling the bathroom. "And I'm falling fast," he grins, "so make sure to catch me."

"I will," the words fall from my lips, getting lost in his mouth as he takes my lips with his, kissing me.

It's different now, more forceful, maybe, filled with a desire and longing like I might turn into mush and melt away in his hold. Despite how much I feel I might do just that, I hold his face and respond with the same force to show him I'm not going anywhere.

He picks me up, carrying me into the shower, where the cold water splashes on his back and shields me.

Milo gasps, his eyes closing as I drop to my feet. He stiffens. "Shit, that's *fucking* cold!" He hisses as water runs down his body.

I laugh, covering my mouth, cackling at his stiff figure under the water, each muscle in him tense and ridged.

He looks up at me. "You think it's funny?" He questions in a playful tone.

He reaches for my hand, and I try to yank it away with a yelp but am too slow. He pulls me towards him and turns us around.

And he was right, it's *fucking* freezing.

I gasp as the water immediately falls down my body, making me shiver and stiffen, just like the laughing man in front of me.

I shuffle out of the way of the shower spray and into Milo's arms. "*Milo*! I hate you."

He nuzzles his face into the crook of my neck, rubbing my wet back. "Oh yeah? Because just a moment ago, you were saying how terribly you're falling in love with me."

I roll my eyes with a smile and turn around, adjusting the water to a lukewarm temperature. It immediately satisfies me, Milo falling in line behind, reaching over to grab the body wash and my loofah, dropping some on it, and softly scrubs my back with the soap.

"Ask me something," he says. "You told me you feel like you don't know me sometimes; that should change."

His hand wraps around me with the loofah and rubs along my stomach. My hand slides up his arms, feeling his muscles flex as he washes me.

"Okay..." A harder question to answer than I'd expect.

I want to know so many things that I don't know where to start. "Why do you teach if you're, Y'know, rich?"

"I don't teach for the money. I teach because I love children. My father's money might not always be with me. I'll have to live off something when that happens. I'd rather it be something I love doing."

I lean my head back on his shoulder, sad that that question led to his father. Even with the mention of him, I can tell the change in his demeanor.

"Your turn."

Turning around as he tilts his head, I explain, "Ask me a question now." I pluck the loofah out of his hand and step around him so his back faces the water, and I'm shielded again.

While water pours down his chest, I rub the soap along him.

"How are you so beautiful?"

I smile. "A *real* question."

"That *is* a real question."

"You *know* what I mean."

"Fine. Where would it be if you could travel and visit one place?"

I bite my lip, my scrub slowing as I think of an answer. "France."

He raises an eyebrow. "Yeah? Why is that?"

"It's beautiful there. At least, it looks like it. I always wanted to see the Eiffel Tower someday in my life. Plus, I took a few years of French in college, and I can speak it pretty well." I'm not fluent, but I'm damn near it.

"No way," he says, shaking his head.

"Yes, way."

He smirks at me. "I don't believe you. Speak a sentence in French."

I take on his challenge to prove me right.

"Alright..." I look down between us briefly, then back at his face. "*Ta bite est énorme.*"

The smile on his face grows immediately, his cheeks burning a bright red with blush. "Fuck."

I realize exactly what's going on.

Gripping my waist and whispering under his breath another curse, he leans his head back, the muscles of his neck showing to me for a moment before he looks back down at my embarrassed face.

I'm such an *idiot*.

I *assumed* he just didn't know French! That he'd never actually know what the sentence I said meant. Clearly, that isn't the case.

Otherwise, I wouldn't have blatantly told him his *dick is big*.

I close my eyes as he lowers his head to the side of mine and grazes his lips on my earlobe.

"*Cette grosse bite est à toi, mon amour.*"

23

Milo

Everything in my life seems to be working against me: my mother's illness, my father's vendetta, and this ordeal with Jenna.

But the sole person who keeps me from spiraling and stopping me from derailing is the woman standing in front of me, water droplets falling from her bare skin—flustered.

She's staring up at me like she wants me to take her completely. To fuck her for hours.

"I..." She clears her throat. "I didn't know you understood French." She moves nervously, turning her head.

I twitch between us as her previous words swirl in my head. Words that set fire to my skin the moment they leave her lips.

I step towards Raelynn, her back hitting the tiled wall. She sucks in a soft breath and looks up at me.

My lungs shake as I inhale, aching for her touch, her kisses, her pussy. Craving her entirely.

"I could say the same to you."

My hands lower to the sides of her waist, gliding my palms up and down her soft, wet skin.

I drop my head to her neck, latching my lips right on her throbbing artery. Her head tilts back.

With a pulse this quick, there's no doubt that she's dripping for me between her legs.

"You are by far," I drag my lips down to her collarbones, my words mushing together into a low muffle, "the most incredible woman I've ever met."

She tilts her head, allowing me further access to her neck as her nails softly scrape down my chest, sending a shiver up my spine as I've just been electrocuted in this very spray of water.

My lips travel right beside the end of her jaw, below her ear, latching on.

"Milo," the words barely escape her. I hum against her skin in question, tasting her. "I'm..."

I smirk, letting go of her neck and slipping my lips directly over her left ear. "You're what, darling?"

I breathe roughly, forgetting that her feet are shuffling and her eyes can't stay open.

The confession of her love and the way she handled my idiotic decisions tonight, she deserves to be pleased to the fullest.

To my surprise, Raelynn lifts my head back with her hands and looks at me with a dazed expression.

"I want to do things to you," she whispers. "Many things."

Between us, the tension causes me to throb.

I latch back onto her neck, and she lets out a soft moan, gripping tightly onto my hair. "You can do it," I grab her thighs, holding her up onto my hips, "whenever," turning off the shower, sucking her skin, "and whatever you want to me."

"Is there anything else you want to tell me?" She asks hesitantly as I walk out dripping bodies to my room.

I think deeply. If there's one thing I learned in my life, it's that that sentence never means anything there's something I should tell her.

But my mind fails to work. I can't think of anything other than her hard brown nipple pressing into my chest.

Her panting chest indicates she needs to be pleased.

My mind races, but its only goal is her lips.

"No," I answer correctly, hopefully.

She stares at me for a long minute, contemplating something, and then kisses me.

Fuck me.

It doesn't take long to press her against my room wall, her hand finding my cock.

I gasp, breaking our kiss, and slam a hand into the wall beside her head as she strokes me.

"Fucking hell," I breathe out roughly. She smiles, pumping me faster in her tight grip.

In moments, she'll be dripping in more ways than one if she doesn't take it slower.

I grab her arm. "You first." Our eyes latch onto each other, her gaze making me rethink myself—nervousness zipping through my bloodstream.

She tilts her head, her pearly whites showing. "Not this time. I should teach you a lesson."

I raise my brow. "A lesson?"

"Yeah." She says pressing her fingers in my chest, so I step back. "I think I have to make sure you never keep a secret from me again."

I watch wordlessly, my eyes following her ass as she turns her back to me and walks into my office. Moments later, she's back, one finger out, handcuffs hanging from them.

A small pocket knife in the other.

"These are yours, right?"

I nod, my heart thumping like a drum against my ribs. The sight of her holding them alone might be enough to drive me insane—no, it does. It drives me insanely mad.

She hums, twisting the key in between her other fingers. "So, have you ever used them?"

I swallow, a nervous sweat breaking an inch out of my hairline. "Uh... yes. A few times."

She opens them, standing right in front of me, my bed at our sides, our faces close. So close.

"Really?" she says in surprise. "So you've had many women in your bed, your room? Pinning you down... fucking you?"

No. "Yes."

She nearly smiles, and it makes her face glow. My lips part.

Have me. Please, Raelynn, take me.

"Don't lie to me," She warns me, and my face runs cold.

"I don't... uh, I don't understand."

The air in here is getting thick. She can't possibly know, can she?

She can't know.

She brings her hand to my face, cupping me in her warm touch, the cuffs and knife hanging from her other hand at my hips. The cool metal makes my thighs tense.

"It's okay, Milo." She lifts on her toes and kisses my lips slowly. "I don't care that you're a virgin. Everyone has fantasies of their own."

My blood burns so hot I can't think of words to defend myself. Do I even need to? I don't want to seem inexperienced.

I want her to know that I know what I'm doing.

But she's right; somehow, she's discovered the truth. I've never had sex before.

It's not like I never wanted to. But I simply didn't. With the arranged relationships and then the permanent reminder of my father's discipline on my back, I never grew the courage.

I lied to her.

About the room. About the people who used my tools on me. It's all for a show, in hopes someone special might come around and these dreams become a reality.

I never actually thought it'd happen.

"Sit in the chair." I follow her finger to the wooden chair at the side, next to a small desk in my room.

I do as she says, walking over and sitting down.

She grins lifting a hand, pulling my bottom lip down with the flat of her thumb. I close my eyes to control myself.

"I think I'll like this," She starts, "you so... obedient."

"I've been at your disposal since the moment you stepped into that elevator, Raelynn. You just didn't know it.

"You could've pressed me against that wall and taken me in your mouth right then and there, and I would've loved every second of it."

I lean back, following her body with my eyes as she walks behind me and pulls my arms behind the chair.

The cool metal meets my wrist, seconds later locking around them.

God, I love the sound of that. The anticipation eats away at me.

"I bet you would've," she curls her fingers around my neck from behind and leans my head back far to kiss me from above—spider-man style.

I feel her pulling away, teasing me with her lips, her tongue slipping in and out of my mouth, playing along with mine that's reaching for hers. Then she's gone.

"But... I'm new to control," she admits, lifting her legs and sitting on my thighs, moaning leave my scratchy throat. "It's been a long time."

"You seem to get the hang of things quickly, love," I say, almost as if I'm in pain.

It drives me far off the rails, having my dick so close to her soaked mess displayed to me, yet not being able to do a thing about it.

It also thrills me.

She grabs me again, our eyes locking as saliva drops out of her mouth and lads on the very tip of my cock.

So, fucking hot. "You're so fucking hot," I repeat my thoughts in words, throwing my head back. Muscles in every part of my body tensed, and she lifts her hips and rubs her clit against me.

She whines and bites her lip. "God, Milo, you're massive," she cries out as my throbbing cock spreads her wet lips apart.

Noise doesn't stop escaping my throat.

Overwhelming feelings rush over me, the need for her killing me like she's oxygen and I'm on one failing lung.

"Do it," I tell her. "Sit on me."

She grabs the pocketknife she set on the desk beside us and shakes her head, examining it. She drags her finger along the blade, and I almost tell her to be careful when she moves it away and softly presses it on my Adam's apple.

My throat tightens, holding still.

"I'm making the orders, remember? How about you tell me what you want me to do with this."

"Down," I whisper, careful not to move my neck against the sharp metal.

She goes up.

I inhale slowly. I'm going to come.

"Raelynn. Don't be a damn tease."

"I'll be whatever I want." She drags the tip of the pocket knife down my neck, a shiver making me squirm.

It travels between my collarbones, down my best, over my abs, all the way to my dick. "I should be careful, shouldn't I?"

"Ruin me. Hurt me. Pin me. I couldn't care any less what you do to me. Just do it."

She presses the knife to my lip to pull it down with enough force to prick me.

I gasp softly, and she does as well as if worried suddenly, her eyebrows arching up to the ceiling. "Milo—"

I grin at her, laughing briefly and sucking at my bleeding lip. The copper taste flooded my mouth. "I'm alright, beautiful. More than."

She places the blade down for a moment and brings her attention to my wounded lip, cupping my head between her hands and taking my bottom lip between hers, pulling and cleaning. Her tongue ran over the wound, soothing the prick of pain.

"Take me," I mutter in her mouth. "Please, just fuck me, Raelynn."

She stays kissing me, a soft moan of hers slipping down my throat as her hand wraps around my cock, and she lifts her hips.

"Look at me," I tell her. And she listens, looking down at me with admiration in her eyes and swollen lips.

And I breathe out my mouth, my tip coming in contact with her soaked entrance, and then I'm engulfed with her entirely.

My body nearly collapsed in this never chair, a loud moan leaving me, whimpers straining along. It's the most incredible thing I've felt: her slick walls contracting around me, the look on her face when my size filled her. I press against her cervix as she sits completely on me, having me deep inside of her, just where I belong.

"A fucking prayer," I tell her. "You hear me? You're a f-fucking pra—" she rises herself before the words can escape me, coming back down with force.

I groan, wanting to touch her, wanting to grip her ass, but my hands are cuffed.

She moves her body in a rhythm that might make me come anytime now. She flexes her falls with every thrust, milking me, owning me.

"I'm the only one you can fuck," she says, quickening her pace, bouncing on me. "I'm the only one who can fuck you like this. Ever. Okay?" She cries out.

"I'm yours, baby. I'm all yours."

I'm stuck in a haze, a highness caused by Raelynn. Every inch of me inserted in her over and over again until I feel myself knotting, my insides melting.

"Coming," I cry out in warning. "I'm gonna come."

She lifts off me just in time to drop to her knees and wrap her mouth around my cock, my release shooting into the back of her throat as she sucks me off.

"*Fuck,*" I shout, throwing my head back. "Fucking shit, you're so good."

She sucks me dry and smiles proudly at me.

"So it was okay? I did okay for your first time?"

I laugh, panting. "Okay? Raelynn, unlock me."

"But—"

"Unlock me. Now."

The tone in my voice makes her move fast, taking the key off the dresser and freeing my hands from the cuffs.

Immediately, I take her in my arms, rising from the chair, and carry her towards my bed, her squeals and laughter following.

"What are you doing!" She giggles as I kiss down her body, down her stomach, down her scarred thighs.

"You've had your little fun," I mutter against her throbbing clit, flicking it just once with my tongue. "I want to have mine now."

I flip her over on her stoma h, grabbing her ass, squeezing her, and spreading her ass cheeks out so her asshole is visible.

I groan at the sweet sight—enough *control for you.*

On my knees, I drop my mouth between her legs from behind, licking her from the soaking hole up to her tight ass.

"I want you in so many ways." I insert my tongue in her pussy, and she cries out. "I want this precious ass. I want your clit," I latch onto the throbbing nerve, and her legs begin to shake.

I spin her over again, falling between her legs. "I want these." I suck on one of her nipples, twirling my tongue around the hard things, painlessly nibbling. She grips my hair.

"I want you." Lining myself with her entrance between us, I shove myself inside roughly, paying back for all her orders, getting back my control.

I lock my fingers with hers above her head and moan her name out. Her mouth, hands wide open, below me.

"Stick out that pretty tongue, Rae."

She does, smiling. And I let my saliva dripping down into her mouth as I thrust into her.

The bed bangs the wall with every movement, our bodies colliding and contracting in every way possible.

I drop my elbows beside her head, railing into her. "This is what you'll always get for being such a bad girl like that. This will be your reward."

She can't speak even if she wants to.

I drill into her, my hardness not dying even with my release minutes ago. Another one coming on soon.

Condoms. There's no condom, I've noticed already. "We're playing a dangerous game here," I tell her as I shift my hips and see her face change. She must like this spot.

"Mhm," she whimpers. "Don't... cum in me."

"Oh, are you sure you don't want me to fill you up?" I play with her, ramming even harder against her cervix as if I've been doing it for years. "Cum first, Raelynn."

She bites her lips, our eyes locked on each other, another level of intimacy unlocking as she leans up and kisses me, barely being able to do so, dropping her head back down.

I bend her legs towards the bed, reaching even deeper than I thought possible.

"Fuck yeah," I sigh, feeling her walls contract at an insane amount against me, her body shivering and shaking, her lip jumping as she oozes around my cock.

"There's my good girl," I praise. "Such a good girl for me."

I hold myself as much as I can for her, then pull out when she's calmed, spilling my cum onto her lower stomach, jerking myself in my hand till I'm milked completely.

She watches in amazement, sitting still as I give her my design.

Then I collapse beside her, our panting breathes connecting, filling the silent room. My nose rubs against the side of her face, and I inhale her.

"I love you," I whisper into her ear.

She turns to face me. "I love you too, Milo."

24

MILO

"Mr. Evans, where is Mrs. Evans?" Haven asks me as I get them ready for dismissal. She taps repetitively on my thigh as I throw on my suitcoat.

It doesn't matter how often I tell them Raelynn isn't my wife. The concept of me not being married seems to be the most bizarre thing to their little brains.

I'm only twenty-six, not an older man with wrinkles, after all. But they know no better, so I just sigh before responding.

"She's working on her flowers, Haven."

"In her flower shop?"

I nod. "Yes, a very pretty flower shop."

I try not to think about our night last night. It was one of the best nights I've ever experienced in my life. Especially since it ended in the place I find my safe haven. Her arms.

Speaking of *Haven*, she's talking in her high tone, repeating a statement I've failed to hear the first time. "Did-did you hear me? I said Mrs. Evans looks like my mommy."

I tilt my head, ignoring the chattering of the other children for a moment as I focus on her words.

"Is that so?"

Haven's mother passed away late last year—I was informed by her father when I realized a change in Haven's behavior. While this little girl with tight, pretty curls and a smile so bright would come in with the longest frown on her face, I knew something was wrong.

And I was right. I always am when it comes to paying attention to my kids.

I bend down to one knee to her eye level, taking her jack at the bottom to help her zip it as she answers me, "Yeah, she has my hair and skin just like mommy did. See?" She points at her face, pulls at a small braid with beads on the end of it, and smiles.

"I see," I say. "You both are very beautiful. That's something else you have in common."

She pokes my nose and giggles, reminding me immediately of Raelynn doing the same thing.

It makes me wonder if this situation with my father and Jenna passes us, will we get any further? Will we have children? How many? Does she even want children after her family drama and what had happened to her? I'd only have to ask, but I suppose it's too early to bring up things like this. I don't want to overwhelm her any more than she is now.

"She'll come back and you'll be able to see her again, alright?" Haven nods and I stand up. "Alright. Grab your bag." I clap loudly, grabbing the attention of the children holding hands in pairs and forming a line at the wall beside the door.

"Are we ready to go home?" I'm met with deafening screams and cheering. I couldn't agree more.

I can't wait to see my home either. Only for me, it isn't a place.

***

"Gen, hello?" I answer the phone as I open my car door.

I was on the way to meet Raelynn at her shop when Genesis called, silent. I can hear a faint sniffle on the other end.

My body drops in the car, closing the door. The silence worries me. "Genesis, what's going on?" My first thought goes to Mum.

"Is it our mother? Is she okay?" I called her this morning, as I do every morning, and she seemed to be pulling along. Her surgery still sits on pause, with each day that Morgan holds off on fucking paying it. I'll have to find a way through him.

She shouldn't pay for the bad blood Morgan and I have.

But Gen hums a no. "Milo," she croaks, her voice thick with sobs. "Can you pick me up, please?"

She should be out of school right about now. Usually she ends the same hour as I do, then goes off to track practice.

I start my car immediately. "What's wrong? What happened?"

"People are being bullies," she cries.

It's not normal to hear my little sister cry like this. My heart speeds up with anger. There's only a few things that pisses me off. But someone hurting my girls is above them all. Whatever happened had to be big. Genesis isn't one to ponder over little things. I start my car, lock the doors, and pull out of the parking.

"Where are you right now, *soeur.*"

She stutters a bit before answering, loud sobs and quivers of her voice breaking my heart to hear. "I- I wanted to go for a swim instead of running tod—" she breaks off to let out a cry. "Today. And the school p-pool was empty, so I did go in, but after my swim, I went to m-my locker. My clothes—they're gone."

I press down on the gas, my grip on the steering wheel tightening.

"It's really cold. I- I don't want to go out there in my cozzie. They're for sure waiting with their *shitty* phones and their *shitty* friends to catch a *shitty* laugh—"

"I'm coming right now," I say sternly, trying to decipher exactly what she's saying through her cries. "You stay put, and I'll handle it all."

"Don't hang up, please," she pleads.

My jaw tenses. "I won't."

I drive over the limit, steady sniffles of Genesis filling my heart. She's crying, I know she is, silently. How long has this been happening?

How long had I not realized? I suppose there have been many things going on, but neglecting to see my sister is troubled shouldn't be something that happens.

"Gen?" I'm nearly five minutes away, but the cries are breaking my heart.

"Mhm," she hums weakly.

"Tell me a joke," I say, hoping to distract her for the remaining time. "I'm sure you have one up your sleeve somewhere."

She's silent for a moment. "Okay," she utters. "How do you know if a vampire is sick?"

I pretend to think hard. "I'm not sure. How?"

"You check if he's *coffin,*" *she giggles momentarily,* and I smile. I laugh for her, and she groans at me. "Don't laugh at my jokes because I'm crying. You always think they're terrible."

"They're so terrible that it makes them funny."

Getting to the school is when I finally hang up on Genesis before she tells me where she is. The pool building is separate from the school building but near the same area. Putting her in a private school was my mother's way of making sure she was protected from these sorts of things. Turns out kids will be—as Gen puts it—*shitty* regardless.

Stopping just in front of the pool building, I eye a group of kids who haven't yet seen my car.

They stand right outside the entrance. Three boys and two girls snickering to themselves, their phones out like she said they would have.

I shake my head, get out of the car, shutting the door, which causes their heads to snap in my direction.

Walking around the car, one of them whispers, knowing exactly who I am.

Before they can run, I speak. "You move, and I'll get every one of you expelled."

They look at each other with their phones behind their backs and their faces resembling a deer in a headlight.

As I reach them, one of the girls, around the same height as Genesis, clears her throat. "He— hi. Milo, right?"

"Where is it." I slip my hand into the pockets of my trousers.

One of the boys says, "Huh? Wh-where's what?" He tries to laugh it of, looking at his friends who don't seem to find it as funny.

They're smarter.

"I know you all are incompetent little twats but pretend for a *moment* that you aren't as stupid as I know you are. Where is my sister's clothing."

I scan their hands, finding that the boy who spoke is holding a black bag. His smile was no longer on his face.

I step forward, right in front of him, my heart bumping hard against my chest with anger. I nod as he hands me the bag.

"I don't know how long you all have been fucking with my sister, but it will stop now." I spit out harshly, yet with a calmness that I remind myself to hold. "You all want to get into college, I assume?"

They only nod, their eyes still glancing at each other.

"Your mouths work, right? *Do you want to get into a college,*" I speak slower this time.

"Yes sir," they all whisper consecutively.

"Right. If I hear another word from Genesis about *any* of you, I'll strip all of your futures away before you even realize it's gone. Do you understand?" My eyes meet each of their eyes.

They nod. One girl with teary eyes clears her throat. "Yes, sir."

"Good." I wave my hand in a dismissive gesture, and they all immediately shoot down the street, soon out of sight and around the corner.

I let out a sigh. Speaking that way isn't my favorite thing, but I'd rather die than have my little sister be a victim of damaged kids.

Wasting no time getting in the building and make my way towards the locker room where Gen said she was. Knocking, she opens the door to peep out.

When she sees me, she gasps and opens the door, running and wrapping her arms around my neck. "Milo!" The tears began again, her voice straining.

I hug her back, her swimsuit on her as she said, her hair drenched, and body covered with goosebumps.

"I got your clothes." I lift my hand as she leans back, looking at my hand.

"You saw them?"

I nod in response.

"What did you say to them?" She grins. "Did you beat their asses?"

I laugh, shaking my head. "No, Genesis. But they won't be a problem anymore, alright? Get dressed."

She lifts on her toes and plants a quick kiss on my cheek, then elbows me. "Love you."

***

Raelynn sits in the back seat of the car alongside Genesis as they scream the lyrics of current pop songs.

After picking up Genesis, I went to pick up Raelynn as well, filled her in on what happened, and she insisted we go on an ice cream date to cheer my sister up. All three of us.

So here I am, with two of my girls in the back of my car, eating Cookies & Cream flavored ice cream as I drive.

"I have an idea," Raelynn says, licking a strip of her ice cream cone. I watch her through the rearview mirror.

"Yes, darling?"

"No, I wasn't talking to you, Milo."

Genesis laughs. "What idea?"

"A sleepover at Iris house," she states. "How is she doing anyway? Is she alright?"

We go silent, not sure how to answer that question. "For the most part, yes."

"How would you know, Milo," Gen mutters. "You haven't gone to see her in ages."

I swallow, gripping the steering wheel. "I've had a lot going on. I call her—"

"She wants to *see* you. She asks about where you are all the time. You never know when she'll just..."

"Enough," I whisper, cutting her lingering words.

I sigh roughly through my nose. It's been hard deciding when I'll go see my mother. I don't want the last memory of her being a bad one, one of her passing, God forbid. I don't want to see her sick and in pain. It'll kill me to know I can't do anything about it.

"I will go," I tell Gen. "I promise."

The next few days that pass, my mind races nonstop. Through the sleepovers, through the silent threat of my father's words that have yet to go anywhere. Through my mother's sickness.

Currently, pacing the living room of my apartment is when Raelynn walks in the front door, speaking on the phone.

She has a new hairstyle, her hair parted down the center, two braids ending in a large curly bun at the back of her head.

I would smile at her, but the concerned look on her face tells me there's something wrong.

"It's not a problem, Gia. It wasn't your fault, moms the way she is."

She looks up at me, handing me the flowerpot of tulips she holds and her bag of groceries.

She sighs. "I'm happy for you, I am. We'll be there."

I wait patiently for her to hand up the phone before raising an eyebrow. "Your sister?" She hasn't spoken about her family since the day of that shit dinner.

She walks up to me, wrapping her arm around my neck. "I thought we had missed her wedding, turns out she pushed it back after what happened. We can still go."

I hug her tightly, sliding my palm over her ass, the thin leggings doing it justice.

"Do you want to?"

She is silent for a few minutes. "Yes. She's my only sister, and she called several times crying to me and asking for me to forgive her when she didn't do anything. It was all moms. I won't let her split us apart."

I nod. "So, a wedding then, hm? When?"

She kisses my neck, and I shiver. "Two days. Quick notice, I know. Are you up for it?"

I haven't heard word from my father for a few days now. I hope he's just forgotten about me entirely. Something tells me he's just biding his time but, in the meanwhile, I don't want to spend mine worrying.

"Of course, my love."

25

RAELYNN

I haven't been here in ages.

Walking up to the garage door of my dad's repair shop, the sound of metal clanking against each other and machines at work meet my ear.

It smells of oil and burnt rubber.

I don't really know what made me want to visit Dad, especially alone.

Well, not entirely alone...

Pausing right before I pass the opening of the garage, I peer behind my shoulder at the Tesla several feet away, Milo in the front seat tapping his finger on the steering wheel. He smiles at me, nudging his finger for me to walk forward.

I smile back, inhale, and walk.

Inside the garage, the annoyingly loud sound of an electrical drill makes me wince. I grew up hearing that and many other sounds like it, with my dad being a car mechanic.

Twirling the rings on my finger and tapping my tongue on the roof of my mouth, I look around the dim room.

Maybe this was a mistake. I don't speak to my dad much, why try now?

He had nothing to do with me being forced to have that abortion years ago. That was mom. He just never intervened, which is just as bad to me.

Speaking of Dad, the bottom half of his body is visible underneath a car I don't recognize; he who he's in the drip and uses another tool that causes a glow to shine on the floor every use.

I knock on the metal garage door.

"Genome, is that you?" Dad calls out for one of his workers from under the car, lying on a skateboard. "Can you pass me the wrench?"

I don't respond; instead, I walk towards the wall filled with hanging tools and grab a wrench, handing it to my dad's open hand. He thanks me.

I wait till he's done, looking around the same place he wishes I take over for him. He's wanted me to work here ever since I was able to work. It was never my thing, don't think it ever will be.

"Raelynn?" I turn to the sound of my dad's low voice. He's sitting up of the skateboard, the metal safety mask lifted above his face marked with oil stains. "What...what are you doing here?"

I push off the desk I was leaning against and slip my hands into my Jean pockets. My eyebrows jump. "I'll just leave then. Clearly, you don't want me here."

I haven't seen him in forever since the terrible dinner, since he found out I was raped, since he last spoke to me. And he asks me why I'm here.

Walking towards the garage opening, he calls out, "Hey!" His gloved hand grabs mine, spinning me to face his tall figure. Sweat trickles down the side of his bronze skin. The same one I share with him.

"You know I want you here, Sweet. I just didn't expect to see you." He exhales, and I stare at him, my eyes stinging just a bit at his sad eyes. "You uh... how've you been doing?"

"Fine." He lets go of my wrist, pulling off his face guard. "Was just gonna ask if you're going to Gia's wedding tomorrow."

That's not why I'm here. In fact, I don't *know* why I'm here.

"Yeah, of course. Are you going?"

I nod, and he folds his arms, trying to suppress the surprise on his face, leaning his body against the car he was just working on. "I'm glad to hear."

"But really, Raelynn," he adds. "How've you been? *You*."

"I said I'm fine, okay?"

"If you were *fine* you wouldn't be here. You wouldn't have visited me." He stands straight, walking towards me. "When you were much younger, you never went to your mother when you were hurt. You came to me. You'd tell me, *Dad, I'm sad. Can we go to the park?*" He laughs for a second, shaking his head. "You knew I'd do whatever you wanted—"

I shake my head. "I don't need a trip down memory lane, alright. Those days are over."

"They don't have to be."

"Well, they *are*, I'm older now." My face turns away at the neighborhood outside, a tear rolling down my cheek.

"And I'm still your father. Your age doesn't change a thing. Maybe it's me you're waiting for to say something, and I..." I look back at him when his words fade, his head dropping into his head as if choking on his own voice. When he looks back up, shiny tears cover his eyes.

I've never seen him cry before, not once.

"Dad?"

"I'm so sorry," He whispers like if he spoke any louder, his voice would crack. Steps closer. "I should've known. I should've protected you."

I shake my head. "I'm fine now."

"Now is not enough. I'm your dad. I should've been there, sweetheart. I did everything wrong. From the moment you told me and your mother about the child, it was like something in me shut down. I didn't know what to do or say, so I let her take over." He squeezes my cheeks with his palms, his gloves now off. "And I'm so sorry, Raelynn. I'm so sorry."

My hands grip his wrist tightly and it's only when the salty tears meet my lips that I realize how hard I'm crying. I didn't think I would hear these words. As I said, we haven't spoken much over the years, and to finally hear them is like a twist to the stomach.

I shake my head, licking my lips. His fingers wipe away tears as I speak, "I felt so alone, Dad," my voice cracks.

I drop my head into his chest, not caring about the oil stains on it or the metal smell he gives off.

My hand grips his shirt. Crying into him as he hugs me tightly. A warm feeling floods my body, one I've never felt before, one that even Milo can't provide me with.

The love of a father is unmatched.

"I know, my little girl." He kisses the top of my head as I cry into him.

I don't know how long we stand like that, sniffles and cries filling the garage, but this moment is something I never want to end.

Lifting my head, I look up at dads face, a smile on it. "So," he says. "That guy you're with. How is he?"

I struggle to find words at first. Guy talk was never something I had with anyone.

"Uh..." I bite my lip, memories of Milo passing across my eyes. Him climbing my fire escape, sitting in my bed, appearing at my flower shop, dropping of his pickle, his sweet words, the way he handles children—

"Lost in thought?"

I jump out of my thoughts and begin pacing, feeling a burst of energy. "I love him."

Dad opens the hood of the car, grunting in surprise. "Love?"

"Yeah, love," I repeat. "He's a really good guy, dad. Not like the ones I used to be around in high school. He's different. Milo at the dinner was just him being protective."

"Hey, I never said he wasn't good. I believe you. But if he ever hurts you, I won't be silent this time."

"I—"

"You don't have to worry about that, Mr Garcia." Milo's British accent causes us to turn our heads to him.

Wearing black slacks and a white button-up with its sleeves slid up his arm, he leans against the garage.

"She's very safe with me," he adds.

I smile at him. "How long you've been standing there?"

"Not too long." He steps up to my dad, who is just about the same height as Milo.

"Milo, ain't it?" He sticks out his hand.

Milo shakes it. "That's correct, sir."

Dad chuckles, nodding. "David."

"David."

I laugh at the exchange, Milo's politeness, and my dad's effort to speak to him.

"Milo, how about you come here and help me with this hood since Raelynn refuses to."

Milo looks over to mess if questioning it, or maybe he's begging me to pull him away.

I grin, nodding.

He runs his fingers through his hair, pushing it out of his forehead, and walks towards the car. "Of course. What do I do?"

"Have you ever used this before, rich boy?" He raises the electric drill and points it to Milo as who looks absolutely on edge.

Milo clears his throat. "No, should I wear gloves?"

"Nah."

"You have gloves on."

"For safety reasons."

Milo glances at me, and my dad bursts out into laughter. "I'm fucking with you. Raelynn, did you see the look on his face?" He walks to the shelves, grabs a pair of gloves, and tosses it into Milo's chest. "Now, if you're gonna be with my daughter, you gotta know how to fix a car. I don't care how expensive they are. They break down. Now..."

Milo listens in as if the world might crumble if he doesn't catch every word my dad says. And dad looks more than excited to share his love for cars with someone willing to listen.

***

"Don't touch me. Your hands are filthy." Getting home late with a dirty Milo and a tired me, we didn't get a chance to buy a dress for the wedding tomorrow.

I feel better going, knowing I'm on good terms with my dad. At least it won't be an entire disaster.

"You think I care whether I get you dirty or not?" Milo challenges. His shirt was covered in oil stains and dirt.

I miss his words; they fly right past my ear as my worry about what I'm going to wear fills my head.

"Are you alright?" Milo asks.

I sit on the bed. "I need to run down to my apartment and find something to wear for tomorrow."

He shakes his head. "Open my closet, darling."

I look at him, confused. He nudges his chin towards his closet across the room, and I walk towards it, opening it.

Right beside all his suits and shirts hangs several dresses. I remember picking out earlier for myself.

"You kept them?"

"Of course, I kept them. You never got a chance to try them on for me." He whispers himself down with disinfecting wipes as he speaks and sits at the edge of his bed. "You can now, however."

I grin at him. Pulling the dresses off the hangers I throw them over his chair. Milo manspreads, leaning back onto one elbow.

"You have to close your eyes so I can get dressed. It has to be a surprise."

"Closing them."

I watch him closely. Seconds later, he peaks one eye open.

"Milo!"

"Okay, alright." He slaps one hand over his eyes, and I laugh, grabbing the first dress.

It's a black dress first, along with a slit. One shoulder is off, and the other is long-sleeved. I undress, putting the dress on.

"Okay," I say. "Open."

Milo drops his hand, and his eyes drop down my body. I pose, turning in a circle so he can see the whole thing.

He licks his lips, his hips rising off the bed for a second.

"You like it?"

"I love it."

"Do you think it's wedding appropriate? Since it's black."

He clears his throat. "Yeah, you should try the others on for me. All of them."

"Okay, close your eyes."

Red is the color of the next one. Short and has slashes on the side that show my hips and thigh. Getting it on, I tell Milo to look.

"I think this one might be a little much."

His lips part. "Fucking shit."

"What? You don't like it?"

"What? No, Rae, I love it. A lot. Give me a spin."

I spin for him, putting my hands on my hip and end with a pose, laughing. He extends his hand, humming as I take it.

"I think you should save this one just for me." He grips my thighs, squeezing me as his hands slides to my ass. He twists me, and bends his head, kissing my hip. "Next one."

Why does he have to be so hot? I squeeze my thighs together for a moment and shake off the feelings he never fails to give me.

I try on two more dresses, each of them getting approved by Milo.

I groan. "You're no help."

"What?"

"You can't say they all just look perfect on me. That's not how it works."

"Well, they all do look perfect on you, love."

"I can't wear them all."

"You're right, you won't. A few are saved for my eyes only."

I roll my eyes. And grab the last dress, making Milo cover his eyes. A cream color dress, reaching my calves, the neckline runs low. I look in the closet mirror. It's pretty, it hugs my hips, and it's simple enough. I fiddle with the straps, trying to get them to look a certain way.

Maybe the straps were a little tighter...

"Beautiful."

I turn to see Milo up and walking to me. His dirty shirt is off now, as he walks behind me and kisses the back of my head.

"I love this one," he says.

"You said that for the past five dresses."

He grips my hips and drops his head between my neck. "Yes, but I think this one you should wear. You look stunning."

I turn my body, standing on my toes to kiss him.

He freezes for a moment, then grips my body, wrapping on arm around my waist to pull me into him.

His head drops, and he sucks on my neck. I gasp. "Shower first."

He hums against my skin, giving my neck a kiss. "Fine. But Raelynn?"

"Hm?"

"I did enjoy the day with your father," he practically whispers in my ear. "I never got to do anything like that with mine..."

I nod, running my fingers through his hair. "I know. You can as many days as you want. He seems to really like you now."

"Yeah?"

I nod, kissing his lips just once. "Now shower. You smell like oil and sweat."

***

I never would've expected myself to be this nervous showing up at my sister's wedding. But I am. And I have no idea how to control myself.

Milo, wearing one of his many expensive suits, grips my hand tightly, noticing how fidgety I've been all morning.

And now, walking into the venue, a sign with a picture of Gia and Dallas, her fiancé on the front. I blow out a long breath.

"Relax, love."

"What if mom tries to speak to me? I don't want to speak to her."

"You don't have to. I'll be at your side if you need me."

I nod, walking into the room full of people Gia had invited—family members I haven't seen in years and friends of Gia's she made in college.

Finding out seat number, we sit down, two rows away from the where Gia will stand. I don't say hi to anyone despite their eyes on me. My moms probably told everyone about our status. News tends to travel quickly in this family. But I couldn't care less.

Milo squeezes my thigh, bringing my attention back to him, and smiles.

He looks different. Whether it's the touch upon his stubble or the way his hair is perfect, there's not a flaw I can pick out from this man.

"I have a question," I whisper.

He raises one of his thick brows. "Yes?"

"Did you ever need milk that day you came up on my fire escape?"

He takes a second to answer. "No." Then laughs. "It was an excuse to talk to you. It worked, didn't it?"

I nod, leaning my head on his shoulder. "It did."

Beside me, someone sits.

I look over to see my mom.

Gia. She did arrange these seats, of course she'd put me beside her. Mom doesn't acknowledge me other than a sorrowful glance at my face and at Milo's. And she stays silent. Not a word spoken to either of us for the entire time till Gia is set to walk down the aisle.

Dallas stands at the front, a few of his friends at his side and a few of Gia's on the other side when the classical wedding music begins.

Everyone turns their head and I glance at my mother sitting in front for a second before looking at the door Gia's suppose to come through.

And she does, slowly stepping out in a beautiful dress, Dad holding her arm at her side.

But there's something wrong. She isn't smiling. Not a real one, at least. It doesn't reach her ears like it should, her eyes are wrinkled at the corners like they should be. She looks almost... sad.

Reaching the front, Dad hands her over to Dallas.

"Do you think she's alright?" I whisper to Milo.

He shrugs. "She looks fine to me."

She doesn't to me. Even though I haven't been around my sister much these past few years. I grew up with her; I know something's wrong.

The priest speaks, Dallas and Gia hold their hands as they repeat his words.

"I do," Dallas says.

The priest looks at Gia, asking her the same thing. If she takes Dallas to be her husband. She's silent for a moment. Her chest visibly rising and falling.

"Ma'am?" The priest questions. Gia scans the crowd, and her eyes meet mine. Teary eyes. Ones that hold sadness and regret. Then she looks at Mom and back at Dallas.

She shakes her head and chokes out a cry.

"Baby?" Dallas whispers.

"I'm so sorry," she cries. "I can't."

I stand up, and so do a few others as Gia quickly walks off and out of the venue.

26

RAELYNN

My eyes follow Gia's as she exits the venue, leaving everyone confused.

Mom in front of me scoffs as everyone begins to mutter amongst themselves. "Don't panic," she voices. "She'll be back. She's just a little scared. It happened to me! I'll go get her—"

I grip her arm as she tries to leave the aisle we sit in. "No, I'll go."

She looks at me. And I mean *really* looks at me. Her eyes say the words I know she wants to say.

I'm her mother, I'm the best person to go.

"She needs my help," she says instead.

She's doing well hiding the anger she's feeling, but I know her. The moment she gets Gia alone, nothing Gia truly wants will be listened to.

Dad beside her stands up as well, putting a hand on her shoulder. "You should let Raelynn take this one," he suggests. "She's her sister."

She ignores him. "I'm sure she wants her *mother* right now."

Delusional. I lean in close so she can hear me very clearly. "The moment you're alone with Gia, you'll turn it into a screaming fit. Trust me, you are the *last* person she wants to see right now. So please, step out of our way."

With lips pressed into a thin line, her eyebrows bounce up, and she pushes her chair back an inch so I can pass after a few more transactions.

Taking Milo's hand in mine, I pull us along toward the exit Gia had run out of several minutes ago.

"Where do you think she's gone?" Milo asks as he meets my pace at my side. We walk in sync through the hallway as I figure out an answer to that question.

"Not sure." I pull out my phone from my purse to call her. No answer, of course. If I didn't want to be found my phone sure as hell wouldn't be turned on. "Can't be far. She's in a wedding dress and high heels. She hates heels."

It doesn't make sense, Gia was so excited about her wedding for months. She planned it all to the T, and her love, in my eyes, was unmatched.

But it makes me wonder if it was all for show. A show that only our mother was here to enjoy and clap for.

We've been looking for her throughout the entire building for nearly fifteen minutes.

Getting into her dressing room upstairs, the last place I haven't looked, my heels click on the wooden floor below my feet.

"Gia! Are you in here?" I push open the bathroom door, empty.

"Darling," Milo says behind me.

I spin to face him, and he points to Gia's wedding heels. They're laying in the corner of the room. I let out a sigh.

She swapped them for sneakers, most likely. Meaning she's outside somewhere.

Sitting down in the pulled-out chair from the desk, I let out a long breath. "She could be anywhere."

"Perhaps we wait till she appears again? The only person who she might actually want to talk to is you, love."

"We don't know that. I haven't spoken to my sister—in a real conversation—in forever. After that dinner..." My words fades. "After the dinner, I didn't talk to any of them until she invited me here. I feel terrible, dropping my abuse on them and then just never speaking to them again. What if she hates me for making her feel guilty? There isn't really anything she could've done to prevent it from happening. What if it's my fault that she doesn't want—"

"Raelynn, my love." Milo walks over and drops to his knees in front of me while I sit.

He takes my hand, and I lift my other one to his beard, stroking his rough stubble.

"It is no one's fault, and certainly not yours. Telling them what happened to you was what you wanted to do. You are not at fault for a shit of a boy not having any self-control. Do you understand me?"

Moments go by, our eye contact strong before I nod softly. "I understand."

He lifts my hand to his lips and kisses the back of it, then rises and kisses my lips while softly pinching the tip of my chin.

The entire day was spent looking for Gia, no one having any luck actually finding my sister. I worried the entire day, but something in me told me she wasn't missing; she just didn't want to be found right now, and that's okay. Right?

After we left the revenue, Milo and I even drove around the city for a while asking if people had seen a woman in a wedding dress before we headed back home.

No one had seen her, or at least no one cared to say they did. It is New York City. After all, people tend to mind their business around here.

"She'll show up, Rae. Lay down, please," Milo pleads as he watches me pace his bedroom for the thousandth time.

"She can't just go MIA like that; I can't lay down until I know she okay, Milo, I can't." I wear a change of clothes instead of the wedding outfit I had on earlier, jeans and a blouse, yet I feel beaming hot to my skin.

"Why is it so *hot* in here?"

Milo lets out a breathless laugh and slips off the bed to crank down the AC temperature.

"There," he says, walking to stand at my back to wrap his hard arms around my waist. "Is that better? Or are there any other ways you'd like for me to cool you down?" He plants a kiss on my neck.

My heart flutters and I smile for the first time today.

I spin in his hands and hang my arms around his neck. "Have you heard from your father yet or from Jenna?"

He shakes his head, his face dropping slightly like he was trying not to think about it all.

"No, I haven't. I've spoken to my mother on the phone, but that's about it. I don't know how long the last treatment will hold for my mother before she can't afford another one. He's just biding his time, is all."

"Have you gone to see her? Iris, I mean?" I remember Genesis asking the same question the car the last time we were together.

He shakes his head. "No."

I nod, hugging him tighter when I feel his hands begin to shake on my hips. "I have something for you."

Pulling away, I walk towards the dresser across the room. I'm not sure why I waited so long to show him. Part of me forgot I held possession of it. Digging in one of the dressers to pull out a pair of jeans I wore the day Jenna came to me, my hand slides in the back pocket.

"What is it?" Milo questions curiously.

I engulf the engagement ring in my hand and drop the pants, facing Milo. His head tilts.

"She gave it to me, just in case we ever need the money to move somewhere. To sell it. I think Iris needs the money more than anything right now, though."

I open my hand and show him the ring. It's a beautiful one, silver with diamonds that probably cost more than anything I could ever afford.

He stares at it, then at me, hesitating to take it like it might send some underlying meaning that he doesn't want to send my way.

"I know it has no connection between you two anymore. You can take it."

"There was never a connection, to begin with." He whispers. "Just a ring."

I nod, and he takes it from me, uttering a thank you and slipping it in his pants pocket.

We'll get passed this, these problems, and troubles. and we'll do it together, we have to.

In my purse, sitting on the bed, the tune of my phone ringing causes the tense moment to break. Milo and I both glance at each other for a moment before I slip around him and reach for the bag to fish out my phone, seeing Gia calling me.

My eyes dart to Milo with a smile, and he gestures for me to answer it.

"Hello?" I say after swiping my finger across the screen.

"RAELYNN!" I jerk the phone away from the eardrum-popping scream. "Are you around anyone?" Her voice filled with hysteria.

"Besides Milo, no. Where are you, Gia? What happened?" I slide off the bed and make my way to Milo. "There are dozens of people worried and looking for you. I mean, I almost called the cops."

She sighs and clears her throat. Then snorts. "Oh, Raelynn..." she starts to laugh. A rough and slurred laugh like she's been smoking cigarettes since she was a baby. That, or she's drunk...

My brows furrow in confusion, and I stand up to pace the room. "Are you... okay?"

"I feel better than ever, Raelynn. I feel... *free*."

I grab my purse and put her on speaker. What the hell is she on? "Where are you? I'm coming to pick you up."

"No, Raelynn, I never want to leave here! I met someone, and he's *amazing.*"

My brows pull together. "Gia, you have a *fiancé*. You were getting *married* not even twelve hours ago. What do you mean you met someone?"

"Oh, come on, Raelynn, you know I didn't love him. Y-you know it was for Mom. It always is." I try to decipher her words as best as I can through the slurs, listening hard to understand. I press my lips together, realizing what she means.

It was a show for her, after all.

"Where are you."

"If I tell you, promise to have fun with us? And Milo — b-because I know your British self is listening — Do you mind buying more drinks?"

Milo shakes his head while laughing silently. "Hell, I think Raelynn and I both need a few drinks after today."

I narrow my eyes, and he raises his brows in innocence.

"Perfect!" Gia shouts. "Guys! My sisters are getting us drinks!" The background is booming with music and several other voices mixed together, making them difficult to make out.

But as Gia gets closer to one of the guys, the one she mentioned she met, I assume, the phone picks up a second of his one deep-toned word.

"Sweet," he says.

My brows pinch together.

Then Gia screams and shouts her address on the phone, to which Milo nods. "I know that bar. I go there myself sometimes with Logan."

I don't acknowledge his sentence. All that swarms my head is the familiarity of the voice that responded to Gia. It was no longer than a second before every other noise drowned him, but even then, it pricked the hairs on my arms up like a chill during winter.

I shake it off, not connecting the voice to anyone I know currently. I'm paranoid.

The sound of Milo's keys rattles through the room.

Ending the call with Gia, I slip my phone in my purse and fiddle with my tongue piercing, sliding it against the back of my teeth. The doctor told me once that it causes teeth damage or whatever, but it calms my nerves. And right now, I need them to calm down.

For what reason, I'm not sure.

"Everything alright?" Milo asks, noticing my shift in mannerism as he opens the front door of his apartment.

I nod and answer with a smile, "Yeah. Everything's fine."

At least, I think so.

27

MILO

I like to think that whatever happens, it does for a reason. Most of the time, at least.

And Raelynn's sister running away from her own wedding, that sure as hell was something I didn't expect to happen.

The night sky is dark, not a star in sight. Only airplane lights that I like to pretend are moving stars and the moon are visible at this time.

I keep my eyes on the road; Raelynn beside me bounces her leg as she looks out the window like her mind is running a thousand miles an hour.

Reaching over, I place my hand on her thigh, and she jumps a little, looking over at me.

"You alright?" I question.

She's acting a bit strange, maybe it's because of her sister's situation. Then again, she's always been but of a jumpy person.

She smiles her pretty smile at me. "Yeah, I'm great. How much longer?"

"We're almost there just a minute or two away."

Logan and I were in this same bar not too long ago, drowning myself in alcohol because I couldn't come clean to Raelynn about the Jenna ordeal. I'm just glad she wasn't the same twat to Raelynn I met all those years ago.

Arrive to the bar, which is now packed to the brim, I sigh and park, shutting off the car.

Music pours out of the door and onto the silent street every time someone opens it. Even with the door close the sound of shouting and male voices blurred together still spill through the walls. It makes it hard to believe Raelynn's sister is here.

"Do you know how long she's been here for?"

Raelynn jiggles her seatbelt, unlocking it eventually. She's mastered that thing now.

"My guess, a couple hours." Sighing as well, she reaches to open the door, but I pull her arm back to me.

"Hey," I say.

"What?"

I cup here chin between my fingers and lean into her. She does the same, meeting me halfway into our tender kiss.

"Don't stress yourself, you're only helping her. Like a good little sister."

Her eyes dart around to a few points on my fac before a small smile rises on her lips. She nods. "I know."

"Come here," I whisper, curling a finger towards me.

She leans into me across the console, and I take her chin in between my fingertips, kissing her slowly.

Breaking it, her eyes part open, and I can tell by the way she squeezes her legs in the seat that I've gotten the reaction I hoped for. The fact that I affect her in such ways makes me feel all sorts of things.

I smirk. Then unbuckle my seatbelt to leave the car.

Raelynn meets me out outside, where our priorities shift back to getting Gia back home.

"You're sure she's in here?" I question, walking up to the bar door where the volume of the noise inside gets increasingly higher.

"This is the location she texted me," her shoulders come up into a shrug.

Let Raelynn enter the bar first in front of me so I can keep an eye on her with so many drunk twats surrounding the place. I wouldn't trust a soul around my woman, let alone any drunk bastards.

I know this place well; people can do any and everything.

I put a firm hand on Rae's waist when she started to walk a little too ahead of me, lowering my head to whisper in her ear, "Stay close to me, darling."

She turns, and I point my ear at her to hear her clearer. "I can handle my own," She jokes.

"Oh, I'm certain you can, but I'm a six-foot-five man that's three times your body weight and muscle; you don't need to handle a thing with me around."

She barks out a cute laugh, her cheeks forming a circle with her smile as she shakes her head. "I almost forgot how cocky you can be."

"It's true, though, yeah?"

"Yeah, yeah," she brushes off. "We're here to find my sister, not stroke your ego." She pokes me on the cheek and turns back around to search.

"Ego?" I whisper to myself. Do I have an ego?

This bar is one of the biggest bars in New York City. Walking in, you only met with the front, tables follow, pool tables, arcade games, being fucking in corners, and even a stripper pole somewhere, I believe.

It's like walking into Chucky Cheese, except instead of children with children's games, it's old drunk bastards and their entertainment.

"Milo?!"

I squeeze Raelynn's waist, and she stops at my action.

Dammit, of course, he's here, I should've assumed. I turn around to face Logan, his blond hair matted and wild like he was electrified.

He throws his hands in the hair. "Oh-fucking-*shit*! It *is* you." He throws an arm around my neck and laughs, stumbling.

He's pissy fucking drunk.

"You smell like pure shit," I mutter, pealing his arm off of my shoulder.

"Hey, bud, you want a dr-ink? What happen with that girl and your crazy ex and—Oh shit! There goes bubblegum."

I pull Raelynn flush against my side, my arm firmly around her. I can tell she's a bit annoyed by it, but I ignore her annoyance.

"We've met before, I'm Logan, Milo's buddy—"

"I know," Raelynn interrupts. "You spilled a drink on me a while ago."

"Yeahhhhhhh, about that. That's my fault, bubblegum. Hey—I have a question: do you taste as good as you look—"

I shove him away from her and grab his collar with my free hand. "That's enough."

He puts his hands up and wheezes out laughs. "I'm kidding, man! *Joking*! *Geez*, I don't want your hot girlfriend. Why are you guys here, anyway?"

I let go of him, and before I can scold him more, Raelynn speaks. "Gia Garcia. My sister was looking for her."

The place is so crowded that we're nudging shoulders with strangers and have to move out of the way of the intoxicated people every few seconds.

Logan's eyes widen, "ohhhhhhhh." He bounces his pointer finger at Raelynn. "Yeah, you guys do look like siblings. Gia's at our table down there."

He walks off instantly, assuming that we follow, which we do.

"I'm sorry about him," I whisper to her. She doesn't hear me despite my lips touching her ear. "Rae?"

She jumps out of whatever state she is in and nods, "It's okay, he's drunk."

"Raelynn! Milo! Over here!" I look towards Logan's booth, where several people I don't recognize sit in a deck of cards in the center and a space for Raelynn and me at the corner. No, Gia, though.

I try to walk forward, but Raelynn is rooted to the ground. This isn't very good, considering there's no pace you can stand still in here for more than a few seconds.

Her eyes are blank, it seems. But she looks a bit off. Perhaps this place is too crowded for her.

"Are you alright?"

She looks up at me and smiles. "Yeah, let's go."

Now she's fine again. I shake my head and take her hand, walking to Logan's table.

I sit beside a guy with red hair, flicking a lighter into a cigar.

Who the hell smokes cigars still? His bloodshot eyes look up at me, and he silently offers me a puff. I decline. That's clearly not the only thing he's taken tonight.

Raelynn follows and sits beside me at the end of the table. Rigid. I look down at her, wrapping my arm behind and around her.

She must not see her sister.

"Everybody!" Logan shouts at the table. "This is my good British friend, Milo, and his girl, Raelynn. She's Gia's sister."

A collective action of eyebrow raises are done simultaneously by strangers.

"Milo, Raelynn, this is Curt," he points to the man beside me.

"Sup," Curt grumbles. Too high to care what's going on.

"This is Jaden." I look at the guy string across from Raelynn on the table's edge. He has a goat T, short hair, and a line of cocaine lined up in front of him. He nods at us both casually, then gets back to lining his drugs with a MetroCard.

I watch him clog one nose, snorting a line and groaning loudly. "Yeah, baby!" Then, he throws his head back into the booth seat, laughing to himself.

A crackhead. *Nice job picking your friends, Logan.*

I shake my head, and Logan introduces the other addicts at the both.

There is an empty space where I assume Gia was previously.

"Logan," I interrupt whatever he's currently rambling about. "We're not here to chat. We're here for Gia."

"Righttt, Gia." She looks around the area and points away. "There she is."

Raelynn and I both turn to see Gia walking barefoot to the circular stage where the stripper pole stands tall.

She has on different clothes than when she left the messing. A cropped top and shorts so small everything will show if she spins on that pole.

"Oh my God," I hear Raelynn whisper as she watches her sister, who has a large grin on her face, wrap a leg around the pole. Dozens of men surround her, money being flung into the air.

I look away and down.

Raelynn gets up, and I grab her shaking hand. My brows furrow. She must be extremely angry with how much her hands are moving. Her unrest eyes continuously blink before she puts her palm to my face.

"I'll—I'll handle it," she says. "It's my sister."

"But—"

"Stay here," her eyes sat away from me to the table, but I don't get to see where before she's off to grab Gia.

Ignoring her request, I move to get out of the booth, but Logan groans. "Come on, bud, she isn't going to go anywhere. You can leave her side for a second."

I go to speak, but Logan passes me a bottle of whisky and raises his eyebrows.

"You said you were buying, and we both know you can."

I look back at Raelynn, now at the front of the stripper pole, successfully getting Gia's attention. Gia gasps and gets to her feet to crouch and talk. Stumbling and clearly drunk.

Raelynn's fine, I can see her from here. I look back at the bottle of whiskey Logan probably put on his tab with no money.

I grab it.

The entire table cheers at my action, and I shake my head and laugh. Today's been a long day. "One shot only."

Logan slides a shot glass over my way and I take it in my fingers, filling it and down it down my throat. The burn is fast, but there.

Raelynn would disapprove.

I slouch lower into the booth, manspreading, thinking.

We'll be gone in no time, yeah? She won't mind me having a drink or two.

I'll be sober before I even start driving back.

***

"Milo." I hear my name being called from my side as I wheeze at a joke the guy beside me made seconds ago. What was his name? Curt.

I look over at Logan who called my name. He's standing up with a bill in his hand, flinging it across the table at me.

My smile fades, and something in me clicks back to reality.

Nearly a thousand dollar worth of shit.

How long have we been drinking? My head spins, but I'm not lightweight. It takes a lot of alcohol to get me to go insane.

I take the bill in my hand and stand up when my mind goes to Raelynn instantly.

Looking around the table, she's missing. So is Gia. And so is that guy who did cocaine earlier.

Raelynn wouldn't leave without me, right? She must be around here somewhere. What if she's hurt? Or endanger, and I'm here drinking?

"What's up, bud?" Logan says, concerned.

"Raelynn," I say. "Where is she?"

"Oh, Gia said she wasn't leaving, so she went upstairs with Jaden. Then Raelynn slipped away, too, like a few minutes ago. My guess..."

The rest of his words don't process in my mind. The mind that's racing nonstop.

How have I been so blind?

Jaden.

Her uncomfortable. Her strangeness tonight since she was on the phone at the house. She's good with keeping things in, and this entire time, I thought it was because she was worried for her sister. Not because the Jaden that's sitting in front of us was the same Jaden that haunted her dreams.

My heart beat races as I close my eyes and shake my head. Please, I need to be wrong.

"Logan," I cut him off as he slips back into the booth. "What is Jaden's last name?"

He makes a face like he is trying to remember and turns to Curt to ask him.

Curt mumbles the one answer I hope he wouldn't have, "I don't know. Caddel or sum'."

I feel my skin begin to sweat in every crack and crevice.

I need to find Raelynn, and I need to find her now. I push my way out of the booth, my sight swaying and bouncing, but I couldn't care less.

"Milo, hey! You didn't pay!"

I ignore Logan, pulling my phone out to call Raelynn as the room around me spins, and my breath shortens.

No answer.

28

RAELYNN

"Gia!"

I climb the stairs to the second floor of this bar, my voice bouncing off the hallway's walls.

I can barely take steps forward because of how much I'm fucking shaking.

He was right there. I recognize him; his face is the same, besides the excessive aging he's gone through. I recognize his voice, the same one that convinced me to go to his bedroom while drinking shitless.

The same man who gave me his baby unwillingly.

He was sitting right in front of me.

No care in his cocaine-filled black eyes. He didn't even acknowledge my existence, let alone recognize me.

It was only two years ago, yet he's completely forgotten my face.

I wanted to reach across the table and dig my fingernails into his face. Brutalize his image like he's done mine from the inside out.

I wanted to scream and make him know the pain and hurt he's caused me the past two years.

He ruined everything, and I thought I'd never see him again. Yet, there he was, at the table.

I wanted to tell Milo or wanted him to realize it. But I was lost for the words to say it.

Milo's drinking didn't help; he's completely oblivious, and It's all my fault.

I should've told him as soon as I heard that voice on the phone.

"Gia!" I shout again, walking through these floor doors.

I'm met with a narrow apartment building-like hallway and silence.

My footsteps make little to no noise as I walk towards one door, realizing it is an empty bathroom, then to another door.

I put my ear against the door just as I hear a scream—Gia's scream.

"GIA!" I shout, twisting the knob and barging into the room.

Panting, I look between Jaden and Gia, holding pool sticks and standing beside a pool table. The entire room seems to be some sort of game room.

Gia looks up at me and smiles. "Raelynn? You wanna play? I just shot the 8 Ball in!"

But my eyes are on Jaden.

And his eyes are on me.

He points at me and tilts his head with low eyes. "Do I know you from somewhere?"

I swallow. He's playing with me. He must remember. You can't just *forget* you've done that to someone.

Gia looks between us. "Do you guy?"

"Gia, can you step out in the hallway, please," I ask, my eyes still on Jaden.

"Uh... sure." She lowers her pool stick on the table and closes the door behind her.

Jaden raises his eyebrows. "We chatting now? Or playing?" He questions. "Or do you have somethin' else in mind?" His smirk makes me want to peel every inch of skin off his body.

"You don't remember, do you?" I try my hardest to keep my voice straight, my nails digging into my palm as I speak quietly.

He leans against the table. "Remember what?"

My eyes sting, but I hold the tears back.

I need to do this.

"That day." I step only a few inches closer, leaving him still across the room. "Two years ago."

He throws a hand up and shakes his head. "College? I got nothin'. You have to be specific. What I do— Rob your house? Steal your drugs—"

"You *raped* me," I barely whisper, my eyes filling with tears., cutting him off.

He stops leaning and squints his eyes as if trying to remember.

"What the fuck are you talking about?" He steps closer.

"At your party. At your house. In your bedroom. I woke up with no c—clothes on. I was drunk and drugged, but you knew that because *you* drugged me."

"I have no idea who the hell you are. How about you go somewhere else with your story because you got the wrong guy."

"Jaden Caddel?" I voice louder. "That's your name, isn't it?"

He huffs and laughs breathlessly, not answering.

I shake my head, a tear unwillingly falling down my cheek. From my heartbeat alone, I can pass out right now and faint, but I pray I don't.

"You don't even remember doing it, do you?" My voice cracks. "You don't remember leaving me with the *scars* I have on my fucking body? The ones your fingernails caused?"

He runs a hand down his hair and inhales, stepping closer.

I step backward.

"Listen," he says, his voice coarse and dry. Brittle and engrained into my head like a drill. "College was a blur for me. But making those accusations—"

"They're not accusations!" I hiss at him. "I remember you—" I break off. "Your face for a moment. It's you. It was you."

I don't realize the tears falling down my face until I can barely see them. blinking several times to clear my eyesight.

"I don't *fucking* remember you! So fuck off!" He shouts back. His voice echoes around the room, it seems. "There were so many girls. You're not the first, alright?"

My eyebrows raise. "There were more," I whisper more to myself.

I don't realize it till now how close he is to me. Only an inch or two away. Tall, just as I remember. The smell of alcohol and all sorts of stenches ooz off of him.

He smirks. "Yeah, there was more. Does that upset you? That you weren't the special chosen one? Hm? You were probably wearing some slutty outfit and leading me on the entire party. Just like all of them. And then complain when I give you what you want. Because that's what I did. I didn't rape you. It's not rape if you were asking for it—"

I scream.

Loud.

And in a flash, I launch myself towards him, knocking us both to the ground.

"You PATHETIC—" I slash his face with my nails continuously, "piece of—" punch, "SHIT!" I scream again, and this time, I'm stopped by a familiar voice.

"Raelynn!" I turn, jumping off of Jaden like he's acid to my skin, and look at Milo in the doorway, Gia behind him, crying.

She must've heard it all and went to get help.

Milo's eyes darken with something I've never seen before when he lays eyes on Jaden on the floor.

He knows now. He knows more than anyone the pain I've gone through. He's seen firsthand the damage the pathetic man on the floor left behind.

Jaden groans like he just got melted by fire, "My *fucking* face." His hands wipe the blood dripping from the scratches on him.

I can't control the anger fuming off me, I wanted to do more.

I wanted to kill him.

Milo walks up to Jaden and kneels beside him. "You're gonna have a lot more to complain about when I'm finished with your ass."

Jaden laughs mischievously. "You fuck me up, and you go to jail, so go ahead. Do your damage. Not like you can prove anything I did."

Milo's chest heaves, and he looks at me as if asking permission.

Even now, when I know everything in him wants as much revenge for what he put me through, he gets my approval.

I slip out my phone from my pocket and look down at the voice recording that's been recording for the past ten minutes.

I end it.

Rewinding to the part that is more valuable than punches ever could be:

"*Yeah, there was more. Does that upset you? That you weren't the special chosen one? Hm? You were probably wearing some slutty outfit and leading me on the entire party. Just like all of them. And then complain when I give you what you want. Because that's what I did. I didn't rape you. It's not rape if you were asking for it—*"

I stop it and look at Jaden. The color drained from his face satisfies me.

I'm finally winning.

And I'm feeling so fucking good.

29

MILO

One to his jaw.

The sound of my knuckles meeting his face thrills me—an overdue action.

Adrenaline pumps through my veins, fueling me like crack does an addict. The blood oozing from his busted lip drips on the hardwood floor below his beaten face.

I don't exactly know the moment I begin my abuse. The moment I found Raelynn, things all seemed to go blurry.

Especially after I heard what he said to her.

His ego seemed a little too high for someone whose life is nothing but taking advantage of women. And each punch lowers it just a bit.

I get one last one off across his cheek before Raelynn puts a delicate hand on my shoulder. "The police are on their way, Milo, Gia called them. That's enough for now."

I shake my head, every muscle in my body tense as I stare at the pathetic excuse of a man lying underneath my tight grip around the shirt of his collar.

If a fire were racing through my body, I'm sure flames would be coming out of every possible hole in my face right about now. Nothing can compare to the speed of my heartbeat.

My gaze goes from Jaden up to Raelynn. I know deep down she wishes I continue. She wishes that I kill him. Send him to his grave for what he's done to her.

But Raelynn is a good girl, no matter how much she pretends to act like a bad one.

Panting I flex my bruised hand and stand up and grab ahold of Raelynns arm, then face, bringing her close to me.

She's crying silently, tears steadily running down her face.

My body softens at the sight of her, and I wipe away the wetness on her cheeks. "Don't you cry, love," I whisper only to her. "You hear me? Don't you cry?"

Her head drops into my shoulder, and I hold her tightly against me and walk us out of the room to where Gia sits on the floor crying as well.

Although I rarely had conversations with Raelynn's sister, I can't imagine how she's feeling now.

She was seconds away from marriage before running away from her fiancé, to unknowingly meeting her sister's abuser all in one day.

Who knows how long before Gia became his next target?

The thought makes my throat burn.

Holding out the arm that isn't wrapped around Raelynn, I invite Gia to my other shoulder.

I found out from Genesis is that hugs are the best form of comforting someone. And right now, these two both need a long one.

Gia stands up from the hallway floor and walks towards me, mimicking Raelynn's stance, her head digging into my shoulder.

I stand there with them both till the police arrive.

Love, Milo

***

It's been two weeks since Jaden Caddel has been put in prison.

Raelynn had his confession on tape, and others had stood up and shared their story along with hers.

The trail was rough to sit through and listen to every detail Raelynn had kept from me about her assault. But I heard every word. And I applaud her for even being able to say them out loud. It was only a few months ago when restating what happened was impossible.

I can see how much she's grown. How much stronger she's gotten since I first met her, panicking in that elevator. How little to no power that bastard holds over her now.

It was satisfying even for me to hear the judge slam down her hammer, sentencing Jaden to twenty years in prison.

And it was freeing to Raelynn, I'm sure, to finally have justice served for the trauma he put her through.

"Children," I call out to my chatting students.

"Yes, Mister Evans?" Haven shouts with a grin on her face, being the only one paying attention.

I sigh and clap a rhythm to which they copy, silencing them.

"It is the *last* day of first grade. Are you all excited to become adults?" I joke.

The classroom erupts in cries and dramatics.

I chuckle at them all, glancing at Raelynn sitting in the back of the classroom with one leg crossed over the other. A tight black dress hugs her body and curves, with an admirable smile plastered on her bronze face, looking just as beautiful as ever.

I send a smirk back before ripping my gaze away from Raelynn and back to my students. "I know, I know, no adulting just yet-"

"Mr. Evans, what happened to your knuckles!" A student calls out from their desk, pointing up to the front.

I look down at my unwrapped hand that I'm waiting to dry after washing my hands. There are scraps all over my knuckles, visual proof of what I rightfully did to Jaden's face.

"Hm..." I hum, failing to come up with a lie. "Good question."

Raelynn's heels click through the room. "See, Mr. Evans is *really* good at saving me from raccoons. So, one day, one attacked, and he jumped in to save me and got scratched up a bit."

The student's eyes light up as if they just discovered that their teacher is spiderman.

I chuckle, recalling the day I killed that raccoon Raelynn's talking about. However, I wasn't the one who left with any wounds.

"So, he's your hero?" Haven asks Rae.

Raelynn looks at me with a smile and nods. "Yeah, *exactly*. You get it. My hero." Her voice lowers as she gets to the end of her sentence, like she's saying it more to herself than to Haven.

I spend the day wrapping up the year with students, finishing their first official year all together.

Sometimes, I wish life was as simple as learning to sing your ABCs.

Enter my apartment, my hand immediately going to the tie around my neck; I loosen it, drop my keys on the coffee table, and turn to look at Raelynn.

She kicks off her heels, and I clip her hoop earrings. throwing them beside my keys.

Her eyes lock onto mine, "Why are you staring at me?"

"I can't stare at my girlfriend now?"

"Not when you look like you're about to start drooling," she tries to hide the smile on her face by turning away from me but I shake my head, walking towards her.

"Maybe I'm just hungry."

Her pace quickens, and she runs into the kitchen and around the island in the center, me on the opposite end.

"Can't catch me," she teases, tauntingly hanging her pierced tongue from her mouth.

I cock my head to the side. "Is this what this is? A game of tag?"

"What? Too slow?"

I dash to one side of the island, and Raelynn does the same on the opposite end, cackling.

I nod. She's in a playful mood. She's been in one for two weeks. And I'm not complaining.

I loosen my collar and unbutton my dress shirt down one.

"Stripping already?" She pouts playfully. "I didn't even touch you yet."

She bends over with her elbows on the table, giving me a full display of her breasts.

My eyes can't help but stick to them both like they're magnets. They're the perfect size: two large handfuls on a sculpted body.

She gasps, "I have a game we can play."

Turning around and digging in my cabinets in search of something, I watch her ass in that dress.

Bloody fucking hell.

As she rises from her tiptoes to increase her height and drops back down, her ass bounces. Every bit of movement makes the remaining space in my trousers dissipate.

"What are you looking for—"

"Found it," she sing-songs, pulling out a bottle of wine from underneath my sink.

Wine, she must've hid there from me at some point.

"Follow me."

She walks towards the living room, and I do as she says, unroll right beside the couch.

I'm not sure what her plan is, but the wine and the look on her face tell me it'll be something I enjoy.

"What are you up to, hm?" I hum.

"We're gonna play Flip, Slip, or Strip. Now sit."

She presses her palms into my chest and pushes me onto the couch. I land, looking up at her between my legs.

Shit. "What's the rules?" I ask her.

"I have a coin," she holds a quarter between her fingers. "I'll flip it, and you have to guess what side it lands on. Heads or tails. Guess right, and nothing happens. You guess *wrong*, and I get to ask you a question you must answer honestly. If not," she tugs on my collar, "one of these come off."

I soak in the rules, nodding my head.

"What's the wine for?"

She shrugs. "Beverage."

I cough out a laugh and shake my head. "Alright, daring, let's play."

Her eyes light up as if half expecting me to say no. She sits down on the couch beside me and holds the coin. "I go first."

Spinning the coin, she slams it on the back of her hand and looks up at me. "Heads or tails?"

"Tails," I guess.

She lifts her hand and twists her lips. "Correct." She rolls her eyes and hands me the coin.

I grin at her, spinning and shaking it in my hand.

"Heads!" She shouts.

I look down at the George Washington facing me. "Correct."

She bounces, clapping once before snatching the coin back and spinning it.

"Heads."

Just by her smirk alone, I can tell I got it wrong.

She shakes her head and bites down on her bottom lip. "What's my middle name?"

I squint my eyes, unaware that she has a middle name. "That isn't fair. You have never told me it."

She shrugs. "Too bad, answer."

I look her up and down and lean back, widening my legs. I'm just going to take a wild guess. Something that suits her.

"Rosie."

"Rosie? Really?" She laughs. "That's the best you can come up with?"

"*What*?" I lift a hand. "Roses are sexy. You're sexy. I merged them together."

She rolls her eyes. "Wrong. I have no middle name."

My lips pet, and my jaw twists, "You dirty little player."

She giggled at me and waves for me to stand up. "Hey, I never said you had to play fair."

I nod, standing up, taking note of that.

"Two can play that, sweetheart," I mutter as I unbutton my dress shirt, throwing it to Rae. She catches and lowers it, her eyes on my chest and abs.

I sit back down, my clear boner now being the elephant in the room. But now, my legs are wide open as I slouch, with a v-line that disappears under my belt.

I whistle, catching Raelynns attention. "My go. Or are you a little distracted?"

She rolls her eyes, tossing me the coin. I catch it spinning.

"Heads."

I look down at the coin and look back up at her deviously. "Tails."

She sits up, ready for my question for her.

"What's my favorite tune?"

She twists her mouth. "Hm." Her finger taps against her lips. "It Will Rain by Bruno Mars?"

I raise my eyebrows for a moment. "Good guess. But no."

She gasps. "What?"

Maybe it's because that song is always playing in the back when we're in the car; I do happen to have it on every playlist.

I shake my head. "You're wrong."

"What is it then?"

"I can't tell you. Now strip. It's a shame you have one piece of clothing on, isn't it? Cuts your game time a bit short, yeah?" I grin as she stands up and walks towards me. "Or maybe that was the plan all along. Was it, beautiful?"

"Shut up and tell me your favorite song." She drops on my groin, and I groan, gripping her waist to where she giggles, laughing.

I stare at her, darting from one eye to the other. "There you go."

"What?"

"My favorite song. You've done it."

"My... laugh?"

I smile crookedly and nod. "I could listen to it on repeat."

Her face softens, and her body drops a little into me, and she smiles. "Ugh," she sniffles. "You and your words."

Getting off of me, I watch her turn around and move her curls from over the zipper of the dress she wears. I stand up flush to her back and slide my hand around her waist, the other taking the zipper in my fingers and pulling it down slowly.

So slowly, I could practically hear her heartbeat with each second I prolonged. Her legs shift each time I breathe against the back of her neck.

"What's the matter?" I whisper.

She visibly swallows and shakes her head.

I smirk, finishing unzipping her, seeing her turn around with just a bra and a thong.

My eyes scare from her breast to the tattoo on the top of her thigh, to the scars neighboring it.

All of it is beautiful.

She sits down, and we continue for what feels like hours.

Each moment she sits in front of me, not allowing me to reach for her or touch her, being achingly long.

But we play until I'm naked, and her final piece of clothing is being removed.

She stands up and walks between my legs. "Take them off." Speaking about her thongs.

I look up at her, and she nods.

Don't have to tell me twice.

I curl one finger around both sides of the thing but halt, bringing my mouth to her lower stomach and sucking on her skin.

She stops breathing, touching my head and gripping my hair.

Rock solid, I drop to my knees off the couch and lower my lips with the material between my fingers, inching closer to her wet vagina.

I look up momentarily to her, and her lips parted, eyes softening.

Until I lick over her clit.

She gasps sharply, and I lick again, separating her lips. Her legs lock together, and I shake my head, pushing her down on the couch where her legs go up and over my shoulders, giving me full access to her pretty pussy.

I waste no time indulging. Flicking my tongue against her clit, sliding the flat of it along her entirely. She squirms and whines and pulls at my hair so tight I think some strands might fall out, but the thrill of satisfying my woman overboard any ounce of pain at the moment.

"Milo," she cries out. "Please."

I raise my head for a second. "Please, what, my love?" And I'm back, slipping my tongue in and out of her, taking turns with my fingers until she can't even finish her sentence well enough.

Until she's shaking uncontrollably at the side of my head.

Until she cries out loud the syllables of my name as she cums on my tongue

"Good job," I praise, leaning up to make out a doll with her aggressively. Her nails big into my back as I move her to hers, leaning over her and positioning my cock between her legs.

"Fuck me," she mutters in my heart.

I moan softly, gripping my cock in my hand, pressing my wet tip against her wetness. "Say it again for me. Nicely."

"Fuck me," she cries. "*Please*."

I slip my tip inside her right hole, and she gasps. "Like this?"

I slide fully inside of her with ease, hitting her crevice and feeling her walls tighten and fit around my size. "Or like this?"

"That," she stutters. "Like that."

"Yeah?" I nearly slide out before slowly giving her every inch of me again, watching her eyes roll to the back of my head, her jaw locked open.

"That's right," I whisper. "You're not in charge all the time, darling."

I slip out, tapping my head against her clip, watching her jerk with each it before ramming back into her, this time having to keep myself from losing control.

I grip the couch beside her and the side of her hip, hammering every inch deep inside until I hear her gasp more harshly at a certain spot.

"There? Is that where you want it?"

I hit that same spot over and over again. Watching as she shakes uncomfortably around my cock, releasing. I let her ride out her joy, before I pull out, finishing seconds after on her stomach.

After cleaning her up, panting and sweaty and long breaths follow, we lay beside each other, both out of breath and tired.

She turns to me. "I love you," she whispers.

"I love you too—"

My eyes flick to the living room TV playing quietly in the background when I see a familiar car and a familiar name on the news channel.

My eyes widen and I reach for the TV remote, turning up the volume.

"This just in, a fatal car accident has occurred here in downtown New York City, and it's said to believe businessman Morgan Evans is one of the victims of this devastating accident."

30

RAELYNN

We were allowed two weeks of happiness.

To escape from the world that we all know is a shit show.

I'm not sure whether I should cheer or grimace at the words Milo had heard coming from the TV. His father was in an accident.

The same father that beat Milo. The same one that threatens him with his own wife's life. The same terrible father is now getting rushed to the hospital.

After dressing and getting out things, I meet Milo in the living room, where he grabs his eyes with one hand and has his phone in the other.

"Genesis, are you alright? What's going on?" He says frantically to his sister on the other line. He glances at me and waves his hand to the door. " I saw the news. I'm coming right now. Just... sit tight, alright? Keep Mother busy till I get there."

He hangs up the phone, and we exit the apartment, getting in his car.

The sun is setting, making the sky look beautifully orange and yellow like a sherbet swirl ice cream and unfitting for the occasion, partly.

Milo drives frantically, his knuckles white with how tightly he grips the steering wheel.

I can't imagine what's going through his head.

Sadness? Happiness? He's more confused about what to feel than anyone at the moment, which worries me. He's said not one word the entire way to the hospital, and I haven't forced him to speak. I know how it feels to be in a position of shock, speechless.

When we arrive at the hospital Located in downtown Manhattan, it seems like dozens upon dozens of press are lined up at the front door: ambulances, police, paparazzi, and bystanders. Morgan was a well-known man.

It seems I underestimated just *how* well-known.

"Holy shit," I whisper as Milo parks the car.

He rushes to unbuckle his seat belt and sighs out a heavy breath before getting out of the car faster than anything I've ever seen.

I'm unsure of what to do.

Do I go out with him? Or do I stay in the car?

The paparazzi are beginning to recognize Milo quickly, and I look at his back facing the car.

Milo turns around, looks at me through the windshield, and holds his hand for me. Who am I kidding? Of course, he needs me here at his side. To these people, Morgan Evans might've been the greatest guy to exist in this world. A kind, generous, wealthy businessman with a wife and two lovely kids. Because that's the image he's most likely crafted for the public eye.

But to Milo. He knows the real Morgan.

And with my hand in his, as we walk towards the hospital entrance, he squeezes me tightly each time a question is thrown at him and a camera is shoved in his face.

"What is to happen to The Evans business!? Will you keep your father's legacy?" One of the paparazzi shouts.

How rude. How desperate can you be for the money that you camp outside a *hospital* after something like this?

Milo gives the man a deadly stare, and his lips part, but before he says anything, I tug at his arm. He looks at me, and his nostrils flair, continuing forward.

Getting through security and In the elevator reminds me of the first time we met.

In that elevator.

That same stupid shitty elevator that caused me to panic to no end. The same elevator that brought the love of my life and me together. I'm still a mess when it comes to small spaces and being claustrophobic. But I've learned to control it, at least when I'm in elevators.

Thanks to Milo, of course.

I squeeze his hand and put my focus *not* on the metal walls encasing us but on my anxious-filled boyfriend holding onto my hand as if his life depended on it. he's probably more scared to leave this elevator than to stay in it. Who knows what condition his father is in? And despite how fucked that man is, it'll still take a toll on Milo seeing him, I'm sure. Right?

"Milo?" The number above the elevator doors slowly inclines as we get to the floor the doctor at the entrance directs us to go to.

He has barely said a word to me since we left the apartment. I'm worried for him.

His jaw twitches, and he visibly swallows before clearing his throat. "Yes?" It's rough, like the singular word struggled to pass through his throat, strangled by the tears he's attempting to hold back.

That's why he won't look at me.

He doesn't want to cry. He doesn't want to show that he still cares for his father, even after everything he's done to him and his family. He doesn't want to seem like a fool for caring.

But he doesn't know that my heart swells even more, knowing he can't help *but* care.

My Milo. Full of nothing but kind-heartedness.

"Look at me?" I request softly.

He drops his head so I can barely see the right side of his face, shaking it. "What if he's dead?" He whispers.

I'm stubble slightly for the correct words.

There are three options I have.

Say what I really want to say. Which is "the bastard deserves to be dead for what he did to you."

Or say what I'm supposed to. These are the comforting words of a girlfriend and tell him everything is going to be okay.

I don't want to lie to him. I've never been on to sugarcoat shit and that's not changing today. But I will also not hurt any piece of this man's heart with my truthful words.

So, option three.

Stay silent.

And that's what I do, pressing my lips close and the truthful words in. *Ding*. The elevator door opens.

***

MILO

I know what she's thinking. Despite her thinking, her silence is saying nothing; it's truly saying everything that's running through her head.

I know it because I'm thinking about everything there is to be thinking about at this very moment possibly. Thoughts and voices swarm my head, and I can't exactly pinpoint any specific ones telling me how to feel, think, and respond to this news.

My father might be dead.

I should be happy. I've always wanted him to croak for his cruelty. There's always been a small part of me that hoped in the future. Morgan would change and be the father I wish he were. And I suppose that part of me is what is showing right now. The part that wishes he could live so I can fill that empty hole only a father can fill.

Just like Raelynn and her's. I hoped it could be Morgan and I.

And walking to his room, my heartbeat triples in speed and I squeeze Raelynn's hand. She squeezes me back.

When we get to the closed door with my father lying being it, I hover my hand over the knob only to see how terribly I'm shaking. What is wrong with me?

Why do I care so much for a man who treated me like pure shit on the bottom of my shoe?

Raelynn's hand falls over mine on the knob, and I finally look down at the woman who's patiently accompanying me through this. Her eyes soften when they see mine. Probably red and puffy. However, no tears have escaped. I haven't let them.

He doesn't deserve another tear of mine. Alive or dead.

With just her silence, I can feel her pushing me, telling me to be stronger. Telling me he doesn't deserve the sympathy I know I shouldn't give him.

Sighing, I turn the knob on, only for a man in a white lab coat and scrubs to be pulling on the other side.

Several other nurses stand inside the room, their voices muttering together into one blob of voices.

"Excuse me," The doctor says. "Who are you?"

I clear my throat of the lump that resided in it. "Milo," I answer. "Milo Evans."

The doctor nods, and the look on his face doesn't ever translate to anything good. "I see. Milo, we've been expecting you, actually."

"Expecting me?" I say with a stutter, glancing at Raelynn.

The doctor nods and waves his fingers for me to follow. Raelynn is instructed to wait outside and not allowed any further in the room. I follow the doctor inside the room to the circle of other doctors.

My eyes scan around, no sight of a body. No sight of a man. No sight of my father.

"Where is he?" I question.

"Milo," a woman doctor walks up to me with a folded paper in her hands. "Your father wanted us to give you this before he disappeared."

My eyebrows lower, and I try to process her words. Disappeared? "What do you mean?"

She looks around at the other doctors as if saying too much might kill her. They all seem to look that way now that I point it out. What the hell is going on? Was the man who crashed not my father?

"Morgan..." she looks past my shoulders to the door, making sure it's closed and lowers her voice. "He hired us and instructed us to give this to you. We don't know what it says, all we know is the orders he's given us."

She holds out the paper and I pluck it from her fingers, unfolding it to reveal a letter in my father's handwriting.

It doesn't make any sense.

These doctors, their words, this... letter.

It doesn't make sense until I begin to read.

Son,

I know we haven't had the best relationship over the past years. It's my fault, I know it is. And you would agree that I owe you an apology.

And this is not one.

This is an explanation and a repayment for what I've done to you, son.

If you're reading this right now, I am dead to all but you and the doctors handing you this letter. But the truth is, I've moved far away, to a place far from you and Iris and lovely Genesis. I'm too ashamed to face you all, to look in your faces that I've failed. So yes, I'm taking this way out, away from you all, away from my businesses, away from the disappointment, the easy way out.

I'm not going to say sorry, it's not what you want to hear, and I know that. You are a strong man, Milo. You've taken the role I failed to play, and I thank you for that, keeping Iris and Genesis intact.

Being held by a doctor are cards in your name, Iris, and Genesis, and yet to be activated. On these, you'll find money. The money that I've kept from you all for so long. All of it. I wish you and the woman who's stolen your heart the best. I shouldn't have tried to choose your path.

Please make sure Iris is well and give Genesis much love.

All I ask of you is that you keep my secret— I am dead.
- Morgan

I'm stuck staring at the last three words. Struggling to process all I've just read.

My father faked his death.

I lower the letter and begin to pace the floor, sliding my hand down my face.

Anger is the simplest term for what I feel. No longer am I sad, worried, or filled with a hot anger that boiled in my blood.

He doesn't get just to leave his responsibilities. He doesn't get just to go and be a fucking pussy.

"This is *bullshit*," I hiss.

"Mr. Milo—"

I strut to them, crumpling the letter in my hand and throwing it across the room. "Fucking bullshit."

I wanted him to pay. Money isn't going to take back the scars on my back or the years of damage he's caused in me. While he's living off in, God knows where I'm here taking care of *his* family.

Go to Hell, Morgan Evans.

I'll keep his secret and take back what's rightfully *mine*.

But I'll forever despise him. I won't have to pretend he is dead because he's been dead to me for years.

"The cards," I spit. "Where are they."

I don't know if I should even call them doctors anymore. They're just working for my father. When you have money, you can do nearly anything. Even take your own death.

One of the men stubbles around, searching his pockets, and pulls out three debit cards, handing them to me.

I take them, reading all three of the names on them.

The first thing I think of is my mother. She's suffering right now, and the one thing she needs has just been given to her.

Money.

Without a word, I go to walk out of the room when I'm stopped.

"Sir, we're authorized to tell you to keep this a—"

"Secret," I grunt. "I know." And walk out where Raelynn is sitting patiently in the waiting room.

She stands up as soon as her eyes meets mine and stalks to my side. "What's wrong?"

"I'll tell you on the way."

When is said his secret was save with me. That included Raelynn.

***

"He's such a bitch," Raelynn curses after I tell her all of what's going on.

Couldn't have said it better.

I sigh. "It's neither here nor there. What matters now is getting my mother what she needs." While walking into my mothers hospital room with Raelynn, I prepare myself with a long inhale.

Raelynn plants a hand on my back knowing I haven't visited my mother in a while. Knowing how I'm pain she always is with nothing in my power that I could do to help her I couldn't have seeing her in such a state.

My poor mum.

"Mum?" I say softly, turning the corner of the curtain that splits the room in half.

Laying in her bed, hooked to several different machines and looking just as beautiful as ever, but also sicker than I've ever seen her, tears swell my eyes immediately.

She's looks fragile, her head turns the way of my voice slowly, as if any sudden movement might end terribly bad.

Her eyes widen and she smiles. "Milo," she says weakly, sounding just as French and . Though I know she's thrilled inside. "Look what the cat dragged in, *mon fils.*"

"Hi mum," I respond with, the words barely distinguishable. I feel just how I thought I would. Like shit.

I clear my throat and wipe my eyes with the back of my hand.

"Oh sweetheart," my dear mother says, scooting over so I can sit beside her on her bed. She taps the spot. "Come here."

I can't hold back the waterfall of tears dripping down my cheeks any longer. "I'm so sorry," I apologize, sitting beside her and laying back, careful not to hurt her in any way. My head lays on her chest and I can hear the steady slow heart beat of hers.

"For what? You done nothing wrong."

"For not visiting you sooner," I croak like a wuss.

"Oh shush," she waves. "I knew you'd come around sooner or later. You're a busy man."

"Not too busy to visit you."

"And here you are, practically in my lap like you never left it 25 years ago."

I laugh at that. If there's one thing about her, she will lighten up any topic. Even the ones you think isn't possible to lighten up.

"So stop your crying." She nudges me. "And look at me."

I sit up, looking at her and she grins.

"You've become a very respectful strong man, Milk. I'm very proud of you and Gen."

I sniff and nod. "I have good news," I say, the corner of my mouth cracking into a smile.

"Yeah? And what's that? Marrying that beautiful Raelynn, yet?"

I cough out a laugh, knowing Raelynn is somewhere near listening behind this curtain. "It hasn't been long enough for marriage, mum."

She rolls her eyes. "I haven't seen you happy in years, Milo. And I say if she makes you happy, this happy, don't lose her. Don't let her go." She puts a hand on mine laying flat. "Not just anyone will put up with your shit."

I smile. "She won't be going anywhere. I'm sure of it. But that isn't the good news."

"Then what is it?"

I pull out the cards Morgan left behind and show her them.

She gives them a puzzled look. "What's this?"

"Money, for your treatment."

She looks up at me, a change in expression. However, I can't tell weather it's a good or bad one.

"Where's the money? I'm sure Morgan didn't just lend you it."

I shake my head. "Never mind where I got it. Here. You can get treatment now," I say, enthusiastically. "The doctor had said it's the one thing that can save your life, so—"

"It had a possibility. Nothing is ever a hundred percent certain, Milo." Her tone has changed. Less humor and now more serious.

I tilt my head. "Does it matter? It's worth a shot, right? The money is yours."

She sighs and gives me a sympathetic smile. "You were always so sweet."

"Mum—"

"It's too late, Milo."

I drop the cards onto the floor.

"W-what do you mean too late? The doctors said—"

"The doctors said that when the possibility of getting better was still available. It's not available anymore."

I swallow hard, tears rushing to the surface of my eyes instantly. "No, stop it."

"It's okay, Milo," her voice cracks. "You are—"

I shake my head getting off of the bed and wiping my face of tears that soon bluer my vision again.

"Stop!" I cry. "I don't want to hear goodbyes, mum."

"I'm not saying a goodbye," she says.

"It sure sounds like one."

"It's whatever you want it to be. Now you either leave this room, or come back here and sit with your mother."

Stepping back to the bed I retake my position on her shoulder and sob. She's been here for everything. She's done everything and has been the best possible for us.

"This isn't the end you deserve," I whisper.

"Oh I know. If it was my choice I'd be invincibl—" she goes into a coup hinge spree and I snap my head up.

"Is everything alright?" Raelynn says behind me, walking around the curtain.

Mum puts her hand up and clears her throat. "Just a little cough." She looks past my shoulders at Raelynn and her face lights up.

"If it isn't the beauty herself, come here too."

Raelynn looks at me as if saying sorry for interrupting but I give her a soft smile to tell her she's alright. Walking to the other side of my mother she lays the same way I am and I laugh at the humor side of it all.

Two grown adults laying like children beside her.

"Now, I know you've been listening, so that saves me another sad reveal."

Raelynn laughs a little, sniffling. She's been crying too.

Mum continues, "I need you both to stay around for Genesis. She's living with my sister and she's just as devastated. Though she's known longer than you Milo, I've told her to keep my secret tight and she did."

Secrets. How I bloody loathe secrets.

"You're a strong couple. And I wish you both healthy children and a long life together, you hear me?"

We both nod. "Thank you," Raelynn says.

We spend days straight for the past two months sitting beside my mum, eating beside her and sharing laughs and cries with her. Genesis had came for most of them as well, a true family bonding moment for us all. It was in these past two months I felt the happiest. The most thrilled to have no problems in my life, the women of my dreams at my side and a beautiful mum and sister. I wish it had lasted for longer. Our time with my mother. However, it had to end. And it did.

Our mother passed happily.

She passed with her children at her side, she passed knowing she was loved so much by the ones who mattered the most.

We made sure to fill her last two months with happy memories and fun times. Raelynn got to know my mother even more before it was her time to go.

And I'm glad it happened in such a way. A way that made me feel at peace. Despite her being gone, I've gotten to say goodbye in the best way possible over these last two months without a shitty speech.

Now, all I have is one single thing left to do to make my mother's wishes feel complete.

Genesis points through the glass at the pretty diamond engagement right in the display. "That one's pretty."

"Ou!" Gia says. "She'd love that, it's gorgeous!"

I tap my finger at the stress and nerves running through me. These two were my best bet at getting the perfect ring for Raelynn.

It's been eight months, and I've never been so certain about someone in my life.

"When you two get married, can I be the flower girl?" Genesis asks. "I'd think I'd make the perfect one."

"That is something you can ask Raelynn. I'm sure she wouldn't mind. If you stop being an annoying brat, that is."

Gen gasps. "You're an ass, Raelynn loves me."

I only smile because that's true. She does love her greatly."

I had to lie to her today and tell her I've gone out to work, but I've called in a substitute to cover for my students.

"Genesis," Gia says. "We're gonna be absolute best aunts."

"Of course we are!"

"You two aren't doing much helping," I interrupt.

But it doesn't take me long for a ring to catch my eyes.

It's silver, the shape of a flower with a large diamond in the middle of it. It's almost like it was made solely for her.

What screams Raelynn more than flowers? What better way to propose to her than with a flower engagement ring.

"Which are you looking at?" Gen asks.

"That one," I point.

They all follow my finger to the ring.

"Oh," Gia says with a high pitch. "Well, isn't that one just damn perfect?"

31

MILO

New York City has its flaws, but its beauty is definitely something worthwhile.

Especially when it's snowing.

This city is at its prettiest in the winter.

A large grin has been plastered on my face the entire way to the ice skating rink located in downtown Manhattan. The one I've begged Milo to come along with me to.

School got shut down for a snow day, and the flower shop I've chosen to close for the day. It's not difficult keeping flowers healthy during the winter with all the tools I have, but that day, Milo promised me something.

"C'mon, Milo, don't be like that," I say to Milo, kneeling on the ground to tighten is skates so he can stop pouting. "It'll be fun! Besides, you're the one that said we can do anything I want today."

He breathes into his hands and rubs them together. "Yes, dear, but I thought you'd say maybe a nice dinner or perhaps a trip to the salon, not glide on ice with blades. I'm a grown man I'm not meant to glide on ice."

I roll my eyes and stand up when I dismiss his laces and extend my hand. "Don't be a grump about it. That's usually my job."

Now that I think about it, I haven't had much to be grumpy about over the past several months.

I try to hide my grin when Milo grips my arms and tries to balance on the floor. The level of concentration on his face is enough to make me giggle out loud.

"Stop laughing at me. We haven't even gone on the ice yet!" He yells in a hushed voice so others around us won't hear.

"I'm not laughing at you," I say, *laughing*.

"Oh yeah?"

I nod, biting my lip to stop. But fail.

He shakes his head, but a small, handsome smirk rises on his lips. His head rocks side to side in disappointment, and he casually takes my neck in his hand and double-checks that no one's looking.

"I better come out unhurt and alive, Raelynn." He whispers to me.

I raise my brows and cross my arms over my chest. "Or what?"

He only smiles and lets go of my neck to grasp my hand. "Come on now." He says with sudden enthusiasm. Since you know how to skate, teach me."

I nod, sliding my beanie lower on my head of box braids, and slowly walk Milo to the ice rink.

When we get outside, big fluffy snowflakes falling in the billions from the sky make almost everything pure white. Everything besides the massive rocker feller center Christmas tree behind the rink.

For all the years I've been here in NYC, I've not once seen the famous 100-foot tree in person.

Only on the television where I also only ever seen the Macy Thanksgiving Day parades and New Year's parades. They looked amazing on TV and this wasn't an illusion. This tree is giant and beautiful.

With lights making it glow several different Christmas colors and slow on the tips of the branches looking couples holding hands, kids falling on ice, and a bunch of people sowing in a circle, it looks like something out of a cheesy rom-com movie.

But I'm glad to be living it out with Milo at my side because two years ago, I never thought going skating for a date on a snow day would actually be my reality.

I look over at Milo, his nose and lips bright pink from the cold. Stubble dresses his cheeks, but if it wasn't, I'm sure those would be red too. "Okay, ready?"

"I'm not sure," he mutters.

I tug him along and get on the ice carefully. "Okay, easy now." I hold both of Milo's hands and force myself to hold back laughter at the clear fear in him at the moment.

He's standing like a starfish.

"Bring your legs closer together," I instruct.

"I'm going to fall, darling."

"You have to trust me."

He looks up from the ice. "I do trust you."

I nod and nudge my chin at his legs. "Closer. And bend your knees a little."

He sighs and brings them closer, lowering an inch down. Sometimes I forget how tall he is, but with these skates on, he's almost taller than everyone on the ice right now.

He wiggles a little as I begin to pull him with me slowly.

"Careful, Raelynn."

"Relax, you're doing it!" I wiggle my fingers in his tight grip, and he squeezes harder.

"What are you doing?!" He panics. "Don't let go of me."

"It's just one hand," I assure him. "I have your other one. You won't fall, I got you."

"If I fall, you're falling with me. And then we're leaving."

I laugh. "Oh, shut up and let go."

He eventually lets go of one hand, and now I skate at his side, one hand losing circulation dealing with Milo and the cold.

"There, see? Not too hard."

Milo grins and looks at me, and nods. I look away but still feel his gaze melting into the side of my head.

"Isn't this place so pretty?" I say as we eventually make a lap around the rink.

He shrugs. "I've seen much prettier."

I look sideways at him and tilt my head. "Really? Tell me what. Because this place is pretty tough competition. I mean, look at the snow it makes it look almost magical like Fairies are gonna come out and sprinkle magical cocaine dust on us and—"

I'm cut short when Milo grips my waist and slides up messily towards the rink's barrier, sandwiching me between me and it.

I gasp briefly and look up at him while laughing. "What are you—"

He bends his head to kiss me, catching my lips like they're his only means of warmth.

We open our mouths to each other for a moment, letting our tongues slip against each other before unlatching, being mindful of the people around us.

"I was going to say you're prettier than this place, but that wouldn't have done much justice." He strokes his cold thumb along my jaw. "You are the most beautiful woman I've ever laid eyes on.

"Sometimes, when I look at you and your smile," he talks low, running the flat of his thumb over my lip, "or your concentration on your flowers. Or how bright your eyes get when you see me after work. It all makes my chest hurt. This place's beauty doesn't make my chest hurt nearly as much as yours does."

My face softens, and I raise my lips into a small smile as my chests burn and defrost from his words. "Thank you."

He cranks his head down and presses his lips into my cheek, giving me a thousand pecks before I shy away with laughs. "Calm down, Romeo, calm down."

We stay at the rink for nearly four hours. Milo had fallen several times, but he didn't make us leave. Instead, he let me help him up and wanted to try again. Eventually, and surprisingly, he got it down fast. I shouldn't have underestimated him, but now he practically skates as well as me, and he's only had four hours of practice. I envy his determination to perfect things.

"That was fun, wasn't it?" I slide my beanie off as we sit in his car.

He nods. "Yes, it was." He checks the time, reading two in the afternoon. "What else is on your mind for today?"

I twist my lips. "Why are you so nice to me today?"

"What do you mean, love? I'm nice to you every day."

"No, I mean really nice. Why are you willingly giving me a day of anything I want?"

He shrugs. "Because you deserve it," his hand drops on my thigh as he starts the car and then looks at me. "And I love you."

***

"Wow..." I turn around in a circle as I stare at the fish swimming all around us, trapped behind glass.

Aquariums. It might be my new favorite thing.

The room glows a deep ocean blue and I hold Milo's hand as I follow the fishes swimming really close to the glass, tapping. It flaps away, and I giggle.

"This is fucking amazing," I whisper. We've been here for an hour, and it still amazes my eyes like a child in a candy shop.

"It is." The sound of Milo snapping a picture with his phone of me touching the class makes me jump.

"Hey! Cut it out," I laugh, reaching for his phone, but he pulls it away, shaking his head.

"Nuh-uh," he hums. "I need these."

"Oh yeah? Why?"

"Because today is a special day."

"What makes today so special?"

He smirks. "Because I have a surprise for you."

My brows perk up. "What surprise? Tell me."

"Would you like to go see?"

I nod frantically; hell yeah, I wanna see it. Whatever it is, it has his voice sounding strange. Did he get me a puppy?

I don't remember asking for a dog, but I definitely wouldn't complain. I hope it's a German Shepard, but then again, Milo is like the huge version of a German Shepard, so I'd have to guess second that wish. Dramatics will be at an all-time e high with those two.

"Alright then, let's go."

He doesn't tell me where we're going, only drives me for half an hour till we reach Central Park. His surprise is Central Park.

I mean, I won't complain, considering I live in this place, but I've been here many times growing up. It's a park, a nice one, but still a park.

Milo walks out of the car and around to my side, where he opens my door and helps me out.

I smile, telling him thank you.

He brings me along the walkway in Central Park, where we peacefully stroll past the frosty iced ponds and the pretty white layered park.

I'm convinced everything is prettier in the winter.

I mean my head on Milo's shoulder while holding his hand. "Thank you," I say.

"For what?"

Seconds go by before I answer. "Everything."

He kisses the top of my head. "Do you remember the first gift I've ever given you?"

I nod and laugh. "Pickles. It had a little note on it that I didn't want to admit it stole my heart, just a little."

He nods, seeming satisfied that I remembered. "Right," he says. "Well, I have another note for you."

I lift my head off his shoulder and look up at him. "What note?"

His eyes dart away from means as we turn a corner.

I stop walking.

In front of me, where the pathway lowers under an archway created by a stoned bridge, stands Gia, my *dad*, and Genesis, all helping each other hold two signs that read into one note that make any heart swell out of my chest. The lamppost lights my pathway to the sign, and golden balloons are tied around each of them while slow flakes drop on us all.

I hitch a cry as I read it repeatedly, a hand to my mouth.

Will you Marry Me?
Love, Milo

"Turn around, idiot!" Gia shouts playfully.

I turn to find Milo on one knee and a small black box holding the most beautiful ring I've ever seen in the palm of his hands.

I gasp again, tears now running down my eyes.

This can't be my reality. My body shakes with cries as Milo reaches for my left hand, and I give it to him to hold.

"You are wonderful, Raelynn. I thank you almost every day that fate has let me to find you in that elevator all those months ago. Even if it hadn't, I'm certain we would've met one way or another because you are undoubtedly my soulmate—" he breaks off with a quiver of a cry, "—and I love you dearly.

"You make me the happiest I've ever been. You make me want to grow as a person, a man, and, hopefully, as your husband. Raelynn Garcia, may you please marry me?"

Without hesitation, I nod, dropping to my knees before him to wrap my arms around his neck.

"Yes, Milo," I sob. "Of course."

I can feel his body deflating, and he pulls back, gently taking my hand in his as we sit in the fluffy, nearly untouched snow and slips the engagement ring on my ring finger. I can barely see it through the tears that blur my vision, but when I blink to clear it all up, I'm amazed.

It's a flower-themed ring.

I look up at him with a massive grin, and he stands up, tightening me up in his arms. From behind, our family cheers and then kisses me.

It's now that I really feel like my life has done a complete 180-degree shift.

I went from my lowest to shutting everyone out to being the girl I hated, the person I despised within myself. To bring at my absolute highest with the love of my life. And I can't wait to spend the rest of my days with this man.

The man who saved me.

And if I ever find myself at a low, there's one thing I'll always be sure about.

And it's that I love Milo.

Epilogue

Five years later

Raelynn

I watch as my husband rises from between my legs.

The distant sound of children partying leaks through the bathroom door from the backyard. Finished with tying my heels over my calves, Milo grips my hips and brings me close to his groin.

"We have a few minutes before everyone starts to wonder where we are. You know that, right?" He drops his head and kisses on my neck, sucking the skin that makes my legs weak to the bone.

"They... need me," I tilt my head, giving him more access despite my words.

"I need you," he whispers, warm breath fanning against my skin. "*Desperately.*"

He picks me up and sits me on the sink, where my legs wrap around his torso. My body erupts into flames, and the self-control in me struggles not to rip the white dress shirt off his body.

He arches my back, leaning me back towards the mirror behind us.

His head lowers, and his mouth glides across my cleavage, palming one of my breasts and kissing the other over my sundress.

I press my head into the mirror and moan out his name.

"We can't, Mi—"

His hand creeps up under my dress and grips my thigh. "A dangerous dress, Raelynn."

I bite my lip. "Maybe That's why I chose it."

He laughs and smirks, shaking his head. "Of course it is. Wouldn't be you without a little lease, would it?"

I shake my head. "Nope."

I look down at my stomach at the obviously noticeable bump. I've been hiding in sweaters and Milo's clothes for so long I almost forgot how big my stomach has gotten.

"Trying to get me even more pregnant?" I joke.

"If I could, you're damn right."

He gently lays his hand on my stomach and presses his forehead against mine before rising to kiss it. "I love all three of you."

"We love you too," I whisper back, blinking away the tears in my eyes.

Why am I so emotional, Jesus Christ? It must be this little human baking in me making me like this.

And at the right time, my stomach shifts just slightly, but enough for Milo to gasp and take his hand away.

Fear crosses his face. "Did I hurt you? I'm so sorr—"

I shake my head, bringing his hand back. "No, that was them! They moved. You just felt a kick."

He watches my stomach like it's the most fascinating thing in the world. Which it is; pregnancy is incredible, even though I'm strolling through hell for nine months.

"That was the little one?"

I nod, "Mhm."

He laughs. "I want to feel it again."

I only giggle. "It's random, really—"

"Mommy! Dad!" Haven, the birthday girl, voice breaks through our quiet time. "Where are you guys? Can I go to the bouncy castle, *please*? I promise I won't throw up this time!"

Milo and I cackle to ourselves, remembering when Haven vomited inside the bouncy castle this morning after eating her large birthday breakfast. It's our fault for letting her go in so early on.

Milo kisses my lips and opens the door, jump scaring the little girl with brown kinky hair and a pretty dress on the other end.

"Dad!!"

"Come here," he runs and scoops her up, twirling her around like the princess she is.

Four years ago, Havens's biological father passed away from a natural death.

With no family to take her in, Milo stepped in with adoption. He made sure it was what she wanted—for us to be her parents. And considering how loud and frantically she pleaded yes that day, it's safe to say she had no problem at all with it. And we were happy to have her as our daughter.

Haven Lenard.

Today, being her tenth birthday party, we decided to throw her a party with all her friends from school who are giving my parents and my sisters his most likely.

"You can go to the bouncy castle," I say. "As long as Milo goes with you.

She looks at Milo with pleading eyes, and Milo sends a glare my way.

I giggle.

"Please, Dad?"

"Alright then..."

"YES!" Haven drops from his arms and grabs him, pulling him urgently towards the backyard.

I follow them out, leaning against the doorframe to watch Milo get bombarded by my tiny humans all the way to the bouncy castle.

It's funny, sometimes, knowing that Milo would do absolutely any and everything for us, his girls. The word no early leaves his mouth to her, and when it does, her pouty face changes that answer faster than I can.

"You look happy," Mom says.

Me and mom have been working on fixing our relationship over the past few years.

We've done pretty well.

Although the past won't change, the future can, and we've made the best of what we have.

I'm glad to have her in my life still.

"I am," I respond.

"He's amazing with kids. A great father."

"Yeah, well, the perks of marrying a first-grade teacher," A breathy laugh leaves me. "He's a natural. I just hope I get better at it all."

She places a hand on my stomach. "You're a great mother, Raelynn. To haven and eventually to this one right here."

He pauses before continuing. "You'll be a hell of a lot better than I had, that's for sure."

315

I give her a sympathetic smile, knowing how sorry she's been over the years and how desperately she tries to make up for it all. and I admire her determination. It reminds me of Milo.

"Mom!" I look away at Haven running to me with her hands behind her back.

"Yes?"

"I have a surprise for you."

"What is it?" I bend down as far as I can to her height, and without any time to react, I'm squirted in the face with a small water gun.

I gasp, and Haven giggles and runs away to where Milo stands, walking towards us, smirking.

Definitely his idea.

He's lucky I have zero makeup on it I'd be killing him right now.

As Milo approaches me, my mom chuckles and walks away to deal with the kids.

"Well, don't you have yourself a little minion?"

He grips my waist with one hand, rubbing the water off my face with the other.

He kisses me for a long time, cupping my head in his palm and then pulling away before any of the kids see.

"I just needed an excuse to return and kiss my beautiful wife."

Acknowledgments

For nearly four years, I've dedicated hours to writing books about silly little romances and happy endings. None of what I wrote gained me any income, though that was the last thing on my mind. It gained me a loyal following filled with readers who now get to hold these silly little romance books in their hands. *Love, Milo* initially resided on a simple writing app, and I'm grateful to see my book grow and become what it is today. It's a special thing to hold my creation in my hands and feel proud of it, so I thank you for reading and supporting it.

I want to thank my best friends, Natalie, Yarelis, and Abigail, for always hyping me up when I send them my achievements, supporting my work, and always being there for me. You guys were there through the beginning of my writing stage, where I only talked about my stories (not that that's changed, though).

A special thank you to all of my Wattpad readers; you guys are MVPs, and I would not have thought to self-publish *Love, Milo* book if it weren't for over one million of you. I always loved logging in to read the funny comments on every line in this book.

About the Author

At seventeen years old in the year 2020, Author Kayla rose started pursuing her dream of becoming an author by writing under the name *kaylarosewrites* on *Wattpad*. Living in the West side of Harlem, New York, she spent most of her time during quarantine typing and making content about her novels while also attending online schooling for her entire senior year of high school. That was just the beginning for her. Now, in the year 2024, near the age of twenty-one and in college to become a financial accountant, she has self-published her novel, *Love, Milo*, which racked up one and a half million reads on the reading app *Wattpad*. While the pen name Kayla Rose is not her true full name, it is her true first and middle name and has become part of her brand.

While reading this, you can always find Kayla Rose writing for free on the Wattpad app and talking to her readers like close friends.

Socials

www.wattpad.com/user/kaylarosewrites
www.instagram.com/kaylarosewrites_
Tiktok.com/kaylarosewrite

Made in the USA
Middletown, DE
25 February 2024